WHEN A MARQUESS
LOVES A WOMAN

By Vivienne Lorret

The Season's Original Series
"The Duke's Christmas Wish" in
All I Want for Christmas Is a Duke
The Debutante Is Mine
This Earl is on Fire
When a Marquess Loves a Woman

The Rakes of Fallow Hall Series
The Elusive Lord Everhart
The Devilish Mr. Danvers
The Maddening Lord Montwood

The Wallflower Wedding Series
Tempting Mr. Weatherstone (novella)
Daring Miss Danvers
Winning Miss Wakefield
Finding Miss McFarland

WHEN A MARQUESS
LOVES A WOMAN

The Season's Original Series

VIVIENNE LORRET

AVON IMPULSE
An Imprint of HarperCollinsPublishers

Excerpt from *Intercepting Daisy* copyright © 2016 by Julie Revell Benjamin.

Excerpt from *Mixing Temptation* copyright © 2016 by Sara Jane Stone.

Excerpt from *The Soldier's Scoundrel* copyright © 2016 by Cat Sebastian.

Excerpt from *Making the Play* copyright © 2016 by Tina Klinesmith.

EPub Edition OCTOBER 2016 ISBN: 9780062446350

Print Edition ISBN: 9780062446374

Avon, Avon Impulse, and the Avon Impulse logo are trademarks of HarperCollins Publishers.

AM 10 9 8 7 6 5 4 3 2 1

For Kim
Thank you for being my friend from the
beginning of this wonderful journey.

April 1820

"Good morning, Saunders. Any noteworthy headlines today?" Max Harwick asked when he reached the bottom of the stairs. As part of a daily regime, the butler waited in the foyer with a pressed copy of the *Post* on a bronze platter.

Saunders inclined his bald head, sunlight from a transient window glancing off his polished dome. "Sure to be a hotbed at the House of Commons this afternoon, sir." Then with a conspiratorial arch of his gray brows, he continued in a hushed tone. "Best walk slowly to the breakfast room."

"Thank you, Saunders." Max eyed the paper with eager interest, opened it with a snap, and began his slow trek. As a rule, no one was allowed to read at the table. Not even a man of four and twenty. So Max had become an expert at navigating the halls while devouring the stories with the most political intrigue. Today was no different. Reading about the uprisings in the north counties and the demands for reform, he took each step by rote, guided by the scents of coffee, salted meats, and freshly baked bread.

"Maxwell," Mother said, clearing her throat.

It was only when he looked up that he realized he'd crossed the threshold already. Then, receiving a pointed glance down to the paper in his grasp, he dutifully folded and tucked it away behind the first of four silver chafing dishes on the sideboard.

Marjorie Harwick was not a strict woman by nature. She was all ease and nurture, with a generous smile and a softly rounded outward appearance to match. Her dark wavy hair was always in some sort of disarray, likely due to her state of constant motion. In all the years of rearing two sons, she'd never raised her voice. However, when it came to breakfasting together in this cozy hexagonal room lined with diamond-paned windows, she was a veritable Yeoman of the Guard. She would have her way, no matter what.

Stepping to her chair, he bussed her cheek, and she affectionately patted his in return. "Good morning, Mother." Then, catching his father's eye, he inclined his head. "Good morning, sir."

Alton Harwick mirrored the gesture, touching a serviette to his mouth. After an absent greeting, he glanced toward the hallway. "Is your brother on his way downstairs?"

To be precise, Bramson Sheffield, the Marquess of Engle, was Max's *half* brother. Four years the elder, Bram was the product of their mother's first marriage. Alton Harwick, having been a friend of the late marquess, had confessed on several occasions that marrying Marjorie—after a suitable mourning period, of course—had been the best way to honor the Engle line.

Overall, he was a kind man and a good father and husband. Many of his acquaintances even considered him affable. In fact, he only had one notable flaw: he kept forgetting that Max was *his* firstborn, his only son by blood, and the one who would carry on his name.

"I believe I saw Bram's valet in the hallway," Max answered. And while he still had Father's attention, he rushed onward. "With the news of the day, this afternoon's session of Parliament is sure to be quite the stir. Father, perhaps we could go to St. Stephen's and watch the proceedings from the gallery."

"Not today, I'm afraid," Father said, pushing a bit of egg on his fork toward the blade of his knife. "Bram and I are heading to Tattersall's. There's a prime pair of grays he has his eye on."

The morning excursion would still leave the afternoon available. But Max made no comment.

"Perhaps another day," Mother added with a cheerful nod as she dropped a dollop of clotted cream onto her scone. Much to her credit, she loved her sons with equal fervor and gaiety. Yet she was oblivious to the biased favoritism toward Bram that confronted Max on a daily basis.

Moving to the sideboard, he prepared a plate. Vying for his father's time was a battle he'd lost too frequently, and familiarity with the defeat caused a numbness that made it easier to shrug off the disappointment. Besides, it was a pleasanter task to think of how he would spend his afternoon. He loved watching the debates at the House of Commons, and hearing those—who might not have had a voice otherwise—seek justice. He'd even thought of standing for a seat but lacked the money and the influence required.

Since he was a gentleman of limited means, the *ton* discounted him, rarely even aware of his presence. In fact, the only time he garnered attention was when someone wanted to ask after Bram, wondering whether or not the marquess had chosen a bride yet.

Of all the questions posed to Max, that was his least favorite. Even though he never offered a definitive answer, he hated knowing that Juliet White was among the candidates on Bram's list. Yet she was far too beautiful not to be included, lack of fortune or not.

The *ton* called her the *goddess* and some even the *hollow goddess*, believing she was nothing more than a gilded plasterwork molded into perfection. Few knew how insightful she was or how she noticed everything and everyone. Even Max.

Unfortunately, she noticed his brother more. Only a blind man could miss the way her eyes lit up like sapphires against a candle flame whenever she saw Bram.

And with that thought, Max's appetite disappeared. He looked down at his plate with disinterest as he lowered his frame into a straight-backed chair.

"I have a good feeling about today," Father said, placing his silverware on the rim of his plate and glancing toward the hallway again.

"Do you think Bram has made a decision?" Mother asked.

"There's a good chance of it. *Ah*—and here's my boy now." Father dropped his serviette to the table as he stood, smiling. "We'd better make haste if you want to land those grays before Knightswold gets his hands on them."

"*That* I shall not allow," Bram said with a chuckle as he strode into the breakfast room. He too held a newspaper, folding it beneath his arm before he gripped Father's out-stretched hand.

Standing next to Bram, Father painted a rather nondescript portrait—straight brown hair, brushed back from his forehead and tinged with gray at the temples; plain brown eyes; and features that were unremarkable.

Max had those same features but also possessed Mother's dark hair and slight olive cast to his skin. Against Bram's pale coloring, aristocratic bone structure, and magnetic charm, there was little Max could do to compete. So he'd always relied on other methods—eldest son to eldest son.

While Bram had the slim, agile qualities of a top-notch fencer, Max's athletic build was created for stamina. When it came to matters of strength and endurance, he could outmatch and outride Bram any day of the week. Unfortunately, Max's skills were better suited to a jousting tournament during days of old. They did him little good here and now.

"After all," Bram continued, "a man cannot become betrothed without the finest pair to pull his barouche, can he?"

Mother gasped, smiling. "You have decided?"

"Indeed." Bram tossed the *Season Standard*—the *ton*'s premier scandal sheet—down onto the table, without receiving a word of reprimand. "This morning's column cleared away any doubt I possessed. They have announced this Season's *Original* and, as luck would have it, the name is the very one that holds a claim upon my heart."

Max stared at the paper. Suddenly, it was like looking at a feral beast on the table, froth dripping from its mouth, claws ready to strike.

Juliet had pinned all her hopes on being named the *Original*. The title was bestowed to the one person who encompassed certain qualities worthy of the *ton*'s notice and emulation. For a gentleman, this frivolous honor could mean that his wit or the cut of his clothes had far surpassed the others. For a young woman, her style and poise made her the most sought after of all debutantes. Most importantly, she would have her choice of husband.

And Max feared that her choice was now standing in the room.

Knowing what was expected of him, Max stood as well and offered a hand to Bram. "Congratulations."

"You don't even know whom I've chosen." Bram cast a dubious glance down to the hand and laughed. Then he reached for the *Standard* and slapped it into Max's grasp instead.

Ignoring the slight, Max skimmed the column. *Proud to announce…this Season's* Original…*a young woman with charm, beauty, indefatigable effervescence…*

"Miss Leonard?" The name left Max's lips on a breath that drained every ounce of air from his lungs. His chest collapsed and then abruptly filled with relief more profound than he'd ever known before. "You're going to marry Miss Leonard?"

From what Max knew about Miss Leonard, she possessed an artful way of boasting her own accomplishments by way of self-deprecation, which tended to earn her even more praise. Yet all he saw was a façade of crafted manners and a false beauty that fed on compliments. Most were blind to her character, seeing her only as a charming, orphaned heiress whose only family was an aging aunt.

"Poor Miss White," Mother said. "I know she counted on today's announcement. Doubtless that was the reason her parents had planned a party for this very evening. I wonder if they will cancel now."

Max moved to the sideboard and slipped the paper beside the other. "Of course not. Mr. White is not a man to show his cards. As he and his family always have done, they will display the utmost grace and cordiality."

Although, rumors were now surfacing that the Whites could not afford to lose their social standing. Apparently, Mr. White had a good deal of debt hanging over his head. Since they were practically neighbors, however, Max wasn't inclined to believe it. There would have been indications, after all— fewer lavish parties, minimal *at home* days, or even wearing clothes out of fashion. But none of that was evident.

"Doubtless, you are correct, Maxwell," Mother replied before she stood and requested that Father join her in the hall for a moment.

"I'm counting on the Whites' cordiality because I plan to make my announcement at their party," Bram said once they were alone.

Max balked. "This evening? Surely your new bride would wish for her aunt to host a party in order to make the announcement."

"By then the news will already have been out." Bram offered a careless shrug as he lifted Max's plate from the table and took a bite of ham. "Imagine the surprise I shall receive at dinner when I stand and raise my glass to toast my upcoming nuptials. The entire *ton* has been waiting with bated breath for my announcement."

"It would be bad form." And it would break Juliet's heart. "I won't allow it."

Bram laughed. "And who are you, *little brother*, to prevent me?"

Unfortunately, neither Father nor Mother had succeeded in dissuading Bram from his plan. Therefore, by the time they arrived at the Whites' townhouse that evening, Max was on a mission to find Juliet.

He'd made several attempts to call on her throughout the day but had been turned away at the door, their butler stating that the household was under preparations for the party and therefore could not receive visitors. Max considered leaving a missive but knew that the information was of too delicate a nature to convey through such blunt means. He needed to see her in person so that she could prepare herself and her parents for what would surely come as a blow to all of them.

From the archway, Max surveyed the room, searching for her face. Dozens of guests crowded shoulder to shoulder, filling the small green parlor. Feathered turbans and elaborate coiffures nodded in conversation. Fans flapped, stirring unpleasant odors and cloying perfumes. Voices merged into a cacophony that made the crystals hanging from the chandelier vibrate and shimmer. But there, at the far side of the room, Juliet stood.

With Miss Leonard.

Both blonde and fair, the two young women angled near one another. While Miss Leonard was pretty, with her ash-blonde curls and almond-shaped eyes, Juliet's beauty possessed an otherworldly quality. Even in a white satin gown that, to him, was like any other, she appeared regal. Every gesture—the tilt of her head, the gentle turn of a fan, a blink—deserved admiration. Her hair was golden spun silk, her features delicate, her complexion the finest cream. Her lashes and slender winged eyebrows were two shades darker, providing the perfect frame for the lovely, keen sapphire irises that never missed a single thing.

It was watching her eyes—as he plotted a course and *pardon me*-ed his way across the room—that gave Max his first jolt of anxiety.

Likely, to everyone else, Miss White and Miss Leonard appeared to be engaged in amicable conversation, but to Max, it was clear that Juliet was distressed. The proof of it lay in her subtle gesture of closing her fan and lowering it heavily to her side, in the slight widening of her eyes, and in the delicate, somewhat halted undulation of her throat as she swallowed.

"I trust that you will keep our secret, Miss White," Miss Leonard said, her voice only reaching Max now that he was within a pace of them. Apparently, Miss Leonard was too eager to share her announcement and chose not to wait for Bram's toast at dinner. Or perhaps she wanted to deliver the news directly to a known rival.

Whatever she had said, he could not forgive her for it. Not when he noted how Juliet had gone still. How only her gaze moved, shifting down to the double strand of pearls adorning Miss Leonard's neck.

Earlier today, Bram had settled the betrothal with Miss Leonard's aunt and her man of accounts. As a gift of promise,

Bram had given his grandmother's pearls. The same ones that Miss Leonard caressed with her gloved fingertips right now.

"I'm certain I do not deserve my good fortune this day," Miss Leonard continued, her eyes flashing with undisguised triumph. "To be named the *Original* and to become engaged to the most sought after of all gentlemen? This must be a dream, surely."

"A dream come to fruition is precious indeed," Juliet said softly, but bravely and without the slightest tremble. "Whenever such blessings arrive, we must believe we are worthy of them or else lose their favor."

Juliet's gaze shifted, alighting on Max. Within the faceted blue depth, he saw the stark fragility hovering there. And though her expression remained flawlessly untouched, if not stoic, he felt as if she were reaching out to him with invisible arms, like a hummingbird in search of a sturdy branch upon which to land—to rest, if only for a moment.

Wordlessly, he inclined his head, prepared to be of service.

Miss Leonard pursed her lips as if in thought. "Wise words, Miss White. I will keep them in mind during the next weeks while I am planning my wedding. In fact—"

The sharp tinkling of a bell and the announcement of dinner cut off her doubtlessly unsuitable statement. That was when she turned and noticed Max in their midst and then looked straight through him.

"Oh! Is Bram about? Do you know what his plans are for this evening? Surely he intends to escort me into the dining room..." Her words trailed off as she stood on tiptoe and began searching the room for the sight of her betrothed.

Then with the acclaimed effervescence that had earned her the *ton's* favor, she summarily abandoned them. Making her way toward the door, she wove through the exiting crowd, offering demure giggles and feigned apologies for every foot she trod upon and every arm she grazed. It was obvious to Max, however, that she cared little for anyone aside from herself.

In effect, she was the epitome of Bram but in a feminine form. They were well matched in that regard.

"And that was the reason you called, I suppose," Juliet said from beside him, her voice wearier than it was a moment ago. "To warn me?"

"It was."

Drawing in a breath, she stared at the backs of the dwindling crowd. "You are a good friend, Max."

He winced, those words just as painful as if she would have said, "You would have made a fine brother-in-law."

Yet if all she would give was her friendship, he would take it. He knew her dreams had suffered two deathblows today. And he also knew she would recover from them in time. Until she did, and ever after, he would remain the strongest branch beneath her feet.

"Would you allow me to escort you to dinner, Miss White?"

With a nod, she took his proffered arm. They trailed the haphazard procession toward the dining room. With a glance over his shoulder, he noticed that they were the last to leave the parlor. In fact, the moment they exited, the servants swept inside to tidy up before dinner ended, when the ladies would return while the gentlemen remained in the dining room for a brief interval.

Max shuddered to think of what it would be like for Juliet, enduring Miss Leonard's gloating all evening. Knowing what awaited Juliet in the next few minutes—the toast that Bram had planned—Max guided them into a slow, ambling pace.

Juliet did not try to hurry him. "I should have thought you would arrive late, having spent your afternoon and evening watching the debates at the House of Commons."

"You know me well," he said, the words ringing with truth beneath his breast. During these past two Seasons, they had attended the same gatherings, shared countless conversations, exchanged ideas, and even engaged in a handful of good-natured debates. "Though I had no appetite for argument today."

She gazed up at him, her eyes glinting with mockery. "Come now, Max, you always have an appetite for argument. I've had ample proof in the numerous times that my family has dined with…"—her words drifted off, taking that glint with them—"yours."

He tried to remain sturdy for her, his forearm tightening as if to infuse his strength into the delicate hand resting there. Yet it did nothing to prevent the sudden sheen of tears in her eyes. For one who prided herself on remaining composed, he knew that revealing her inner anguish to the other guests would be the last thing she would want to do.

Without thought, he steered her quickly through an open doorway off the hall—the library, as it turned out. The room was empty and dark, aside from the light filtering in through the partially open door. They would only have a minute to be alone, but it might be long enough to allow her to recover.

He produced his handkerchief and gently touched it to her lower lid. "I do believe an errant turban feather has made its way into your eyes. Horrible nuisances. They make my eyes water too."

She offered a small laugh, slipping the handkerchief from his fingers and blotting away the evidence. "How gallant of you to ignore my foolishness and what a hen-wit I've become."

"You are neither fool nor fowl but simply human."

"Hush," she said, swatting the center of his gray waistcoat with the folded linen. "Practically everyone here believes I'm nothing more than a hollow shell. You must keep my secret."

"Then it is *our* secret." He took the handkerchief from her. Propriety demanded that he release her at the same time or at least step apart from her. Instead, he did what seemed more appropriate and curled his hand over hers. And the moment he did, he knew this was the right decision. Her small, soft hand fit perfectly within his, as if her bones had been chiseled from his own. "They don't even deserve to know the truth of your nature."

Curiosity, and perhaps even surprise, lifted her brows, her head tilting slightly to one side. "What truth is that?"

"That you are clever, and your wit is subtle but sharp. Nothing escapes your notice," he said, stroking his thumb along the seam of her glove. "And you possess more grace and poise than any other woman in all of England."

As he continued his declaration, her gaze drifted from his eyes to his mouth, as if to see the words he spoke for better understanding. But her focus stirred him. The heat of his body rose ten degrees at least. The air between them—what little there was of it—warmed and turned fragrant. A sweet and earthy scent of rose and sandalwood, made of her perfume and his shaving soap, filled his nostrils. Their combined fragrance merged with the leather-bound books and the faint tangy citrus of the furniture polish, creating a unique and thoroughly potent aphrodisiac.

For the second time, he told himself that he should put distance between them. And if she would have given the barest hint of discomfort, he would have done so. Instead, his feet ignored this command and shifted closer to stand on either side of her slippers, the soft folds of her skirts tucked between his thighs.

Still holding her hand, the length of her forearm now rested at an angle between them. Her white gloves puckered slightly at her wrist, and he worried his thumb into the crease, thinking about how this kid leather was the only thing between his touch and her bare flesh.

His gaze shifted to where the sleeve of his coat brushed the outer swell of her breast. All he saw was another barrier. And in that instant, he hated his tailor for having sewn this coat. Hated society's strictures that forced him to don clothes at all.

A somewhat confused-sounding puff of air escaped her lips. "Anyone else would have remarked on what they saw of me on the outside."

"And they are all fools."

By the fresh clarity in her gaze, he knew she was seeing him. When a fond smile curved her lips and she lifted her face, he knew she saw more too.

He was not like everyone else. He was not merely Bram's insignificant half brother. He was not his messenger either. In fact, Max was...

Kissing her. His mouth descended to her soft, dewy lips with a sudden impetuousness that left him reeling. He wasn't even aware of moving. Yet somehow he released her hand so that he could frame her face—a tender gesture that did not match the quick escalation of need within him.

Her mewl of surprise stopped him, however. He drew back marginally, breathing hard and heavy after only a moment, and prepared an apology in his mind. "Forgive me. I—"

But before he could finish, she made that throaty sound again, gripped the lapels of his coat, and pressed her lips to his.

Juliet. His blood cheered her name. His mouth slanted over hers, urging her lips apart. At first, her tongue shyly waited behind her teeth, tentatively bumping against his, only offering the barest hint of sherry flavor that lingered there. Then a tremor quaked through her. He felt it when she arched into him—breasts, stomach, and hips all tantalizingly close. And in that moment, Max hated white satin as much as he hated wool.

But honestly, ridding her of this dress after a first kiss should have been the last thing on his mind. The first thing should have been the fact that they were both at a dinner party. Her parents were the hosts. They would not serve dinner without them and likely would have noticed their absences immediately.

Unfortunately, none of those thoughts occurred to him until he heard a man cough and clear his throat. Juliet must have heard it too because she broke away from their kiss with a gasp, her gloved fingertips covering her lips as if to hide the evidence.

But it was too late.

Lord Granworth, an impossibly wealthy, elderly states-man, stood in the doorway. Over his shoulder were three other guests—apparent late arrivals, who were all being escorted by a wide-eyed maid who kept looking from Juliet to Max as if they were Adam and Eve caught naked in the garden of Eden.

If given another few minutes perhaps…

No. Max refused to think of that now. He needed to keep his head about him.

With this one ungoverned act, he'd just ruined Juliet. Tainted her virtue in the eyes of society. And there was only one way to make amends—they would have to marry.

For a short duration, they would be pariahs. However, in time they would be welcomed back into society. Since he was a man without means, he would learn a trade to find an income, the same way that his friend Jack Marlowe had. Then Max and Juliet would find a modest house and begin a family. He could see it all, their lives laid out perfectly before them.

Max took a breath, certain of his course. All in all, it was almost a blessing that Lord Granworth had stumbled upon them when he did.

The baron sent his party and the maid on ahead and dis-creetly stepped back into the hall, while still providing his chaperonage, albeit *after* the transgression.

Standing in front of Juliet, Max took her hand and bowed over it. "I will set matters aright. I promise. We will marry." Saying the words aloud caused a surge of elation within him. He was breathless with it. "With your father's permission, we will ride to Gretna Green in the morning."

Juliet turned pale. "*My father*—no. I cannot do that to you."

A smile touched his lips as he shook his head. Did she believe he was merely being gallant again? Surely even she knew the gravity of their situation.

"This was a mistake. I'm sorry, Max." And before he could stop her, she ran from the room.

Max moved to follow, but with Granworth there, and Juliet rushing toward the stairs, which likely led to the family chambers, he stopped.

By the time he turned around, he saw Mr. White striding toward him, a glower knitting his brow. Obviously, he'd heard—and likely every other guest had as well.

Max straightened his shoulders. "With your permission, Mr. White, I request an audience."

"It would be better if you left. Immediately." White's glower turned harder, revealing his anger and immeasurable disappointment. Then, lifting a shaking hand, he raked it through his hair. It was the only time Max had ever seen him without his composure intact. In fact, White's entire being seemed to vibrate with impotent rage.

Max felt as contrite as possible. "Yes, sir. I understand, however—"

"You may return in the morning when I have a cooler head."

Hearing the edge of desperation in White's voice, Max stowed his request. After all, it would do him no good if his future father-in-law loathed him. "Of course. My apologies, sir."

With a bow, Max turned on his heel and left the party. By tomorrow, he would have a plan to offer. The interim hours would also allow Juliet to ease into an understanding of the situation. They would marry and, most important, Max would make her happy. No matter what.

It wasn't until the following morning that Max learned of Juliet's elopement.

"The family has gone to Lord Granworth's estate in Somerset, sir," their butler said at the door.

Max refused to believe it.

He shouldered his way inside, prepared to demand an audience with White. Max wasn't going to leave here without Juliet. He had a carriage waiting, a satchel packed, and just enough money for them to stay a few weeks at an inn until the gossip died down. Damn it all, he even had a sapphire ring in his pocket!

But as he took in the scene around him—the maids and footmen bustling about, draping linens over the furniture, lowering the main chandelier to cover it as well—he realized it was true.

And Juliet was gone.

"Sir, if I may," the butler said, extending his hand, a missive pinched between this thumb and forefinger. "This was supposed to go out with the post, but since you are here…"

His name and address were looped elegantly on the small square of parchment. Numbly, he took the letter and opened it.

Max,

I apologize, both for what I am doing and for what I did last evening. I cannot begin to explain my own actions and

profound regret at their results. I hardly know myself any
longer.

The clarity I'd hoped to find this morning is still absent,
and so I made the choice that better suits all parties involved.

~~Yours affect~~

Warmest regards,

J

Max stared down at the letter and then slowly crumpled it
in his fist. He'd been wrong about Juliet. If she could believe
a word she'd written, then she never truly saw him. Worse,
she left without giving him a chance to prove her wrong, dis-
counting him like all the others had.

And he would never forgive her for it.

CHAPTER ONE

May 1825

The Season Standard—the Daily Chronicle of Consequence

This humble paper fears a messenger's fate as we report the latest news from our illustrious committee. Once more, as one month wanes and another waxes, we are left in want. This Season's Original has yet to be named!

Hold fast, dear readers! For we have received the news that we shall have our Original at month's end. Even more scintillating, we have learned that there remain only two candidates on the list. Two!

We are all eagerness!

Yet even our anticipation must pale in comparison to that of our Marquess of Th— and, resident goddess, Lady G—, who, by all accounts, have wagered on the outcome. Scandalous! Though we are not certain what the stakes could be, we do know that our contest promises to be quite the show!

" '**Q**uite the show,' *indeed*," Juliet Granworth grumbled to herself.

Lowering onto one of two silver-striped chairs, she cast a withering glance down at the newspaper that taunted her.

It was bad enough that Cousin Zinnia's butler saw fit to leave the *Standard* on the foyer table so that it had been the first thing she'd read in the morning. But this evening, another copy sat on the low oval table in Marjorie Harwick's blue parlor.

Juliet couldn't escape it. Therefore, arranging her emerald green skirts, she did her best to ignore it.

"*Botheration.* Who left this dreadful paper on the table?" Marjorie asked, bustling into the room. Immediately, she picked up the scandal sheet, pinching it at the corner like a rat by the tail, and scuttled it from the room.

In the meantime, Cousin Zinnia—*Lady Cosgrove*—progressed in slow, refined movements toward the blue damask settee. Seemingly, she took little notice of Marjorie's activity. Her finely lined countenance remained lovely and serene, her focus solely on the art of pedestrianism.

"There now. Much better," Marjorie said as she returned an instant later, flitting past Zinnia—the proverbial tortoise and the hare. The two friends couldn't have been more different from each other.

For Marjorie, it was common to see tendrils of gray escaping the loose, dark coiffure, and typically, an easy smile lifted her rounded cheeks. Zinnia Cosgrove, on the other hand, never left her chamber with a flaxen or silver hair out of place. Her posture was faultless, her smiles hard won but worth the effort.

At seven and twenty, Juliet was more than twenty years younger than they were, but even so, she found a comfortable companionship with them. She would like to think that her own demeanor was a perfect blend of these two.

The truth was, however, that Juliet was more reserved than approachable. In fact, from what she'd been told, most of the women in her family were the same—elegant, outwardly aloof, and renowned for their beauty. But Juliet often wondered if they all shared something else—an overwhelming desire to go mad.

Some days Juliet wanted to fling open the nearest window sash and scream.

And it was all Max's fault.

"Good evening, Saunders." A familiar baritone called from the foyer and drifted in through the open parlor door. Max.

Drat it all! He was a veritable devil. Only she didn't have to *speak* his name but simply *think* it for him to appear. She should have known better than to allow her thoughts to roam without a leash to tug them back to heel.

"I did not realize Lord Thayne would be attending dinner this evening," Zinnia said, her spine rigid as she perched on the edge of her cushion and darted a quick, concerned glance toward Juliet.

Marjorie looked to the open door, her brows knitted. "I did not realize it either. He said that he was attending—"

"Lord Fernwold's," Max supplied as he strode into the room, his dark blue coat parting to reveal a gray waistcoat and fitted blue trousers. He paused long enough to bow his dark head in greeting—at least to his mother and Zinnia. To Juliet, he offered no more than perfunctory scrutiny before heading to the sideboard, where a collection of crystal decanters waited. "The guests were turned away at the door. His lordship's mother is suffering a fever."

Juliet felt the flesh of her eyelids pucker slightly, her lashes drawing together. It was as close as she could come to glaring at him while still leaving her countenance unmoved. The last thing she wanted was for him, or anyone, to know how much his slight bothered her.

Marjorie tutted. "Again? Agnes seemed quite hale this afternoon in the park. Suspiciously, this has happened thrice before on the evenings of her daughter-in-law's parties. I tell you, Max, I would never do such a thing to your bride."

Max turned and ambled toward them, the stems of three sherry glasses in one large hand and a whiskey in the other. He stopped at the settee first, offering one to his mother and another to Zinnia. "Nor would you need to, for I would never marry a woman who would tolerate the manipulation." Then he moved around the table and extended a glass to Juliet, lowering his voice as he made one final comment. "Nor one whose slippers trod only the easiest path."

She scoffed. If marriage to Lord Granworth had been easy, then she would hate to know the alternative.

"I would not care for sherry this evening," Juliet said. And in retaliation against Max's rudeness, she reached out and curled her fingers around his whiskey.

Their fingers collided before she slipped the glass free. If she hadn't taken him off guard, he might have held fast. As it was, he opened his hand instantly as if scalded by her touch. But she knew that wasn't true because the heat of his skin nearly blistered her. The shock of it left the underside of her fingers prickly and somewhat raw.

To soothe it, she swirled the cool, golden liquor in the glass. Then, before lifting it to her lips, she met his gaze. His irises were a mixture of earthy brown and cloud gray. Years ago, those eyes were friendly and welcoming but now had turned cold, like puddles reflecting a winter sky. And because it pleased her to think of his eyes as mud puddles, that was what she thought of when she took a sip. Unfortunately, she didn't particularly care for whiskey and fought to hide a shudder as the sour liquid coated her tongue.

Max mocked her with a salute of his dainty goblet and tossed back the sherry in one swallow. Then the corner of his mouth flicked up in a smirk.

She knew that mouth intimately—the firm warm pressure of those lips, the exciting scrape of his teeth, the mesmeric skill of his tongue…

Unbidden warmth simmered beneath her skin as she recalled the kiss that had ruined her life. And for five years, she'd paid a dire price for one single transgression—a regretful and demeaning marriage, the sudden deaths of her parents, and the loss of everyone she held dear.

By comparison, returning to London to reclaim her life as a respected widow should have been simple. And it would have been if Max hadn't interfered.

She'd been set on purchasing the townhouse where she had once lived with her parents on this very street, willing to pay any amount to the current owners in order to do so. To her, it was the ideal place to begin anew. Then, as luck would have it, that very house had been up for sale after having been abandoned. It was as if the Fates were guiding her home. Or at least it had felt that way until Max had bought the property out from under her nose.

Why did he have to hinder her fresh start?

Of course, she knew the answer. She'd wounded his ego years ago, and her return only served as a reminder. He didn't want her living four doors down from his mother—or likely within forty miles of him.

But that decision wasn't his to make, or anyone else's. After the deaths of her parents, she'd asked Lord Granworth to purchase their townhouse for her, but the tyrant had refused, just as he had with any request she made.

And now, Juliet wasn't about to be cowed or manipulated by another man. Not for as long as she lived.

"And speaking of marriage," Marjorie interjected, her tone a touch gayer than usual, "Wolford's wedding to Miss Pimm was quite beautiful, even for a last-minute affair. Wouldn't you agree, Zinnia?"

"With the pear trees in bloom just beyond the chapel, I daresay I've never attended a prettier ceremony." Zinnia looked to Juliet, as if in commiseration. "A grove of lilacs would also make a fine setting. They'll be in full bloom by week's end."

Juliet's thoughts were in a muddle at the moment—all thanks to Max—and she was trying to guess how they'd landed on the topic of the Earl of Wolford's recent marriage to Adeline Pimm.

Though perhaps, she reasoned, they were merely speaking of weddings in general because of an upcoming event. "I don't recall receiving an invitation to a wedding ball or breakfast this week. Have I forgotten one?"

"Perhaps Lady Granworth requires a meadow of forget-me-nots to aid her memory," Max quipped as he took the chair beside hers, when there were two others open that were a more comfortable distance away. This time, he lifted his own glass of whiskey in a salute but only after a pointed glance down to the one still untouched, for the most part, in her grasp. Then he directed his attention to the others. "Though, to be honest, I do not recall who is to be married this week either."

"No one that I know of," Marjorie answered with a careless wave of her hand. "I simply remarked on your friend's wedding. And since you are in search of a bride, perhaps you would give thought to asking Wolford for the use of his chapel."

Max shifted in his chair, no longer looking quite so smug. "Right. Well, since I have not yet begun to court any debutante, the pear trees will have lost their petals by the time I have decided on one."

"But you'll want to decide soon," Marjorie said, setting her glass on the table. "We are surely past mid-Season."

Unable to resist a chance to needle Max, Juliet chimed in. "Never fear. You have weeks before the peonies bloom. Though you should be warned of the insects—those blossoms are crawling with ants. Hardly the most romantic of flowers." She shook her head slowly and tsked. "It is a pity, really, that in your haste to be married, you will likely have peonies at your wedding."

"That would be unfortunate," Zinnia said with a sage nod. They had both read Charlotte de la Tour's *La Language des Fleurs*, and peonies represented shame.

In truth, they would have been the perfect flowers for Juliet's own wedding.

Max glared at her, his dark brows lowered, the flesh between them furrowing into three distinct vertical lines. "I am more concerned with finding the most *suitable* bride for me than with the frivolity of the foliage in bloom."

From their sordid history, Juliet knew his statement was meant to be a jab at her. The blasted man loved to argue. Regrettably, he had a knack for knowing the pressure points to incite her ire. "I feel sorry for the *poor dear* already. She will likely be married in winter, with nothing but dead twigs sticking up from the ground on her path to the church."

"But no," Marjorie said quickly. "Max wants to be married by summer before settling into his estate in Lancashire."

This news surprised Juliet. She knew that his search for a bride had intensified since he'd recently inherited a marquessate, but she didn't know that he planned to leave London.

Quite an interesting development, to be sure. "Then you will have no need for a house in town."

Which posed an opportunity for her to finally buy hers back from him.

"You are mistaken. I will have every need for a house in town when I am here." Max stood and turned slightly to loom over her. "You had your chance…"

Max paused on a breath, the gray mixture in his irises turning steely. In that instant, Juliet thought he was speaking of his forced-by-circumstance wedding proposal five years ago. And she might have even noticed a sharp twinge of regret beneath her breast too…until he continued.

"But you lost the wager."

Then, before she knew what he was about, he slid his middle finger into her glass and slipped it from her grasp.

She clenched her now-empty fist, fighting to hold on to her composure. "I did not lose—*neither* of us won. There is a difference. You knew that I had intended to purchase that house, but you used your influence to swindle it from me."

Taking a step back, Max made a point of draining her glass in front of her. "The banker holding the deed liked my price better."

As a wealthy widow, Juliet could have had the deed to the house in her possession if the old curmudgeon, Mr. Woldsley, hadn't detested discussing business with a woman. He'd pushed aside her offer for weeks, likely waiting for the first man to come along and outbid her. In fact, he probably would have sold to any male who underbid her as well.

"It still was ungentlemanly of you, Maxwell," Marjorie chided and offered a sympathetic headshake to Juliet.

"Which is why I gave her fair chance of winning the wager." He lifted the two empty glasses in a helpless gesture. "But now our wager has concluded, and there is nothing to be done. I have already hired laborers to improve the structure. They work several days of the week, earning a wage to feed their families. My conscience would not permit me to sell it."

Oooh! Max goaded her terribly. But the only witnesses attesting to this fact were the fingernails cutting into the soft flesh of her palm. He was the reason she'd entered into that foolish wager in the first place.

He'd claimed that anyone could be named the Season's *Original*. All the while, he knew how much that title had once meant to her. Not because she'd wanted to be the most sought-after and admired member of the *ton* but to have her choice of any husband she desired. *And* he knew very well that, years ago, she'd wanted to marry his brother.

Juliet couldn't help but wonder how different her life might have been if she had.

So, two months ago, when her dear cousin Lilah had volunteered to be transformed into the *Original*, Juliet had wagered against Max without thinking of the repercussions of failure. All she'd wanted was to give Lilah the chance to make the choice that was right for her. The choice that Juliet had not made for herself.

Fortunately for Lilah, it worked.

Yet Juliet still needed to forge her own path. And it mattered that her new beginning start in the place where she had once believed anything was possible. Therefore, it had to be that house.

"The *Original* has not been decided, so the wager is not exactly over," she reasoned. "Even today's edition of the *Standard* agrees." Though apparently, the editor failed to realize that their initial bargain was over, with neither Juliet nor Max the victor.

His brows lifted dubiously. "But we know that our choices will not be named."

As it happened, both of the people they had chosen in their wager were now married, which left them ineligible to be named.

"True," she hemmed. "However, there is something we both desire—I want my house, and you want me to leave London."

"Correct."

Finding it more amenable to address a problem when her blood flowed unhindered from head to toe and back up again, she stood and moved toward the back of the silver-striped chair before continuing. "Then I propose another wager."

Max set the glasses down on the table and folded his arms across his chest. A familiar tension coursed through him, the superfine wool pulling taut over his biceps and shoulder blades. He knew better than to enter into any bargain with Juliet. Yet if he didn't know any better, he might think that he'd purposely goaded her for this exact purpose.

And if that were true, then he must be going mad. "A new wager, when the last one is not cold in its grave? I humored you once but no more."

"'Humored' me?" She offered him a cool, practiced smile that she had mastered during the past five years. "The previous wager was all your doing, if you'll recall."

Nothing in her lovely countenance gave away that he'd struck a nerve. No unbecoming red blotches marred her flawless complexion. Her tone remained melodious. Her bearing, ever-poised. And yet, there was a flash of something in her eyes that reminded him of the woman he used to know. Irritation? Anger? Passion?

He couldn't be certain. All he knew was that he loathed the part of him that stirred because of it.

"The first challenge was more about satisfying a curiosity. I'd wondered if this was merely a game for you or if you truly desired that house for a more personal reason." He waited a beat for her to fill in the blanks. When she didn't, he shrugged and continued. "Though it couldn't mean too much to you if you were willing to leave London altogether."

"Is not the first step of a new journey the most fearsome, yet promising the greatest reward?" Mother asked, offering a nugget of wisdom in Juliet's favor.

Max knew that Juliet was not one to take such risks. She preferred the ground beneath her feet to remain perfectly paved and without a single rut to set her off balance—like marriage to a man with no fortune would have done.

"I had every intention of winning." Juliet lifted her hand from the back of the chair, pointing one manicured fingernail toward the ceiling. "And moreover, your stipulation was that I could not buy a house in London, not that I had to leave."

He caught his gaze straying for an instant—nothing more than an unbidden skim down the elegant column of her throat, a cursory sweep over the ripe swells rising above the gold embroidered edge of her green bodice—to the petal-soft hand that had so recently brushed his. But there, he noticed tiny, red, crescent-shaped impressions from her fingernails pressing into her palm. Perhaps she wasn't as cool and composed as she wanted to appear.

Yet the instant he registered her words, his chin jerked up. She had just admitted to twisting their bargain to suit her own desires. "You were not even planning to honor the wager."

"*Au contraire*, to the very letter," she said with a quick tsk of reproach. "However, you never said that I was to be banished from London altogether. Do try to be more specific next time."

He clenched his teeth. "Then I would draw up a contract, so that there would be no misunderstanding."

"And I would be amenable to that. An unbreakable bargain, to which we both must adhere."

That *something* flared in her sapphire eyes once more, causing his breath to stall in his throat and cutting off his immediate reply.

His mother spoke before he could. "Then what is your proposal, dear?"

Juliet arched a brow at Max, as if to gauge his willingness to listen. He offered a nod in response.

"The *Standard* claims that the contest is down to two candidates," she began. "As there are two of us, the matter is simple. I shall write down a name, as will you. Keeping our guesses secret, we hand them to an outside party and witness"—Juliet gestured to his mother and Lady Cosgrove—"who then take those names and place them into a box, locking it tightly for safekeeping until the *Standard* posts the results…whenever that may be."

"Undoubtedly there will be an *Original* by the end of this month," Mother said with a certainty that he would question later. "My concern, however, is for you, Juliet. I fear what will happen should you not…win."

"Leaving London would be a heavy price, indeed," Lady Cosgrove added with a dignified shake of her head.

Juliet batted a defiant glance in his direction. "I am too determined to give up, no matter what *obstacle* stands in my way."

Max chuckled, for he was equally determined to see her live anywhere else. He would never give in. Letting her live in the house where she'd once spurned him, only to eventually see her take another husband, was the last thing Max would concede.

"What should you do if both of you choose the same candidate who is then named the *Original?*" Lady Cosgrove asked.

Juliet tapped her finger against her chin. The gesture drew his attention to the purse of her lips and the plumpness of the bottom one. He remembered the silken texture of that flesh, the flavor...how it felt between his teeth. *Damn.*

It was pure folly to allow his thoughts to venture to that one moment. It had been years ago, after all. Surely, he would have forgotten about it entirely if Juliet had stayed in Bath. But with her return, the past had come flooding back, threatening to drown him in that single memory.

He was willing to do anything to put miles between them once more.

"In that event, it would be a draw," Juliet said in response. "Since both of us cannot win, then neither of us would. I would remain a thorn in Max's side, and he, the bane of my very existence."

Unable to help it, he grinned at her flippant quip. "But when I win, you will find another part of England in which to live."

"Oh yes, I hear that Lancashire has some *fine* properties," Juliet answered immediately, almost as if she'd given thought to following him to his country estate and making his life a living hell.

Max's arms flexed, and he was about to warn her that he would not take kindly to such an action, when she suddenly laughed.

"What a temper you have, Max," she said, proof that her observational skills had not diminished. A prim smile curled the corners of her mouth. "You needn't worry that I will scamper about the country looking to needle you. Once this has concluded, we will go our very separate ways and be all the happier for it."

"Hmm…" Mother murmured, standing. "But what if neither of you wins? This could go on for years."

"Absolutely not," Max argued. He couldn't survive it. "Once this is over, it will be finished for good."

"It would be another draw," Juliet said, ignoring him and answering Mother's question. "Therefore, Max will want to choose his candidate with great care to have a chance at all."

He fixed her with a hard stare. "One month, Lady Granworth—that is all. *And* I will list that in the contract."

Her hesitation lasted only for a minute before she surrendered a nod.

"Good," he said. "With such a reward, I will only accept victory."

In fact, with the name he had in mind, there was no way he could lose.

Chapter Two

Bright sunlight shone down over the manicured park at Lord and Lady Minchon's estate. Rows of boxwood lined the long, grassy avenue, with ivy and moss-shrouded statues at every forty paces. The manicured garden was in the design of a *patte d'oie*, splitting off into three directions to form a giant goosefoot upon the lawn. One lane hosted a Grecian folly. Another, a shaded, tree-lined arcade. And the last was a mystery because the large fountain at the intersection blocked Juliet's view.

Taking the advice of a nearby alabaster nymph with grayish green ivy draped over her brow, Juliet lowered the pink netting from her wide straw bonnet.

Several of the young debutantes in attendance carried lace parasols. As soon as the footmen brought trays of miniature pastel cakes and tea around, however, they would learn their error. One cannot enjoy a garden party without the use of both hands.

Experience came with age, she supposed, and both had their advantages. For instance, when she was younger, it would have bothered her to arrive at a party unaccompanied. Having a friend or even her parents on her arm had helped her to endure the not-so-subtle whispers about her appearance. Because of her features and coloring, the *ton* had labeled her the *goddess* during her first weeks in society. And by the time she'd reached her third year, she'd become the *hollow goddess*, with many believing her to be shallow and unfeeling. Even her late husband had possessed that idea about her.

Few took the time to know her. For if they did, they would know that an empty shell would have crumbled during the terrible years of her marriage. Oh, but there were so many times she'd wished to be hollow. That way, the demeaning statements, the threats, and the degradation would have slipped right through her. Instead, they'd settled inside her, firmly latched like insect larvae feeding on the underside of leaves. The more Lord Granworth's words had filled her, the emptier she'd felt.

"Attending the picnic alone, I see," Max said from just over her shoulder, adding a cluck of his tongue.

She started, her heart and lungs lurching free of those dark musings. Of course, outwardly, she revealed nothing. Concealing her reactions had become an art she practiced. Her parents had taught her that a lady never revealed her true feelings. That was bad form. But what had begun as a lesson in good manners had quickly turned into an act of rebellion shortly after her debut. She had vowed never to let society know that their lack of true friendship and scornful monikers ever affected her.

Stopping on the lawn beside her, Max touched the brim of his tan willow-weave top hat with his gloved fingers. The pale shades of his camel coat and buckskin breeches accentuated his dark features, making his complexion swarthy and exotic compared with the pale, ruddy-cheeked gentlemen in attendance. Though, handsome or not, at least none of those gentlemen were smirking at her.

"And your companion is in your pocket, I suppose?" She glanced down at his green waistcoat toward the folded horizontal slits cut into the cashmere. A stray gold thread at the corner of his pocket wanted her attention, practically begging for her to pinch it off with her fingers, but doing so suggested an intimacy that not even her husband would have permitted when he was alive.

Besides, it would also make tongues wag. As it was, heads were already turned in their direction.

"Perhaps," Max said, turning marginally toward her. "The pockets are too small for me to search, though you are welcome to discover their contents."

If it were any other man, she might imagine that he was flirting with her. Since this was Max, who hated her above all others, however, she knew better. Therefore, she chose to ignore the thread *and* the comment. "I was to attend with Zinnia and Ivy, but the former was concerned that the abundant sunshine would cause spots, and the latter was unwell."

"Nothing serious, I hope." And to Max's credit, his sincerity was evident.

"An effect of her delicate condition," she said, referring to the baby that the Duchess of Vale was carrying. "I am told that the early stages are a trial for some women."

Of course, Juliet had no experience in such matters, nor any opportunity to hope for such. Lord Granworth never wanted anything, even pregnancy, to alter his most prized object—*her*. She'd been for display only, to admire but not to touch.

Thankfully, Max did not comment further on the topic. He stirred again, shifting his stance and staring out across the park. "Yet you still chose to attend, even without an escort. One might wonder at the reason. *Or* if you'd planned to meet someone."

"Are you intimating that I have a lover here? That I chose the Minchons' park for a tryst?" A wry laugh escaped her. "I could say the same of you, as you spend your afternoons in the gallery of the House of Commons and not attending social events. Are you here for a clandestine meeting or perhaps even for a bride?"

His mouth quirked in something just short of a smile. "We have a wager to think of, have we not? Perhaps I am here to ensure my candidate's success."

Three days had passed since they'd signed the contract and cast their ballots for this Season's *Original*, handing them over to Mr. Saunders for safekeeping. At first, they had intended to entrust Marjorie and Zinnia with the task. Yet after careful thought, they decided that the honorable butler was the better choice. Mostly because Saunders would not inadvertently use his position in society to influence the outcome.

Since that day, Juliet had not found herself at an engagement where Max was present. And the only reason she'd noted his absence was the simple fact that the past two events had been rather dull. So much so, in fact, that even an argument with her nemesis would have been preferable.

"And perhaps I am here for the same purpose," she said, using her most aloof and mysterious tone. Yet, admittedly, she was curious over Max's selection. Though passing a glance over the guests at large, she did not see a single debutante or gentleman to shake her confidence.

Her own candidate, Viscount Ellery, was not in attendance. Therefore, if Max was here to spy on his own, she was certain that they had chosen different names. And even more certain of her own victory.

"Then again, perhaps I am merely here to take in the fine weather," Max said, his tone dipping lower into an aura of mystery as well. With a sideways glance, he suddenly shook his head. "Though it is a shame that you have come unprepared. I see that most of the other women have parasols to protect their complexions. One single spot, *Goddess*, and you could lose your moniker."

He was trying to spark her ire, she knew, and she fought all the harder to remain unaffected.

"I am amazed at how you can still underestimate me, Max." Proving her point, a dozen footmen in bright cerulean livery descended the terrace steps, toting silver trays. She gestured to the bronze-handled walking stick beneath the grip of Max's large hand. "I hope you are adept at balancing a saucer on your hat."

By the sudden twitch of his jaw, his gaze on the servants, she saw the instant his foible occurred to him. But Max was nothing if not quick-witted and decisive, for he summarily tucked the stick beneath his arm.

He dusted his hands together. "Every problem has a solution."

She pretended to turn her attention to the seam of her lace mitts and, in that split second, spied Max's gaze sweep down the length of her pink-and-white striped walking costume. A surge of heat, that had nothing to do with the sun, filled her stomach and radiated outward. She was accustomed to being watched and scrutinized by men and women alike, so it shouldn't have made her feel anything at all. Yet there was something in the way that Max studied her that caused the unbidden response.

She wasn't entirely sure what it was. Though perhaps the reason stemmed from knowing that he disliked her but seemed to observe her against his will. A peculiar sense of triumph filled her at the thought.

"Mmm…" she mused. "You are clever, to be sure. Yet you missed a perfect opportunity."

"And what was that?"

"Why, to ask me to feed you cakes, of course." With a jaunty wave of her fingers, she left him to stand there, as she relished the stunned, somewhat slack-jawed expression on his face.

Max stared after Juliet's retreating figure. Her hat was tilted enough to show her eyes dancing with delight beneath the pink netting as she glanced over her shoulder at him. And he might have laughed as well at her cleverness if he hadn't been distracted by the view.

Her dressmaker should be sent to gaol for such a design. The gathers and pleats revealed the perfect delineation of her narrow waist and the slight flair of her hips, as if she wore no garments at all. He felt as if he'd fallen victim to a mesmerist's charm, which swayed ever-confidently back and forth.

Still recovering from her suggestion that he should have asked her to feed him cake, he couldn't seem to banish the image from his mind. Correction—*images*—for several, highly detailed visions instantly formed, including various methods and positions in which to indulge in cake.

Fighting against these errant thoughts, he reminded himself that *one cannot eat his cake and have it as well*. Not with Juliet. Besides, given their rivalry since her return, he doubted that her comment was intended as a flirtation. More likely, it was a device of distraction, the same way that members of Parliament argued against a bill by attacking their opponents on a more personal level.

And if Max knew anything at all, he knew that Juliet was a skilled adversary. As a widow as well as an experienced player among the *ton*, she knew exactly how to use her wiles. He wondered how many others had fallen under the same spell, only to have found in the end that it was all a ruse.

Abruptly, his mood darkened. He didn't want to think about the past and how he'd once thought she was a different person. Nor did he want to imagine all the other men who'd been lured by her…cake-feeding skills.

But *did* she have a lover? He couldn't seem to rid his mind of the question.

There had been no whispered allegations regarding that fact. In truth, since her return, the only name hers was linked to was *his*, which was confirmation that the *ton* was frequently misled and misinformed. Clearly, society hadn't an inkling of the insurmountable animosity between them.

Still, that did not stop him from wondering if her sly wit wasn't the only thing sly about her. Hadn't she already admitted to wanting to skirt the stipulations of their previous wager? So was her remark just now truly a flirtation and nothing more? Or a means of distraction?

The answers shouldn't matter to him, but for reasons beyond good sense, they did.

Of course, it was easy to imagine that she was merely trying to ensure her victory over him. Perhaps her candidate was, indeed, in attendance.

In direct line of his thoughts, Juliet paused to greet the Earl of Dovermere and his eldest daughter, Lady Piper Laurent. They shared an acquaintance because Dovermere was now father-in-law to Juliet's cousin Lilah. It seemed likely that they were merely exchanging pleasantries. However, it could also be that Juliet had chosen Lady Piper as her candidate for the *Original*.

Max mused on the idea and found that it wasn't a terrible plan. After all, a month ago Lady Piper had made one or two appearances in the *Standard*, which listed her as a favorite for the *Original*. And now, with Dovermere's son, Jack Marlowe—lately Viscount Locke—in good standing among the *ton*, Piper had a sporting chance.

She was poised, pretty, and refined, as most debutantes were. And having been Jack's friend for years, Max had spoken with Piper from time to time and found her sharp wit was like her brother's. The anonymous committee who selected the *Original* could make a worse choice and, in the past, had done so. Though to Max's mind, Lady Piper Laurent did not have a chance against the name he'd written on his ballot.

Thinking of his certain victory, he smiled to himself.

Glancing around the park, he studied the faces beneath the shaded brims. Every gaze seemed to flit toward Juliet. Young women were fussing with their parasols, closing them and setting them aside to sip their teas, and all the while staring with transparent envy at Juliet as she progressed, unencumbered, down the avenue toward the fountain. The men wore expressions of admiration. Of course, some were far too admiring, bordering on blatant lust, as if she were walking solely for their pleasure. And Max had a sudden desire to blacken a few eyes.

Not out of jealousy, he told himself. This surge of roiling heat in his gut stemmed from the desire to teach those young bucks a lesson in manners. After all, they were entirely too obvious in their appreciation of her figure.

Normally, Max would laugh and pity them because they did not know what wreckage Juliet tended to leave in her wake, what utter destruction to a man's soul. Today, however, he found that his temperament was not inclined toward humor, sardonic or otherwise.

He blamed it on her, of course. If not for her flirtatious comment, he would be enjoying the fresh air and sunshine while keeping a surreptitious eye on his candidate. In fact, he should be thinking about finding a bride. Instead, he could not stop thinking about cake and wondering if, perhaps—

"M'lord," a footman said, interrupting his thoughts and stopping in front of him with a confection-laden tray.

Max cast a cursory glance over the lace serviettes that were smaller than the palm of his hand. Were gentlemen expected to pick up one of those dainty bits of frippery merely to eat an iced cake that was no larger than a single bite? He chuckled to himself, prepared to send the footman away and to return to his prior thoughts. Then, suddenly, it occurred to him that an opportunity lay before him.

No doubt, Juliet thought she had bested him with her parting words, expecting to take him off guard. And she had. But perhaps it was time he called her bluff by issuing a challenge of his own.

Removing his gloves, he took a serviette and *two* dainty pink cakes before setting off in her direction. Not wanting to give the appearance of pursuit to any of the other guests or to his prey, he ambled about, admiring topiaries and pausing to nod a greeting to those whom he encountered.

Since he'd inherited his title, the *ton* had taken a sudden interest in making his acquaintance. The marquessate was bestowed on him after the death of a fourth cousin, whom Max had never met. In fact, his late father had never spoken of the connection either. Suddenly, however, this tragedy had made Max interesting enough to garner all sorts of invitations, gaining the attention of those who'd peered right through him for years. Then again, the fortune and land he'd inherited had likely helped. Society was nothing if not predictable.

By the time Max reached the fountain, Juliet had parted ways with Dovermere and had strolled down a side path dotted with conical cypress and spirals of juniper. Most of the guests were promenading down the other two paths, either along the shaded arcade or in the opposite direction toward a Grecian folly. Though with nothing more than a large moss-covered urn, a hedgerow cabinet at the end of the alley, and no reprieve from the glaring sun, only he and Juliet walked here.

With every step, the soles of his boots sank into the plush grass, effectively muffling his approach. She wasn't too far ahead of him, her pace slow as she took time to study the gardener's work. Lifting her hand, she brushed her fingertips over the evergreen fronds. A breeze stirred, casting a sweet, piney fragrance in his direction. He drew in a deep breath, filling his lungs with it.

He'd always enjoyed the outdoors and knew it was something he had in common with her. Yet there were days he wished he could forget those things.

"Lady Granworth," he said when he was near enough and earned the quick turn of her head. Unfortunately, the shadow beneath the brim of her hat concealed any other reaction that might have slipped through. Though with her next words, he could guess fairly well that it hadn't been a smile of delight.

"Are you determined to spoil my afternoon?" As she squared her shoulders, her chin lifted, exposing a column of creamy skin down her slender throat. And just beneath the edge of that pink netting, her unsmiling lips captured his attention.

As he neared, he could see her narrowed gaze watching him carefully and her quick glance down to the arm he held behind his back.

"How very ungracious of you," he tutted. Now standing before her, he revealed the prize he carried. "I procured those cakes you mentioned earlier. I must say, you piqued my interest as well, for I cannot wait to sample one."

Those lips parted on a soundless gasp. "I will not feed you cake, Max. Imagine the spectacle it would cause."

Then, as she typically did, she turned on her heel to leave. Yet she must have forgotten that there was no escape behind her.

When he saw her steps hesitate, he grinned to himself. "If that is your primary objection, then allow me to point out that we are virtually alone."

"Which is also enough to put our names in tomorrow's *Standard*." Once she reached the urn, her head turned, her hat angling to the left and right, as if she were searching for another exit. When she came to the apparent conclusion that there was none, she finally faced him.

"Our names will be there, regardless." He spread his arms out in a shrug, cakes in one hand, walking stick in the other. "Now, as you can see, I am utterly helpless"—he paused at the sound of her scoff—"and unable to taste the cake that you offered to feed me."

"I made no such offer."

"Then I cannot think of what I heard moments ago unless…"—he lowered his voice—"you were *flirting* with me. But you, the ever-composed Lady Granworth, would never do such a thing."

He wanted to see her color rise, her ire flash, anything. Damn it all, he needed to ruffle her feathers and crawl under her skin. It was the least she owed him.

"I would not even know how to flirt," she boldly lied and without batting an eye.

Wasn't every nuance of flirtation woven into her being? Every downward sweep of her lashes. Every subtle curl of her lips. Every slash of her tongue. Every single breath!

"Oh, I'm certain that is a false statement," he said, keeping his tone smooth and even. "All you have to do is admit to flirting with me, and I'll be on my way."

"I. Admit. Nothing."

He held out his hand. "Then feed me a cake."

She stepped forward so suddenly she nearly startled him in the process. "Fine."

The crisply enunciated word tolled a warning bell within him, advising caution. He had anticipated their continued banter and even her eventual retreat, but not her acquiescence. Instinct told him to be wary. And yet curiosity fixed him to the spot.

Lifting her hand, she slipped the serviette into her delicate palm, the edges draping over fingers. He stared, paying close attention to every movement, noting how her lace mitts left the entire length of her slender fingers exposed. No doubt, like her dress, they were designed for a purpose, bringing to mind thoughts of bared limbs.

Then, with a delicate pinch of her thumb and forefinger, she picked up the first cake.

Anticipation thundered in his chest, neck, and ears simultaneously. She could still balk. Still storm off in a flurry. He was prepared for such a response but no longer assured of it. Perhaps challenging her wasn't the best idea after all.

His gaze shifted from the cake to her eyes, over and again. Her gaze, on the other hand, remained fixed to his as she slowly lifted the cake—

And popped it into her mouth. Then she closed her eyes, a smile curving her lips, while emitting a low murmur of sensual delight.

Max couldn't breathe, couldn't think, couldn't move if someone were to set him on fire. The pulse that had pounded so hard an instant ago abruptly dropped to his trousers, banging like a drum as blood engorged his flesh.

The tip of her pert tongue slipped out to tease him further. The taunt transformed into torture when she licked the pink icing from her fingertip and then her thumb. When she finished, her eyes opened, the blue a brighter, deeper hue than the sky overhead. He found himself unable to look away.

"Delicious," she purred. "So good in fact that I think I'll have another."

She pinched the second cake, her lips parted. But before she could lift it to her mouth—before he knew what he was doing—he seized her wrist.

He was half-tempted, half-wild with the need to kiss her, to lose himself in the silken texture of her lips once more. To haul her into his arms and feel the curves of her body with his hands.

It took every shred of control he possessed not to give in. At least, not completely.

Watching her all the while, he lowered his head and took the cake into his mouth.

He swallowed it without fanfare or appreciation. The dessert he really wanted was still waiting.

He slipped her finger into his mouth next, the dainty pad at the tip more silken and sweet than marzipan. In slow, searching swipes, he laved her flesh, mapping the route of every fine impression, wicking away every last bit of icing. He would have stopped if he was frightening her. Hell, he was startled by his own actions. But when he saw her pupils dilate, her gaze drifting down to his mouth, and then heard the quickening of her breath, he knew she was not afraid of him.

She was one of two things—either wholly, explosively angry or…wholly, explosively *aroused*. And since he'd been the recipient of her temper before, he wagered it was the latter.

A surge of triumph merged with the unleashed desire coursing through him. She could pretend she was cool-headed and aloof all she wanted, but he knew better. Five years ago, that same passion had slipped through the cracks in her composure.

He wanted more. Greedy, he curled his tongue around her, drawing her flesh deeper, and gently grazing the delicate furrows of her knuckle with his teeth.

"*Max.*"

His name shuddered out of her lungs and past her lips, sending a tremor through him. Yet the tinge of vulnerability in her passion-laden plea swiftly brought him to his senses.

With a quick tug, he pulled her closer. Still holding his walking stick, he touched the handle beneath her chin and tilted it up. "Perhaps you should reconsider flirting with your enemy in the future."

CHAPTER THREE

Juliet felt as if she'd barely managed to hold herself together since the moment she stormed away from Max. For heaven's sake, she left the Minchons' party without even a word of farewell. And now, as she closed her bedchamber door, she sagged against it, gasping for breath.

The things he did to her! He'd incited her temper on purpose. He'd just kept needling her and needling her until—like one of Professor Faraday's balloons—she'd exploded.

There was no other way to explain her behavior. She'd never flirted so shamelessly in her life!

Then again, she rarely encountered a gentleman who listened to her long enough for her to make an attempt. Men spoke to her but seldom engaged her in conversation. They were all full of charm, much like the clerks at a haberdashery, and eager for her fortune. Either that, or they were like her late husband and merely wanted a pretty object to hang upon their arms.

But not Max. He was her rival in every sense, but he listened intently to what she said—even if solely to find his next argument.

Forcing her to admit to flirting with him? The gall of that man! Was his ego so fragile that he could not stand the notion of her getting the better of him for one single moment?

Apparently so. For he certainly set out to ensure she would think twice before doing so again.

Pushing away from the door, she tossed her hatpin and hat onto the tufted bench at the foot of her bed. Feeling over-heated, she went to the washbasin in the corner. She needed to press a cool cloth to her throat and the back of her neck.

Stripping off her mitts on the way, she stopped when she caught sight of a pale pink stain on the white lace. Drawing it closer for examination, however, revealed that it wasn't a stain at all. It was icing.

Juliet covered it with her other hand and closed her eyes, trying to banish the fresh memory that assailed her. But it was no use. She remembered every moment as if it left an indelible mark upon her flesh, seared into the whorls of her fingertip.

For an instant, when Max had taken hold of her wrist to stop her from eating that cake, she'd thought he was going to kiss her. And worse than that was the knowledge that she wouldn't have stopped him.

What he did instead was far more wicked. That mouth of his, that tongue, those teeth…were diabolically thorough. Even though he'd only taken one finger into his mouth, she'd felt as if he'd laved her entire body. Of course, she'd never had a man's mouth on her entire person, so the shameful sensa-tion was merely supposition on her part. But now, because of Max, she couldn't stop imagining what it might actually feel like. Hearing conversations from other women, Juliet knew that some men enjoyed the practice. And with the thought, she was suddenly wondering if Max were one of those men…

Behind her, a soft knock fell on the door in the same moment that her maid opened it. "Madame, I have finished the alterations to your gown for this evening," Marguerite said, each word slow and precise but unmistakably accented with her French tongue.

Even though Juliet had given her leave to speak her native language, Marguerite only did so when she was upset. At five and thirty, she was an émigré who was determined to leave her old life behind and wanted, above all else, to be English.

The instant Juliet turned to see the gown, Marguerite made a sound of distress and dropped the lustrous silver garment.

"Oh! But you are *rose*." Beneath a ruffled cap and a coiffure of raven black hair, a spray of fine lines appeared at the corners of Marguerite's eyes. And currently, her hands were gesturing over her throat and voluptuous bosom before shooing Juliet to the standing mirror. "*Oui, rose.*"

Juliet stared at her own reflection. Beneath her jawline and all the way to the beribboned trim of her bodice, her skin was decidedly pink, nearly matching the stripes in her gown. She touched her hand to her flesh, noting the warm temperature. "I must have taken too much sun."

But in the same moment, she also saw that smear upon her glove again, and gradually the pink of her throat turned to a deeper shade.

Suddenly, she wasn't entirely certain of the cause.

She swallowed. "I must be overheated. Please, help me remove this dress."

As the garment gradually fell away, however, Juliet had a startling discovery. From the neck down, her skin was pink...*everywhere.*

Alarmed, she started unlacing her corset. Next came her chemise, even her stockings. Yet still, every inch of her was pink—her slender arms, the globes of her rose-tipped breasts, her ribs and the valley of her stomach, her softly rounded hips, the flesh surrounding the pale downy curls over her sex, and even the tapered length of her legs down to the tops of her feet.

The sun had not done this.

"I do not believe this was caused from the sun, madame," Marguerite said, mimicking Juliet's thoughts. Then she placed the back of her hand on Juliet's forehead and clucked her tongue in distress. "*Vous êtes très chaleureux. Je devrais appeler le médecin.*"

Juliet shook her head. "I do not need a physician. I know perfectly well what has caused this. My temper."

Moving toward the washbasin, she proceeded to explain the afternoon's events, Max's goading of her, his demand for her to admit she'd been flirting with him...but leaving out a few of the details toward the end.

"*Ce bâtard!*" Marguerite spat. "What should it matter if you were flirting? A woman has every right. He cannot force you to admit it."

"Precisely," Juliet agreed, pressing the flannel over her damp flesh.

Marguerite angrily swiped up the garments from the floor. "I hope you shoved that cake in his face."

"I ate it." *At least one of them,* she thought, and drat it all if the memory of what happened to the second one did not sweep over her again.

"Ha! Even better—*Oh!* You are rose again." This time, Marguerite did not drop all the garments but stared quizzically into Juliet's eyes. "And then...what did you do?"

"I, or rather, *he* ate the other cake"—Juliet's voice wavered, and she began to fan herself with the edge of the flannel—"from my fingers."

A slow grin lifted Marguerite's lips, settling into her dark, dancing eyes. "Ah! Now I begin to understand."

Juliet shook her head, adamant. "I'm certain you do not."

"You forget, madame, I know of these things." In France, Marguerite had worked as a skilled modiste in her aunt's shop, which also operated as a brothel for a select group of gentlemen. Marguerite had never hidden her past from Juliet, nor had she once spoken of any regrets. To her, sexual congress was as basic to men—and women alike—as breathing or eating. In fact, Marguerite had frequently suggested that Juliet take a lover, both during and after her marriage to Lord Granworth. "And I know your husband never once colored your skin."

Marguerite's statement was even truer than Juliet cared to admit. To anyone. It was her secret that went to the grave with her late husband. When she had married him five years ago, the only thing she had known about the relationship between husband and wife was what her mother had told her in haste. *"Your husband will lie with you the first night, and then you will be his irrevocably."*

Juliet had shyly confessed as much to Lord Granworth the night of their wedding after he inquired about her level of knowledge. And dutifully, he had lain beside her in the same bed for the duration of the night.

It wasn't until it was already too late that Juliet learned of the contract her father had signed with Lord Granworth. Apparently, Lord Granworth's marriage bargain had stipulations. He'd agreed to pay all of Father's debts for as long as Juliet pleased him, but when her beauty inevitably faded, he would abandon her, albeit arranging for a house and property. Always thinking of ways around contracts, Father hoped that Juliet would give Granworth an heir that would bind them together for a longer duration.

So when Juliet had told her mother, the morning after her wedding night, that Lord Granworth had indeed lain with her and that she hadn't slept a wink because of it, she had unknowingly confirmed that the marriage had been consummated.

What a simpleton she had been! It wasn't until months later, upon hearing the wives of Lord Granworth's sycophants speak of their husbands, that she realized the truth—there was more to consummation than simply lying atop a bed at the same time.

When she'd confronted Lord Granworth, he laughed at her, calling her his *empty-headed ninny*—the least of all his insults—and then stated, matter-of-factly, that an imperfect bride held no appeal for him. He only wished to keep her *preserved* so that he could enjoy the sight of her all the more. And every night, he did. He'd come to her room, asking her to undress for him, pose for him, walk for him. Sometimes he would spend hours looking at her, candidly remarking on how jealous other men were of him. Evidently, when having abundant wealth was not enough to fulfill his need to incite envy in others, he had decided to take a bride who would.

Having purchased a barony solely as a matter of feeding his insatiable ego, he had no desire for an heir either but planned to settle the bulk of his fortune on those who fawned over him the most. He firmly believed that all the other people around him were put upon the earth for one purpose alone—to please him.

Lost in his own arrogance, he likely never imagined that his death would happen without fanfare or an audience to remark on the magnificent spectacle. In fact, the physician claimed he had suffered a heart seizure in his sleep and drifted off peacefully.

The reading of Lord Granworth's will drew a crowd of hundreds of sycophants, all vying for a piece of his fortune. Most of them had left disappointed, tearless, and angry for having been forgotten. In truth, there was only one soul who mourned his loss—his beloved valet, who had been his constant companion for two decades.

Aside from Lord Granworth's valet, actors and artists were the primary recipients of cash monies. Juliet too received a sum of sixty thousand pounds, in addition to the entirety of his collection. The wording of his will—read for all of their social circle in Bath—had been his final act of degradation. *And lastly, to Juliet, Lady Granworth, the exquisitely preserved centerpiece of my art collection, I hereby bequeath…*

Thinking of Lord Granworth and the miserable years she'd endured, the vibrant color drained from her flesh.

"As I said," Juliet reminded her maid, "I was flushed because of my temper. Max brings out the worst in me."

And it was true. Even though Lord Granworth's cruelty had left her feeling hollow, she still had maintained control over her reactions to him. With Max, she felt positively volatile, and that terrified her.

Therefore, as long as she didn't think about this afternoon, her *temper* would not resurface in such dramatic fashion.

Marguerite kept smiling but turned back to her task. "And what should you do if he *brings out the worst in you* at dinner this evening?"

Drat! She hadn't thought of that. Marjorie Harwick had invited both Zinnia and Juliet to dinner again.

And the instant she imagined seeing Max, the color returned.

"Juliet sends her regrets this evening," Lady Cosgrove said to Max's mother as Saunders took her fringed wrap. "Too much sun, I'm afraid."

Max was just heading to the parlor from the study when he'd heard the knock at the door. All afternoon, anticipation had filled him with exhilaration, wondering what Juliet would do to get the better of him. She'd laid the gauntlet down, after all. He'd merely picked it up.

Now it was in her hands again—or at least it had been until the lovely little coward dropped it by refusing to make an appearance. He supposed he should feel somewhat guilty for his part in all this. And yet, he couldn't summon an ounce.

He blamed his lust for competition in addition to his desire to settle matters between them once and for all. Without an adversary, however, his prospects for this evening seemed rather dull.

"You are quiet this evening, Maxwell. Has all that buzzing about you did this afternoon taken its toll?" Mother asked from the settee a short time later.

Standing across the room to refill his glass, he contemplated a suitable response. But then, apparently deciding she did not require an answer, Mother continued.

"Zinnia, he was practically grinning like a madman when he returned from Lord and Lady Minchon's garden party. Usually, I only witness this from him after a rousing argument at the House of Commons. So there must have been some *on dit*, but do you think I could get a peep from him? Not a word, I tell you."

"Now you have me wondering the same, for Juliet was out of sorts and kept to her rooms," Lady Cosgrove replied and then continued in a whisper. "However, I believe it must have had something to do with her exposure to the sun, for she issued a peculiar request for Mr. Wick to send for a block of ice."

"Sunburns can be terrible nuisances. I hope it was not too severe."

"That's just it, Marjorie. She claims that her hat was a sufficient guard but only that she was overheated."

Standing at the sideboard with his back to them, Max held back a laugh. She'd had to order a block of ice in order to cool down? Oh, he could not wait to taunt her about this. Again, he wondered if it was because of her lack of parasol, her temper, or something else altogether.

Unfortunately, just like earlier, his mind interrupted, forming several images of just how she would apply the ice to cool her flesh…

"Strange, I thought it was rather mild today when I was out in the garden. Though perhaps without a cloud in the sky in such an open park, it felt different." Mother raised her voice from their hushed exchange. "Max, you were not overheated this afternoon, were you?"

He exhaled a thin stream of air, banishing the scintillating visions. And reminding himself that he was in the room with his mother and Juliet's cousin did the trick.

He turned away from the sideboard and walked toward their circle. "There were a few unexpected moments of warmth, but otherwise no. I found the day remarkably pleasant."

"Did you happen to spy Juliet?" Mother asked. "I know that you are rivals, but as a family friend, it would still be a kind gesture if you looked after her welfare."

Feeling too restless to sit, he stood behind a silver-striped chair and rested his hand along the back, drumming his fingers. "We spoke for a moment, and by all appearances, she seemed in fine health." *Very fine, indeed.* "In fact, our main topic of conversation—albeit briefly—concerned cake."

Mother's lips pulled into a frown directed at him. As her son, he knew that this expression meant that he was guilty of a crime. He swallowed and made sure that his grin disappeared with the whiskey.

"Considering how your conversations typically end, I suppose that *cake* is all the pair of you can speak of in order to avoid a public display."

He coughed, imagining how their *display* might have turned into another scandal, should anyone have happened upon them. Or even happened upon him, standing there alone and with blatant evidence of his arousal straining against the fall of his breeches for a full ten minutes afterward. He'd had to sing hymns in his head in order to walk at all. But when he'd made the mistake of licking his lips and tasting sweet icing, he'd had to start all over again.

By now, he should have built up a healthy amount of regret for his actions, but he could not summon any. If given the chance, he would still do the same, even if only to hear her gasp of surprise and see her eyes dilate with passion. And he didn't want her to forget either.

Suddenly inspired by a wicked idea, he left the room to speak privately with Saunders. When he returned, he bowed to his mother and Lady Cosgrove. "As an act of unfettered civility on my part, I have asked the kitchens to send over a slice of cake to Lady Granworth, along with the best wishes for her quick recovery."

It wasn't until they'd begun pudding and were eating that very cake that Saunders came to his side and informed him that a parcel had been delivered from Lady Granworth's tiger.

Excusing himself for a moment, Max went to the study, where Saunders had left it on the desk. Eager to see what she'd written, he opened the sealed missive first.

Dearest foe,
Thank you for the cake. Since I never require silverware
when eating such confections, however, I am returning
that which you sent. Please feel free to find a better place to
keep it. Should you require suggestions, I would be more

than happy to direct you to stick the tines firmly into your posterior. Repeatedly.

    Your most ardent enemy,

    J

He barked out a laugh that echoed off the paneled walls and marble-fronted fireplace before sifting down into the carpet. Upon reading the note again, his laughter continued until he was out of breath. He already knew what he would find in the package. But unwrapping the brown paper only enhanced his amusement, for he found a fat silver fork tied at the neck with a pink ribbon.

In this moment, he could find no reason to bring forth his animosity. He merely enjoyed their well-matched rivalry.

Then he sobered. He knew better than to allow himself to laugh or thrill at anything she might do. Hadn't he made this error once before and to his own detriment?

Juliet was too good at pretending that nothing affected her. So good, in fact, that what happened today might have been only an aberration. And therein lay a temptation to prove there was more lying in wait beneath the surface once and for all. But where would that leave him?

He'd traveled that road before and knew that it led to nothing. What he truly needed was her absence from London before he made a fool of himself again.

CHAPTER FOUR

A dozen flower bouquets, twenty-three invitations, and one small crate arrived the following morning. Since the first two were everyday occurrences, Juliet had little interest in them. After removing the cards, she typically sent her tiger to deliver the flowers to the patients at the sanatorium. Then, while sipping chocolate in the morning room, she would respond to the invitations before embarking on her daily walk. The crate, however, was something different altogether.

"Was there no card?" Juliet asked Mr. Wick, standing near the rosewood table in the foyer.

"No, my lady. None other than your name," he said, indicating the plain white card with *Lady Granworth* in a scrawled sideways slant.

Curious, indeed.

Truth be told, a small thrill sprinted through her. None of her admirers had sent her a gift before, not even when she'd been a debutante. Oh, certainly, she'd received plenty of flowers, but they had lost their appeal during her marriage. Lord Granworth had only presented her with flowers when she was amidst a gathering of people and only for the purpose of hearing their praises at what a fine husband he was. Pretending to be the gay bride each time, especially when she knew what he was like in private, had grown tiresome.

Both she and the butler were still staring down at the crate when Zinnia came upon them.

"Whatever is that?" she asked.

"I'm not entirely certain, though it could be a gift," Juliet supposed and explained that the sender was a mystery.

Zinnia's fine brows arched like handles of shepherd's crooks. "And the reason you have not opened it is because you are wary of the contents?"

"Not at all." Juliet laughed. "Merely speculating what it could be."

She knew it was ridiculous, but she was savoring the moment. Though it was difficult to admit to herself, she'd felt nearly as excited when the domed platter had arrived last night. At first, she'd had no idea what it contained. And even when the enormous slice of cake was revealed, the exhilaration did not fade. In fact, she'd found herself oddly enthralled by Max's jest. But since they were enemies, as he'd so aptly reminded her yesterday, she could not reveal it. Not even to Marguerite. Therefore, in the privacy of the seldom-used, moldering upstairs sitting room, she'd penned her scathing retort to Max, all the while grinning from ear to ear.

"As you requested, Mr. Wick," Mrs. Wick, their housekeeper said, handing a short iron lever bar to her husband. And with a glance around the foyer, Juliet noted that the downstairs maid, Myrtle, had also come closer. Her polishing cloth—which was likely for the silver—now smeared circles on the tabletop.

It seemed that Juliet was not the only one surprised and excited about this new occurrence.

"With your permission, my lady?" Mr. Wick asked.

Juliet inclined her head, holding her breath.

The lid came off with a screech, the nails yanked from the wood sending a shiver down her back.

Zinnia was the first to speak. "Is that…ice?"

And sure enough, within a bed of straw sat a glistening, wet block of ice.

Confused, Juliet first wondered if this delivery was made in error, and she would need to return it. After all, ice was too precious a commodity to waste, and they still had plenty left over from yesterday's delivery…

Then something occurred to her. "Zinnia, did you happen to mention my ice order at Harwick House last night?"

Her cousin hesitated a moment and then offered a nod. "Only to allay Marjorie's concerns for your health, though I was careful not to be overheard, as Lord Thayne was across the room."

Juliet wanted to growl. Of course, Max had overheard. She'd been in that parlor often enough to know that if a person sighed on one end of the narrow room, the rounded ceiling would carry the sound all the way to the window and flutter the curtains.

"This isn't Marjorie's handwriting," Zinnia said, examining the card. "In fact, I'd say it appears rather masculine—*Oh my!* Do you suppose that Lord Thayne did overhear and sent this out of concern for you?"

Her cousin's keen eyes were sparkling a bit too brightly for Juliet's taste. "Hardly. Max is no more concerned for my well-being than a wolf is for a rabbit's. This was merely an error in delivery, and we will return it to the ice house."

Even though she was certain it had been Max looking to taunt her, she decided it would be far better to pretend otherwise, before Zinnia took hold of any romantic notions and then—*heaven forbid*—shared them with Marjorie.

Juliet had overheard the two widows, along with their friend, the Dowager Duchess of Vale, proclaim credit for recent successful unions. Among those were Cousin Lilah to Jack Marlowe, Viscount Locke; Ivy Sutherland to North Bromley, the Duke of Vale; and Adeline Pimm to Liam Cavanaugh, the Earl of Wolford.

The last thing Juliet wanted was to give them the smallest inkling of an idea that either she or Max were anything other than sworn enemies. She had no time to fend off matchmaking schemes from the determined trio. After all, she had a wager to win and a candidate to groom.

"Look at all these invitations, Maxwell," Mother said as she entered the study.

"Hmm…yes, very nice, elegant script, fine paper," he said, giving the toppling stack a cursory glance. Then he resumed making a note in his ledger—a bill of sale for a certain block of ice delivered to Hanover Street this morning. Grinning to himself, he wondered how his *gift* was received, having little doubt that Juliet had figured out the identity of the sender. However, his ruminations were disturbed by the clicking sound of his mother's fingernails tapping on his desk.

He looked up, fairly certain he'd mentioned everything he was supposed to about something as trivial as a stack of cards. "You are giving me that perturbed, impatient glower that tells me I've forgotten an important task. Yet, for the life of me, I do not know what it might be."

She gestured to the cards as if the answer were obvious. "You have yet to tell me if there is a certain debutante's company you favor. Surely you would want to become well acquainted if you are to be betrothed by the end of the Season."

"As of twelve hours ago, when we last had this conversation, I have not had the opportunity to meet any potential candidates, if you'll recall. Therefore, I will agree to accept any invitation where debutantes with more than half a brain are in attendance." There, all settled.

He returned to his ledger, scratching out a sum. Recently, he'd hired a steward to look after Mother's accounts and to see to the running of the estate in Max's eventual absence. He kept his own books separate, even though he was the one responsible for providing his mother the funds she required. Her annual allotment was already spent this year, her money sent to Bram to help with the apparent repairs he needed for his country estate in Devon. Though why he'd requested the funds sent to his chalet in France, Max didn't know. And he wouldn't ask either.

"Here is an invitation from Lord and Lady Simpkin. They have two daughters," Mother said, shuffling through the cards. "Tell me, are you partial to fair-haired young women, or would a brunette suit?"

An errant vision of golden spun silk and dancing blue eyes flashed through his mind before he was aware of it. The instant he was aware, however, he purposely thought of dark hair, auburn hair, and brown eyes. "I care not."

"Are you certain? Because that would help to narrow down your selection."

"You would only ask me which shade I prefer next. Black as the ink in my pot, brown as this leather blotter, red as my chestnut mare, or blonde as golden"—as the words tumbled out of his mouth, he felt as if his mind and tongue had conspired against him—"spun silk."

"Hmm…Strange that you would use those words, for that is exactly how I would describe Juliet's hair. It is a most becoming shade." She hummed to herself, looking at the cards that she'd already considered. "I do not believe there is another debutante that is her equal."

"As a widow, she is no longer considered a debutante." He grumbled.

Mother offered an absent shrug before she flashed an invitation in front of him. "Here is one from Colonel Owen. Miss Owen is intelligent, though she has bright red hair and freckles. Does that bother you?"

Was she even listening to any of his responses at all? "Not in the least."

"You are quite unlike your brother. Bram only wanted to pursue the pretty girls."

"Only those deemed pretty by the *ton*. Aside from that, I don't know if he ever had a preference. He was set on marrying the *Original*."

"Yes. Terrible business. Usually, the *Original* is a fine representation of the tradition, but Miss Leonard turned into such a wild creature after they married. And with Bram so determined to have her, and she him, I thought their natures would balance each other out after a time. However, I'm no longer certain of it. When Bram writes—which is not often enough—I hear less and less about her. It makes me wonder if she is still traveling a great deal with her friends, as she had been inclined to do from the beginning." Mother released a tired exhale. "I'd hoped that, by now, I might have been a grandmother."

Max had thought as much as well. After all, Bram had been married five years now. Yet there was no silencing the rumors that Lady Engle had become a favorite in France with both female *and* male companions. "Perhaps it is time for him to return to England and think about his responsibilities."

Bram had inherited a seat in the House of Lords, but he'd never taken advantage of it. He cared too little for the longevity of their country and the lives of the people who resided within it and too much about seeking his own pleasures. As for Max, he spent the majority of his day garnering support to repeal the Corn Laws, believing that a reduction in food costs was the first step for lessening the financial strains in the north counties.

"He is not like you, Max. He has no desire for politics." She stacked the cards together, gathering them in her hands. "For him, arguing is pointless unless certain victory awaits."

Max chuckled. "Everyone enjoys winning an argument."

"True," Mother agreed with a smile. "You, however, enjoy all of it, from the inception to the end result. You will need a bride who is not only intelligent but of mild temperament as well."

Max shook his head in disagreement. "I would want my wife to be someone who is unafraid to speak her mind. There is no enjoyment in a one-sided argument."

Mother lifted her eyes to the ceiling. "It may come as a surprise to you, but most people do not enjoy conflict. Unless members of the *ton* begin hosting debates instead of balls, I fear you will encounter difficulty finding any debutante who fills your short list of criteria."

"Capital notion!" he quipped, gesturing to the invitations in her grasp. "Find a debate in any of those cards, and I would be glad to attend."

She wagged the stack at him. "This is no time for jesting. Surely you are eager to settle into your estate in Lancashire. You have only been there once since you inherited and not even for a sennight."

The reason he'd left so soon was because he'd been inundated with visits from nearly every country gentleman with a daughter, *or five*, requesting his attendance at dinners and assemblies.

At first, Max had been thrilled by the prospect of meeting so many of the people living near his estate. But soon it had become apparent that they only wanted him to marry their daughters. Max, on the other hand, wanted to know their thoughts, their concerns and issues, because he wanted to represent their interests in Parliament. But in such circumstances, he had received little more than an abundance of politeness coming forth with all the cordiality of a suitor courting a debutante.

"As I have said before, I will return when I have found my bride."

"It seems to me," Mother began, pausing as one does while wielding a hammer, sizing up the head of the nail before continuing, "that you spend far more time thinking about your wager with Juliet instead."

"I can manage both at the same time," he proclaimed but wasn't sure he fully believed it. Since Juliet had returned to town, he'd been distracted. He'd bought a house on impulse, found himself in a wager with her, hired a troop of laborers to repair the house, entered into another wager with her, licked cake from her fingers, caught himself thinking of cake quite often, and now ice… "Besides, once I have won there will be no more distractions."

Mother crossed her arms. "And no more debutantes, if you are going to wait until month's end."

He crossed his arms as well, reclining in his chair. "Then you had better make a decision about which event I'm escorting you to this evening."

She narrowed her eyes. "We will be attending Lord and Lady Simpkin's ball. I've been told by Lady Simpkin herself that their ballroom can hold two hundred comfortably and four in a crush. It opens to the garden as well, which I know appeals to you. Since it promises to be a lovely evening, I'm certain everyone will be in attendance. Perhaps even someone who enjoys debating every topic as much as you do."

While Max knew of no debutante who matched that particular description, he knew of a certain widow who did. Once again, instinct warned him to stay away from such events where Juliet might be present. Yet it paled in comparison to the galvanic expectation buzzing through him.

CHAPTER FIVE

The rumored enormity of Lord and Lady Simpkin's ballroom was vastly overstated. Juliet should have known better than to be lured by Marjorie Harwick's enthusiasm when she'd dropped by for tea earlier. There were no more than a hundred bodies crushed into the ballroom space and another hundred milling about the torch-lit garden. And these two hundred guests were four times more than what ought to have been invited.

Unfortunately, there was nothing that could be done of it now, when Juliet had declined the other invitations for this evening. Besides, Viscount Ellery was here, and he was Juliet's primary focus.

In fact, most of the notable members of the *ton* were present, all but one. Strangely enough, Max wasn't here. Was he at another engagement, possibly one where he could watch over his own candidate? Hmm...Not for the first time, she wondered whom he had chosen. Though surely it was no one as admired as Ellery.

Even now, her candidate was surrounded by a bevy of blushing debutantes, standing by the large sundial in the center of the walled garden. All the while, a scattered constellation of approving mothers watched on with eager anticipation. Ellery was not simply one of the most sought-after bridegrooms, but he was also well liked by every gentleman he knew.

A sense of certain victory washed over her like a cooling rain after a storm. Already she'd begun to imagine dressing each room of her townhouse in new silk wallpaper, stunning Axminster carpets, and freshly upholstered furnishings.

"Ah, there is Marjorie now," Zinnia said from beside her, smoothing a pleat down the front of her modest pistachio green gown. "Though I do wish she would have directed Lord Thayne to enter through the garden gate as we did, to avoid the gauntlet of guests."

Juliet's gaze whipped to the far side of the ballroom and suddenly spied a familiar dark head, his mother on his arm. Marjorie looked elegantly disheveled in her bronze-colored gown and the tiered earbobs that swayed as she shook her head at the crowd. Max bent his head in conversation with her, the line of his broad shoulders turning slightly within his impeccably tailored slate gray coat. The color was quite dashing on him, simultaneously accentuating the whiteness of his cravat and the darkness of his striking, rough-hewn features. Of course, Juliet would be the last to tell him how well he looked.

"No doubt, Marjorie tried to warn him, but he chose not to listen," Juliet said.

Evidently sensing her study, Max shifted his gaze toward her. Juliet did not look away, not even when her thoughts and senses were suddenly flooded with the erotic memory of sweet, sun-warmed cake. As if he knew, his mouth quirked at one corner, and he inclined his head. She did the same and, with a lift of her brows, she wished him luck with traversing the crowd.

Yet if there was a way through that horde—even if only for the purpose of goading her into some sort of disagreement— Max would find it.

All the while, she did her best to ignore the subtle warm tingles that started at her fingertips and crept like scandalous whispers along her arms. After all, the last thing she wanted was to turn bright pink in this crowd.

Opening her fan with a snap, she took a precautionary measure. The action sent the gold pomander at her wrist in motion, giving off a pleasant aroma. Normally, she filled it with rose water alone but had recently taken to adding a drop or two of sandalwood. She found the combination pleasing as well as helpful. Right this moment, it aided in drowning out the unpleasant odor from the gentleman nearest her.

Zinnia clucked her tongue. "Gentlemen of a certain age rarely heed the advice of their mothers, but a subtle word or two from a wife would have made a difference."

"Max would no more listen to his wife than he would a rib of celery." Juliet laughed. "He is far too enamored of his own opinion. Any wife of his would need to be impossibly skilled in the art of discord."

"There aren't many debutantes who could measure up."

"Yes. They are all too eager to please their husbands." Much to their own detriment, as Juliet knew from firsthand experience. "I would hate to see a green girl saddled with such a stubborn ox."

"Then perhaps you could aid Marjorie. She has been compiling a list and trying to steer Lord Thayne in the direction of the women most suited to his nature."

Juliet felt something stir inside her. "Is that why they are here this evening?"

When Zinnia nodded, Juliet began to cast her gaze to the debutantes in attendance, looking for the ones with the strong-willed temperaments. Spying a rather formidable pair of havoc-wreakers, she felt her temper rise. This Season, both Miss Ashbury and Miss Leeds had made every attempt to trample the other debs in their paths through spiteful attacks and spreading detestable rumors.

"Ah. I see the direction of your gaze," Zinnia said with quiet vehemence. "Though after the way they treated our Lilah, I do not know how kind I could be to either of them, were Lord Thayne to choose one for his bride."

Juliet agreed. "As much as Max irritates me, I would not wish him to suffer such a fate. Deep down—somewhere quite far away—he has a heart, which I'm certain he would give to his wife. But if he were paired with a termagant, she would only eat it up and leave him with nothing. There are certain types of people who should never marry." Cruel young women were on that list, of course. But there was also a place marked for a debutante who lacked a sense of worth and married a man who treated everyone he knew as an object.

Juliet had often wondered if she'd have been better off living with the shame of ruination. However, hers had not been the only reputation facing destruction. At the time, her father had been only days away from debtors' prison, and so she had done what was expected of a dutiful daughter.

"I believe I will speak with Marjorie on the topic. Would you care to join me? Your opinion would be invaluable." Zinnia made a motion to Marjorie to take the gallery stairs at either end. "It will be overwarm to linger at such a height, but at least there will be air to breathe."

Juliet's gaze was still with Miss Leeds and Miss Ashbury's progress into the garden. It seemed their current target was Viscount Ellery. They'd even managed to frighten away all the other debutantes. And Ellery, with his quiet demeanor and a chivalrous nature, didn't stand a chance. Clearly, he needed rescuing.

"I think it would be best if I kept my opinion regarding Max's prospects to myself. So I will stay in the garden and wend my way to the stone bench at the far side." It just so happened that she would have to circumnavigate the sundial on her way.

As she drew near, Juliet knew it was no wonder that Ellery had gained so much favor among the *ton*. Not only was his character impressive, but he was also quite handsome, possessing a head full of wavy blond hair and soulful eyes. While he didn't have Max's dark, exotic handsomeness or his aura of virility, he did have an understated regality about him. Likely, he would never argue a point but simply hold his tongue when his thoughts were not in line with another's. What a refreshing notion!

Already Miss Leeds and Miss Ashbury had outmaneuvered their competition for his attention and now flanked Ellery on either side, casting withering glances at any who dared approach.

Juliet quickly formed a plan of action, which would not only provide Ellery with a viable excuse to abandon his current companions but would also shed the most favorable light on his character.

Surely tomorrow's edition of the *Standard* would all but seal his nomination for the *Original*. And, most importantly, assure her victory over Max.

Max left his mother in the gallery and descended the stairs near the double doors leading to the garden. Making his way through the crowd, he kept watch on Juliet the entire time.

As usual, she wore a gown that flattered her form in every way imaginable. He wondered if her modiste chose only the fabrics that would cause a man's fingertips to itch from the desire to touch it and to feel the woman beneath. As it was, a sheath of fine lace covered an apricot silk that clung to her body. *A criminal design*, he thought, believing she should have worn a voluminous sackcloth gown instead. Then again, Juliet was perhaps the only woman who could make that appealing as well. He clenched his fingers into a fist to ward off the stinging sensation at his fingertips.

Then Max spied her slipping the fan from her wrist and surreptitiously dropping it into the shrubbery. Slyly, she gained Ellery's attention, gesturing to the barbed branches as she carefully brushed her hands down the front of her gown. Both were a ploy, Max knew. After all, what man could resist coming to her aid?

She was flirting, of course, and effectively drawing Ellery away from two other young women. Was it because she wanted him all to herself?

Max's mood darkened as the obvious answer came to him. He had already wondered, at Minchon's garden party, if she had a lover. And if she did not yet, apparently she soon would.

Ellery sprang into action, reaching through the shrubbery to find Juliet's fan. Shortly thereafter, he presented it to her with a courtly bow. In return, she laid her hand upon his forearm and smiled at him as if he'd saved all humanity with one small gesture.

A growl rose up Max's throat at her obvious coquettish display, flaunting her interest in Ellery in front of a horde of people. If she wasn't careful, by tomorrow morning, the *Standard* would label her as Ellery's affianced.

Not that Max cared one way or another. She could marry whomever she chose or simply have a slew of lovers. He was only thinking about his wager with her. After all, he would hate for her to have an incentive to remain in London.

She had made her choice to leave everything behind once, and when he won, Max would make certain she did the same again.

Perhaps it was time for him to make that perfectly clear.

Juliet never lingered too long in one gentleman's company in order to avoid the possibility of winding up in the scandal sheets, with rumors of a betrothal to follow. Therefore, after thanking Ellery for his gallantry, she ambled off toward the stone bench, steering clear of the rose arbor so that she wouldn't snag her skirt on a thorn.

She had glanced down for a moment—a moment too long, it seemed—when a familiar nasal tone caused Juliet to pause midstep.

"Ah, there you are Lady Granworth," Lord Pembroke said, every syllable pinched through his rather substantial nose.

She wondered briefly if it would be rude to continue onward or if he would pursue her regardless. Since the man resembled a lanky Afghan hound in both face and figure, it was likely that he would give chase. And here she was, with neither stick nor bone in hand to lead him astray. In his case, however, the quick toss of a coin purse would surely do the trick. It was unfortunate that she was without that as well.

Therefore, she held back a sigh and offered something of a smile. "Lord Pembroke. How are you enjoying this fine evening?"

The flesh stretching over his long face was bone white and glistened with a sheen of perspiration. Absently, he swept back thin wisps of lusterless brown hair from his forehead. "I don't believe we finished our discussion on the mining venture in South America."

Oh, drat. That had been five days ago, at least. The man would likely pinpoint the exact break in their conversation from the ball at Lord Tremaine's townhouse. And yet, he did not appear to notice that she'd asked him a question. Even though it was nothing more than a courtesy, the least he could do was acknowledge it. After all, she had listened to him drone on and on about this investment opportunity for nearly an hour.

Not feeling quite as charitable this evening, she looked past his shoulder and toward the house. "I was actually just heading inside to find my cousin."

"As I was saying, before Lord Markham interrupted us..." he began, again not hearing her. It was as if the rules of conversation had taught him that all he must do was wait for the other party to utter a handful of syllables before it became his turn to speak again. And while he spoke, Juliet wondered if she could say something wholly nonsensical with him none the wiser.

"One can never mine enough silver, after all," he said with a snort of amusement.

Juliet nodded in agreement. "A nuthatch whispered that very thing to me this morning from the windowsill."

Lord Pembroke didn't even bat an eye at her absurdity; he merely continued. He even had the audacity to lean closer, his breath sharp and pungent as old cheese. She opened her fan and began waving so vigorously that he was warned to retreat to where he'd stood a moment ago. When he did, she set her gaze on the perfect route to liberation. If she maneuvered along the outside of the garden toward the brick-lined path beside the house, she could easily enter through the front door and make her way to the gallery.

"Forgive me, Pembroke, but my cousin is expecting me," she repeated and took a step toward freedom.

"Quite interesting, to be sure, but as I was saying..." Pembroke had the audacity to block her path.

This act of rudeness went beyond the pale. She was just about to give him a proper set down when Max appeared, his brow furrowed with those three distinct vertical lines above the bridge of his nose. She was never so happy to see his glower.

Inspired suddenly, she closed her fan with a clap. "Lord Thayne, I seem to recall your rather fervent interest in silver mines. Perhaps you could offer a bit of advice for your friend."

This time, her words—likely the mention of silver—startled Pembroke from his recitation. Max continued his severe frown and looked very much as if he wanted to throttle her. But before he could, the ever-dogged Pembroke caught his scent.

"Lord Thayne, I was unaware of your interest. Had I known, you would have been the first…" and so it began.

Juliet waved her fingertips at Max and made another sly escape.

Max wondered how much of his life was spent watching Juliet's retreating figure. Too much, for certain. And yet, the view was not entirely disagreeable.

Beside him, Pembroke attempted to gain his attention. "There is immense wealth to be had, and for only a small investment of a few thousand pounds…"

But Max's focus lay elsewhere. Juliet made her way toward the house with her usual grace and fluidity. He was beginning to wonder how she planned to enter the crowded ballroom when she abruptly turned onto the narrow passageway along-side the house instead.

Every nerve in his body went on alert. Since the path was well lit with torches, he wasn't concerned for her safety. What bothered him was that, moments ago, he'd seen Ellery disappear through the same corridor. Instantly, he was reminded of his purpose for seeking her out in the first place. She should know better than to flaunt any romantic involvement beneath the *ton*'s watchful eye.

Max turned to go but stopped when the monotonous whine of his companion buzzed in his ears. He'd almost forgotten that Pembroke was there. Yet he didn't forget about the way Pembroke had crowded Juliet, having the gall to block her retreat. For an instant, Max had been tempted to lift Pembroke up by his scrawny neck and toss him over the garden wall. But then Juliet had handled him with aplomb.

Max laid a hand on Pembroke's shoulder and pinned him with a dark look. "Pembroke, if you think for one moment that I've forgotten what a sniveling, manipulative rat you were in school, you are mistaken. And if you ever bother me with your ludicrous scheme or so much as breathe in Lady Granworth's presence, I will seal you in a crate and ship you off to South America."

Knowing that he'd made himself clear by the nervous bobbing of Pembroke's Adam's apple, he strode out of the garden.

After her unpleasant encounter with Pembroke and the way he'd cornered her, Juliet felt the need for space around her. So she didn't return to the ballroom. Instead, she went into a darkened room off the main hall and collected herself for a moment in the quiet.

With so many in attendance, it shouldn't have surprised her that her privacy would be invaded so quickly, but too soon, she heard footsteps behind her. Turning, she had an excuse at the ready to leave without appearing rude. "Forgive me, I—*Oh.* It's you."

She should have known Max would be the one to disturb any small moment of peace.

With the light behind him, his expression was nearly unreadable, aside from the arch of one dark eyebrow. "Expecting someone else, Lady Granworth? A lover, perhaps?"

That mocking tone grated on her, causing her shoulders and neck to tense. She darted a glance around him to the open doorway, knowing that they were far from alone. "Hush. Someone will hear you."

He strode toward her, not stopping until he was close enough to loom over her, his mouth set in a grim line. "I just saw Ellery in the hallway."

"Is this a game, Max? Am I now to tell you who I saw in the hallway?"

The ogre did not relent. "Is he your lover?"

She skirted away from him and out of direct view of the doorway. The last thing she wanted was to be discovered in here, alone with Max. Widow or not, tongues would most certainly wag. "You're going to cause a scene. And I don't see that it is any business of yours."

Max turned toward the sound of voices from a group of people passing by and followed her to the far side, effectively shielding her with the breadth of his shoulders. But the suddenness of his close proximity forced her to take a step back. Directly into a bookcase.

"Library," Max said under his breath, shaking his head. "Of course."

Suddenly, memories swarmed her of his hands on her face, his mouth on hers, his body warm and solid. Now, she felt the heat of him, eclipsing her, blanketing her. And her own skin responded in kind.

She was thankful for the darkness—otherwise he would surely see how pink she was becoming. And suddenly she knew, without a doubt, that it was not her temper making her feel this way.

Drat! She'd truly hoped that it was only his ability to anger her that had caused her unprecedented reaction the other day.

Yet even as she disparaged the certainty, her blood began to hum in her veins. His fragrance reached her nostrils—the scent of clean shaving soap, a powdery essence of shirtfront starch, and a tantalizing aroma of fading sandalwood and musk that was decidedly male. Having used sandalwood oil in her pomander, she knew it did not smell this intoxicating on its own. There was something about the way Max wore it, warmed by the heat of his body, that demanded she take a deeper breath. And so she did.

"I happen to enjoy libraries," she said on exhale, attempting to sound completely composed. It took a moment for her to realize how that statement, given their particular history, could be misconstrued as a flirtation. But Juliet was not one to bumble out an excuse. So instead, she lifted her chin and studied how Max would interpret it.

One corner of his mouth twitched, and his gaze dipped to her mouth. "Is that so?"

"I might even plan a tour to study various libraries—the architecture of the rooms, the spines of books, the structure of the shelves…" Her words trailed off as he stepped closer.

For an instant, the only sound in the room was the sibilant whisper of the silk of her skirts pressing against her legs, giving way beneath the force of his.

As if her pulse were trapped inside her body and looking for a way to escape, it flitted from one place to the next, from her wrists to her throat, to the fingertips gripping the shelf behind her, to her stomach and then to her lips. She fought the urge to press them together, not wanting to give any indication of the direction of her thoughts.

Then he lifted his hand, his fingers cupping her jaw. Slowly, his thumb swept against her mouth, inducing a riot of tingles that begged for a firmer pressure, a nip of teeth... "And would *Ellery* be accompanying you on this tour?"

Only now, as Max pinned her with his hard stare, did she realize his intention all along. All he wanted was an answer to his preposterous question! He had no intention of kissing her. Not that the knowledge disappointed her in the least. In fact, she was quite relieved, because she, most certainly, did not desire to be kissed by him.

Not only that, but she wasn't about to admit her true interest in Ellery as that of her chosen candidate. Since Max was typically cleverer than this, however, she didn't want to give him any reason to think that Ellery was anything other than her lover. Perhaps there would be a victory in a small deception via omission.

"Unless you want your thumb bitten, I suggest you lower your hand."

"And if you do it, there will be consequences." He stroked his thumb across her lips once more and leaned in, goading her, tempting her. But he must have thought better of it,

because he shifted his stance. Now, both of his hands brack-
eted her, gripping the shelves at either side of her head.

She flashed her teeth in a smile that might have been
sweet, if not for the seething anger bubbling up inside of her.
"To which act are you referring—having Ellery as my lover or
biting your thumb? Because now that you have planted the
idea in my mind, I find both entirely tempting."

If this were any other man, she would never speak so
boldly. Moreover, if this were any other man, she would be
eager to flee this prison he was forming around her. She
hated to be blocked in. And yet, with Max, for some strange
reason, even though she despised him to his very soul, she
had the impulse to wrap her arms around his waist, squeeze
him tightly, and press fully against him. She wanted to climb
inside the sleeves of his coat and bury her face in the spot
beneath his jawline and the top of his cravat.

It made absolutely no sense at all.

Once again, she felt as if a maddening scream were building up inside of her. One day, she feared she would be unable
to stop it.

"You should save your bite for someone whose teeth are
just as sharp. Continue to leave those with more tender flesh
alone," he said, the heat of his breath brushing against the
shell of her ear.

It wasn't until she saw his grin that she realized what she'd
just admitted—that Ellery was not her lover presently. The
urge to bait Max further by pretending an interest in ensuring it
gathered inside her like a mob of greedy relations at the reading
of a will, clawing to gain the upper hand. However, she needed
to keep Max's thoughts away from her candidate. Therefore…

"Surely your mind would be better engaged on finding a bride, rather than on who I take to my bed."

His countenance darkened, those mud-puddle irises brewing a storm, as if she'd struck a nerve. "Make no mistake. My sole concern is only that you do not find a reason to stay in London. I should hate for you to fall in love with your paramour, only to have to leave him behind at month's end when I have won our wager." Abruptly, he lowered his arms and straightened.

She released her grip on the shelf. Had this encounter been all about their wager, and because Max wanted her absence more than anything?

Part of her knew it was true. He had made it perfectly clear since her return that he would do whatever it took to rid London of her. Had refusing him all those years ago truly made him despise her so much that they couldn't even live within the same city?

Regrettably, she'd had ample proof of the answer.

A fair amount of hurt pierced her, cooling the heat in her veins. Years ago, he'd been her friend, and that night, he'd consoled her as any friend might. Didn't he realize that she could not have taken advantage of that and forced him into the world of her father's debts?

At the time, and even now, she knew she'd made the best decision. But apparently, Max saw her refusal as an act of war.

Then so be it.

Former friend or not, she had no intention of letting him win. This was too important to her.

CHAPTER SIX

The Season Standard—the Daily Chronicle of Consequence

The chivalry of our Viscount E— knows no bounds, for he was spotted last evening at Lord and Lady S—'s soiree, risking his fine Corinthian blue coat to brave a prickly thicket. Not only did he spare the Belgian lace netting over Lady G—'s awe-inspiring gown, but he rescued her fan as well, and there were no small number of sighs at the sight of the event. One must wonder if our resident goddess was equally affected.

It wasn't until Max stepped through the door of Hatchard's Bookshop that he realized he'd been stalking Viscount Ellery all morning.

Purely by chance, they'd passed each other on Rotten Row. Or rather, Max had passed Ellery, *after* urging his horse to a full gallop and nearly making a spectacle of himself around the bend.

In the end, he'd received a few congratulatory comments on his fine horsemanship, queries as to if he was practicing for a race, and if there was a waiting page in the betting book at White's. Unbeknownst to the onlookers, he won the race, albeit against an oblivious opponent. Ellery was even among those who'd congratulated Max. And he felt foolish for such a hollow victory.

Then, instead of returning home to brush down his mount, he found himself on Piccadilly. And standing not four feet from him in this shop was none other than Ellery.

Realization struck him like a blow to the back of the head, catching him unawares. Whyever was he engaged in a pseudo-competition with Ellery?

Like before, Max assured himself that he was *not* jealous. That he had *not* spent the remainder of last evening wondering if Juliet had plans to pursue Ellery for the purpose of an affair. That he had *not* practically demolished the master bedchambers in the second floor of his house because he could not stop imagining her sharing those rooms with her paramour. Which was ludicrous on many levels—mainly because she wasn't going to win the bloody wager, and therefore she wouldn't live there.

Satisfied with that bit of logic, Max turned to leave.

"Lord Thayne. We seem to have the same list of errands today," Ellery said with an amiable smile.

Suddenly caught without a ready excuse for being here, Max picked up the nearest book and lifted *The Tempest*. "Apparently so."

Ellery held up a trio of leather-bound books with romantic titles. "These aren't necessarily to my own taste. However, it has recently occurred to me that my library is rather dull for anyone other than a fanatic of Surrey history, as well as the flora and fauna of the region."

Max frowned. Juliet also had an interest in plants and gardens. Ellery's library might appeal to her, just as it was.

Turning to the shelves, he replaced the book in his hand and pretended to search for another. "I always find books on battle strategies engrossing."

Ellery chuckled. "Undoubtedly. Though my aim is to appeal to a more tenderhearted reader. I want my library to be welcoming to my future bride."

This was news, indeed. Abruptly, Max's dark mood cleared.

He turned, extending a ready hand. "Congratulations. You must forgive me, for I had not heard."

"Thank you, but no," Ellery began with a shake of his head. "I did not mean to imply that I am betrothed at the moment. As of yet, I am having little luck finding a bride this Season with such a vast selection of suitable young women. A mutual acquaintance of ours—Lady Granworth—suggested that hosting a house party tends to narrow the field and that making a list of guests would bring several to mind."

A shiver of foreboding doused Max's limbs.

"Ah. A reasonable suggestion." Max nodded. Stowing his congratulatory handshake for the time being, his thoughts were distracted and dark once again. Ellery wasn't the type of bloke to hunt for a mistress. He was a quiet gentleman, looking for a wife. Suddenly, the nightmare that had compelled Max to demolish the bedchambers seemed a little too possible. "Do you plan to invite Lady Granworth?"

"And Lady Cosgrove, of course. I have the utmost regard for both of them and would never think of inviting one without the other. A woman's reputation is to be treated with care."

Bugger it all. Everything the *Standard* printed about him was true. Max wanted to despise him, but this man was a veritable saint. "Typically, those rules do not apply to widows. After all, no one would think less of Lady *Cosgrove* for attending without Lady Granworth."

Max adopted an insightful tone, hoping that his inference—that Ellery should view Juliet and her older cousin as one and the same—was subtle.

Ellery, on the other hand, stopped smiling. He straightened his shoulders, his chin and gaze set with a determination. "True. However, Lady Granworth is a woman of marriageable age. Very much so, indeed."

And that was the moment when Max realized that—while he wouldn't necessarily enjoy ripping out Ellery's throat—he would like to spar with him in a ring at Gentleman Jackson's and bloody his nose. *Very much so, indeed.*

"How right you are," Max said, all politeness, even as the distinctive rubbing sound of his own leather glove tightening into a fist reached his ears.

This reaction wasn't out of jealousy. It was because of Ellery's audacity at pretending to know Juliet better than he did. Max knew she was still of marriageable age, but he also knew that she wasn't interested in marriage.

In fact, Max would wager that Ellery did not know that Juliet purposely filled out her dance card with indecipherable scrawls so that she wouldn't have to dance at a ball but could still politely refuse. And if she ever were interested in marriage, she would do as she had done with Bram and save all her dances for her beloved.

"Perhaps I could send you an invitation as well. I should like to have a rousing discussion on battle strategies," Ellery said with a lifted brow, his expression revealing that there was more than gallantry and courtly charm to this quiet gentleman, with the way his blue irises sharpened to steel.

Mistakenly, Ellery might believe that Max was a rival for Juliet's affections when that was far from the truth. The only interest Max had in Juliet was her absence. That was all.

And the more he kept telling himself, the more he was sure to believe it.

"I would like nothing more than to accept. However, I am planning my return to Lancashire at the first of summer."

"A pity. I have a lake simply brimming with perch. And the carp make for some fine sport."

Max inclined his head. "Perhaps another time."

Turning to leave, he spotted a book sticking out of the shelves a little further than the others. The green spine and golden lettering caught his attention first, but it was the title that made him grin from ear to ear.

It was perfect.

"We have received a letter from Lilah," Juliet informed Zinnia later that morning.

In the months since Juliet had come to stay with her cousin, they had adopted the habit of sitting in the morning room each day around ten o'clock to read mail, contemplate invitations, and answer correspondences.

It was a comfortable schedule that one would imagine had come from years of acquaintance—something just shy of two old, doddering women set in their ways—but instead was born of an instant friendship after a lifetime of familial discord, which had been in place before Juliet's birth. Zinnia didn't speak of it, but Juliet knew that it had something to do with an unfair division of assets from their late grandfather's estate. Juliet knew all too well how money or the lack thereof tended to taint relationships, even with her own parents.

Zinnia looked up from her own letter, quill paused over the blotter and a fond smile upon her lips. "Will Lilah be returning soon?"

"They are in Hampstead now and will make their journey to London by Monday next." Juliet handed Zinnia the letter.

As for herself, she couldn't wait to see Lilah. Even though they too hadn't known each other overly long, there was an immutable bond forged between them. Juliet found that she was even closer to Zinnia and Lilah than she had ever been to her own parents. It was a matter of acceptance, she supposed. Her cousins liked her for who she was, not for what they could gain.

Zinnia sniffled, her eyes glistening. "She writes here, 'I never knew that my heart was capable of loving someone so much. And he...well, he loves me just the way I am.'"

"Of course he does. She is perfect in every way." Feeling tears sting the corners of her eyes as well, Juliet slipped a lace handkerchief from her sleeve.

And in the same moment, though with a handkerchief from her own sleeve, Zinnia dabbed at her own eyes. "I am glad Lord Locke found her."

"He is family now, Zinnia. I'm certain it is perfectly proper to call him *Jack*." It was no secret, however, that Zinnia disapproved of the way that Juliet referred to Max by his given name. She, on the other hand, thought it was a bit pretentious to call him Lord Thayne, or even just Thayne, considering their sordid history and the fact that everyone knew of it.

"I suppose you're right, on both counts." Zinnia looked off toward the window, a dreamy quality to her gaze. "Did you know that Jack was my late husband's middle name? *Theodore Jack*. I would sometimes say his names together when I pretended to be cross with him for being too bold. And then he would set about altering my opinion." A slight blush tinted her vellum cheeks the powdery color of a ripening peach.

While most people knew Zinnia as a reticent woman who took great pride in her daily exercise and firmly believed that her form and stature served as an example for all, they were not aware of her secret. Likely, there were few who could ever imagine seeing her without a rigid spine. But they would never know how soft she became—her shoulders bowed forward, her head tilted to the side—each night when she visited the portrait of her late husband in the first floor gallery. In those moments, there was also a frail exhaustion about her, a loneliness so keen that it seemed to drain the light from the taper she carried.

"You were happy?" Juliet could already guess the answer but was enthralled by this rare, loquacious side of her cousin.

Zinnia drew in a deep breath and pressed her handkerchief to the lower rims of her eyes once more. "The happiest. Even after we'd been married for ten years, he accused me of placing each of the stars in the sky so that they would complement my eyes and leave him unable to look at any other woman."

Juliet felt her heart pinch with envy. She'd never had that with Lord Granworth. While he regularly admired what he saw on the outside, his words were hardly romantic. He approved of the quality of her voice but dismissed anything she said as meaningless. He cared nothing for her interests, nor did he bother to endure polite conversation with her. She was either to listen to him or to praise him, nothing more. He treated her as if she were an empty vessel, and after a while, she'd believed it.

It wasn't until recently that she'd begun to feel like *someone* again. A whole person.

"He sounds as if he was a wonderful husband," she said to Zinnia.

"Every woman deserves such a love to cherish."

Juliet sensed that the remark was aimed at her but decided not to acknowledge it. Skimming the correspondences, she hoped to hide the fact that she'd spent too many years of her life without a single ounce of self-worth, deserving of nothing. And it wasn't only Lord Granworth or the *ton* who treated her as if she was a *hollow goddess.* Even her parents had.

Not at first, of course. They were the doting and loving parents that any child could hope for…until they saw profit in her beauty. Once she had come out into society, earning high praises, members of the *ton* frequently commented on how her face and poise could gain a wealthy husband.

Soon after, Father's gambling had increased. He'd begun to wager exorbitant sums on credit. Mother too had become caught up in the whirlwind of town life, exceeding her accounts at all the shops and seeing the admiration for Juliet as a means to gain the most coveted invitations. And knowing what was expected of her—to make a beneficial match—Juliet had resigned herself to the fact that everyone saw her as an object.

It wasn't until the moment that Max had kissed her all those years ago that she had a startling realization that *not* everyone saw her the same way.

He had always been her friend, willing to converse with her whenever his brother was off dancing or talking to the other young women who vied for his attention. Much of the time, their conversations had been the only part of those engagements that pleased her. He always drew her into discussions that required more than a bland, indifferent response, ones that called for her opinions. The topic of politics was typically frowned upon and thought too coarse for polite society, but Max had never been one to speak of the mundane. Juliet had assumed that was simply his way, and he spoke to everyone with the same intensity.

Yet in that moment in her parents' library, she'd realized something else entirely. Max didn't see her as a *hollow goddess*. He saw her as woman of flesh and bone. Not only that, but he'd treated her as if he expected to find a shared desire, a passion. And it was such a difference that it shocked and frightened her.

She'd run from it, confused, and suddenly unsure *and* aware of the person residing in her own skin. It wasn't until later, after it was too late, that she reasoned Max had only been consoling her. He'd pitied her because Bram had chosen someone else. Nothing more. Otherwise, they might still be friends.

She only wished she could stop thinking about it.

Juliet paused in her card shuffling, drawn away from her thoughts. "Here is a letter from the Dowager Duchess of Vale. Strange, but it is addressed to me."

"Perhaps Edith is immersed in one of her projects and requires your assistance."

Projects was a euphemism for matchmaking. After having married off both of her nephews, the dowager duchess was determined to find a match for her niece. Unfortunately, Miss Desmond had a terrible black mark against her name. If this was her venture, Juliet did not believe the dowager duchess had much hope of success.

"I can think of no reason why she would ask for my help." After all, Juliet had only managed to free herself of scandal by marrying one of the wealthiest men in England at the time. Unfortunately, there wasn't a surplus of those lying around.

"Have you not noticed how well received you are among the *ton*?"

Juliet dismissed this compliment as rose-colored nonsense from a family member who could no longer see her flaws. It was actually quite sweet of Zinnia. "I have noted their reception of me each morning in the *Standard*. I am merely a curiosity, or worse, a scandal waiting to happen once more."

She was still grateful that no one had spotted her in Max's embrace at Lord and Lady Minchon's party or again in Lord and Lady Simpkin's library. No one else would have understood that those instances had only been part of their continued, if not escalating, animosity.

Mr. Wick cleared his throat from the doorway, putting a halt to her musings. When she looked over, she noted that he was holding a rather large package wrapped in brown paper.

"For you, my lady," he said, placing it on the table before her.

There was nothing other than a red stamp of ink in the upper corner. There was no name. "It is from Hatchard's, only I don't recall placing a book order. Are you certain it is for me?"

"If I may, the delivery boy was something of a street urchin and not one of their usual runners. Nevertheless, he was quite insistent that it was for you, my lady."

"Curious," Zinnia said with a lift of her brows. "Much like that block of ice."

With the reminder, Juliet wondered if perhaps...

And before she could even finish the thought, a wayward thrill took flight within the walls of her stomach, lifting it ever so slightly.

Outwardly keeping her composure, she set about untying the string with the unhurried patience of a centenarian on a final birthday, reveling in the moment and knowing that whatever it might be—even a mistaken delivery—it had already surpassed her expectations.

The moment she parted the paper and saw *Lady Granworth* in the familiar slanted scrawl on a small white card, Juliet knew it had not been a mistaken delivery. And the moment she read the title, she also knew it was from Max and no one else.

The Regal Traveler's Guide to Notable Libraries

She wanted to laugh. Their rivalry was certainly an oddity. And while he likely thought he was taunting her, she was secretly delighted. If her enemy was the only one who listened to her, then she would like to keep him as her enemy forever.

CHAPTER SEVEN

As the Dowager Duchess of Vale requested, Juliet went to tea that afternoon.

By the firm set of Gemma Desmond's pert features, it was clear that she was attending the tea under duress. Even so, the dowager's niece was lovely—her skin slightly tanned from having lived abroad in southern climes for many years, her eyes a bluish myrtle green, made all the more compelling by a rim of black lashes. Her inky black hair, however, was pinned into such a confining coiffure that the sight of it made Juliet's scalp ache.

They had been introduced before, and even then, Gemma had not appeared overly pleased to be in society. Fortunately for her, her lips naturally followed an upward tilt. Otherwise, she might have had quite the formidable countenance.

"Lady Granworth, I'm so pleased you could attend," the dowager duchess said, the penciled line of her brows slightly pinched with worry. "There are many—aside from my dear friends, of course—who would not think of stepping beneath this roof until the scandal of my brother-in-law's misdeeds have died down."

Albert Desmond had become a notorious criminal in these past weeks after the knowledge of his forgery scheme came to light. Allegedly, he'd been robbing people of their fortunes, claiming to sell priceless artifacts and works of art. But his criminal acts turned violent when he'd kidnapped and nearly murdered Adeline Pimm after she'd caught him in the act.

Even though Adeline was a dear friend of Juliet's, she did not hold Gemma responsible for her father's treachery. "As you know, I am not unfamiliar with scandals."

"Precisely," the dowager duchess said with a pleased smile, as if a debutante caught kissing a gentleman in a library was a trifling occurrence.

Though in many ways, Juliet still felt like that same unprepared girl she'd once been, not truly knowing what had come over her in that all-too-brief moment in the library. "It is fortunate that the *ton* possesses more ardent curiosity than censure. I am thankful that my return inured the former and only a touch of the latter. Given enough time, I imagine all will be forgotten."

Miss Desmond's posture softened in what could only be described as hopeful relief. "Would you agree that your hasty marriage aided in your acceptance?"

"Undoubtedly," Juliet said with a nod but proceeded with caution. She did not want Gemma, or anyone, to rush into marriage solely to expunge a scandal. However, in Gemma's circumstances, she could see no other option. "Otherwise I would have been ruined, leaving a stain upon my family name."

Of course, her father hadn't been too worried about his own behavior. He'd counted on Juliet marrying well. Yet even he had known that the good fortune he enjoyed, at her expense, would not last. Otherwise, he would not have tried to conceal the gold pieces from the highwayman who'd ended his and Mother's lives.

The dowager duchess waved her fingers in the air, moving on from those particulars. "Just so. And given the right circumstances surrounding an event, the *ton* can be quite forgiving."

Gemma shook her head, her slender hands clenching into fists. "My father is guilty of numerous crimes, not the least of which is the attempted murder of a young woman. I doubt the *ton* will be quick to forgive, let alone forget."

"Yes, well, our task is monumental, to be sure, but not impossible."

"I apologize for disagreeing, Aunt Edith,"—Gemma stood—"but it is *quite* impossible."

Then she turned to slip through the space between the gold chintz sofa and chair, no doubt heading toward the door.

"Not entirely," Juliet heard herself say and wondered what she'd just gotten herself into.

Gemma stopped, issuing the quick exhale of exasperation as she looked over her shoulder. "Lady Granworth, forgive me, but your kissing scandal pales by comparison."

A younger version of herself might have become irritated by a comment that wholly dismissed her own trials too, but her wiser self saw this as a way to help a young woman facing a dreadful circumstance. "Please call me Juliet, and if I may…Gemma?"

The petulant debutante inclined her head without hiding any reluctance and gradually resumed her seat.

Juliet continued. "Have you ever heard of Lord Corilew?"

While Gemma shook her head, the dowager duchess's eyes went round for an instant before a small smile curled her lips.

"Lord Corilew was once simply Jonathon Tibble, a disinherited younger son. He was renowned for his gambling and womanizing, so much so that he could have begun a *Duels at Dawn* club, with an extensive list of cuckolded husbands as members." If there was one thing Juliet knew, it was the simple fact that learning of another's ruin always took one's mind off one's own. She was hoping this distraction would be just the thing to help Gemma open her eyes to new possibilities.

"Then one day, he altered his quarry from the wives of the *ton* to one of the innocents, a debutante in her fourth year." Juliet shook her head solemnly before she continued. "There was little hope that Mary Brightwell would marry at all. You see, when she was younger, she'd suffered a terrible kick from a horse to her jaw, leaving her with a bit of a scar and speech impediment. Though it just so happened that one fateful morning, Tibble was caught"—she glanced to the dowager duchess and received a nod to continue—"leaving Mary's bedchamber window at the break of dawn." As Juliet hoped, the subject held Gemma's rapt, unblinking attention.

"Of course, we know nothing of their romance or how it came to be. All we know is that her father, Lord Sharpton, was immensely wealthy, and Mary Brightwell was his only child. In addition, we know that by the end of the first year of their marriage, Mary Brightwell gifted her husband with a son, and thereby her own father with an heir.

"Furthermore, it was rumored that Lord Sharpton was so grateful to his son-in-law that he bestowed a substantial gift upon him, providing enough funds for Tibble to purchase an estate, complete with barony. From that point forward, the scandalous Mr. Tibble became Lord Corilew." Juliet had chosen this story, in particular, to show Gemma that there were ways out of ruin, and to convince her not to lose hope. "So you see, it really is nothing more difficult than a name change."

"And to change my name, you are suggesting that I marry?"

"I would never make that suggestion. Such a decision must be yours alone and for your own reasons," Juliet said, concealing a rise of regret from her own mistakes. "It is my guess, however, that you are looking for an answer to clear away the mark on your name. Otherwise, I doubt your aunt would have called me here to speak on this topic."

Gemma glanced at the dowager duchess and nodded. "We have spent so many years apart, and I…" She cleared her throat. "Aunt Edith is like a mother to me, and I do not want her tainted by my name."

The dowager duchess reached over the arm of the chair and patted Gemma's arm. "As I said before, it does not matter to me. I'm merely happy to have you here, where you belong. I was under the impression that you wanted to be married. Was I wrong?"

"I want to put the past behind me. That includes my father and *all* that he has done." Gemma spoke with the type of firm vehemence that paired well with layers of mystery. And Juliet was fairly certain that she would not be the only one to feel her curiosity piqued. Therefore, she would need to offer a word or two of caution to her new friend. But first things first...

Juliet brushed her hands together as if the matter were settled. "Then we'll simply find a man so taken by—what we'll call—your *charm* that he'll sweep you off your feet."

Gemma laughed softly at the euphemism. "As you might have concluded, I am not of a romantic nature."

"Romance is highly overrated. I'm told it wreaks all sorts of havoc with the heart. Instead, it is far better to think of marriage as a mutual understanding." And, at least with this, Juliet could offer firm advice. "It comes down to the matter of the marriage contract. In order to have everything you expect and nothing you don't, precise wording is essential."

At last, those myrtle eyes brightened. "A marriage contract. I hadn't thought of that."

The dowager duchess smiled and rested back into the chair. She silently mouthed a *thank-you* to Juliet.

"When do you propose that I begin my search for a new name?" Gemma asked, proving herself to be single-minded in her goal, which—in Juliet's opinion—was highly admirable for a young woman in the bloom of youth. In fact, with her determination, her intelligence, and her poise under duress, she would make a fine *Original*, flash of temper notwithstanding.

Hmm...that line of thought made her think of her own candidate, and suddenly an idea sprang to mind. It was perfect! After all, Ellery had made it known that he was in search of a wife. And he wasn't the only one. Max too wanted a wife, and soon.

Yet something about the latter thought did not sit well with Juliet. Certainly, Gemma had already proven herself to be a woman of strong character and not easily manipulated. She had her own mind and possessed the qualities that would make a fine match for Max. Still…Juliet could not picture them together. Her mind simply refused to place them side by side.

Therefore, she would concentrate her efforts on Ellery instead.

Armed with a list, Juliet withdrew it from her reticule. "I believe that Lady Haguelin is hosting a ball tomorrow evening. She is a friend of mine and would surely extend the invitation to include you." In fact, nearly everyone would attend, even Max. "It would be the perfect venue to show the *ton* that you are not in hiding."

Not only that, but with Gemma's presence at her side, Juliet would be able to show Max that she had no intention of going anywhere.

"What ever happened to Lord Corilew?" Gemma asked after they'd settled the particulars of tomorrow evening's event.

Juliet was sure to swallow her tea and offer a smile. "Oh, he was killed in a duel. However, I heard his son became a highly respected parish curate who garnered absolutely no interest from the *ton* at all."

Gemma laughed aloud. "Splendid."

CHAPTER EIGHT

"Surely there are several young women in attendance who are worthy of consideration," Mother said with undisguised impatience from the gallery of Lady Haguelin's ballroom.

Leaning a shoulder against a Corinthian column, Max skimmed over the faces at large, many quite pretty. Some were even known to have sharp intellect and possessed all the graces that one would expect of a debutante. And yet, he wasn't drawn to a single one.

Spotting Juliet as she emerged through the ballroom doors sent an unwelcome jolt through him. And abruptly, he knew that a deep, consuming attraction of mind, body, and spirit would only lead to another disaster.

With his history, he would be better off to make do with any of the lot before him. "Are there any who hail from Lancashire? That would certainly save me the bother of having to journey too far to visit her parents. Better yet, are there any orphans among them, to save me from any relations whatsoever?"

"Tush! Maxwell, I am ashamed to hear such from you," Mother exclaimed in a stage whisper. "Whatever happened to that gentle heart you've always possessed?"

Straightening, Max took a quick look around, seeing a few sideways glances from the nearby matrons standing amidst the potted palms and marble pedestals. Then he replied in a lowered tone. "And what mother have I that would insult my male pride with such a claim?"

"Oh, certainly, you were always finding yourself in one scrape after another, challenging the boys who were bigger than you. But don't forget who caught you feeding a litter of kittens with a makeshift milk dropper after their mother was crushed by a carriage wheel. And you nursed those wee creatures better than any—"

Max gritted his teeth. "Mother, we are in public. It is one thing if the servants hear these remembrances of yours, but I will not have them bandied about, only to appear in tomorrow morning's *Standard*."

"It wouldn't hurt for any of these young women to know of your softer side. You glower so much, half of them are afraid of you."

"I glower because the only reason they know of my existence is due to the fact that I inherited a marquessate and a fortune. For years no one knew my name."

She tsked, flipping her hands in a helpless gesture. "My son, the dramatic. Oh, what a melancholy existence to have scores of young women willing to overlook your lack of charm and think of their own security." Turning her head, her dark gaze met his, and her tone altered to the same one he heard when there was a newspaper in the breakfast room. "You forget. Women possess a good deal of sense, and most are here for the same purpose—because they need a husband while they are still pleasing enough in looks to find one. In a few years, a third of the women here will become burdens to their families. Men have the easy part of it. All you need do is offer a smile, and you'll have at least three debutantes swoon at your feet."

"Then I should have brought my walking stick or perhaps a broom." Even though it was a jest, his thoughts were on what his mother had said about wanting security. He knew that had been the reason she'd married his father. It was no secret that theirs had not been a love match but more of an understanding. But whenever she spoke of her first husband—which she had done to Bram each night in the nursery—her face would take on an otherworldly expression, and her voice would soften.

Now, three years after Max's father's death, whenever she spoke of him, it was with fondness and appreciation but little more. And that, he supposed, would be his own experience. He was marrying for the sake of checking a task off his list before returning to Lancashire, in the same manner that one packed for a long trip.

Of course, he would allow his bride to ride inside the carriage and not a trunk...

His thoughts drew a laugh from him. By the disapproving look Mother gave him, he imagined that she would not find his aside overly amusing.

"Do your poor, anxious mother a favor, hmm?"

He sighed, waiting for her to continue.

"Think of them all as kittens."

"What a pity. It does not appear that Viscount Ellery is in attendance," Juliet said with genuine regret. She was certain that an introduction between him and Gemma would have benefited them both. For Gemma, being acknowledged by the *ton*'s recent favorite would have ensured her success for this evening. And for Ellery, the gallantry of offering a courtly bow to one with such a black mark against her reputation would surely earn him even more favor. At least, she'd hoped it would. But all those hopes were for naught.

On the bright side, Gemma looked stunning this evening in white satin, her skin taking on an exotic glow, her hair drawn up in a white ribbon with black ringlets escaping. "Is he a particular friend of yours?"

"Ellery is a friend to all who know him. He is amiable, intelligent, handsome, and most importantly," Juliet said with a grin, "looking for a bride."

Gemma's gaze darted out across the room. "I'm still not certain that I'm looking for a husband. Marrying for the sake of requiring a new name seems so dishonest."

"It might be if your reason were a secret. As luck would have it, however, everyone already knows."

Gemma laughed wryly. "Oh, yes. I often think to myself how providential my circumstances are." Then she issued a small sigh, her gaze flitting to the gallery, where her aunt stood with Zinnia and Marjorie, before returning to Juliet.

"But aside from that, if your friend Ellery is perfect, then why do you not want him for yourself?"

"I have no need nor the smallest desire for a husband. Though if I did, be assured that Ellery would top the list," she said instantly. Yet as the words left her lips, she knew they were a lie.

Of course, she hadn't intended to fib just now. After all, it was true that Ellery was everything a sensible woman would love, but for Juliet, he was a bit too agreeable, if such a thing were possible. He had no discernible flaws, no temper, and no argumentative nature. In fact, she expected that marriage to him would be the most harmonious of all existences.

The idea should be appealing. After her first marriage— her *only* marriage, she quickly corrected—a husband like Ellery was exactly what she should desire. Loving him would likely be easy too, like walking. One foot in front of the other, and all the while knowing that someone was always there, should you stumble.

By contrast, loving a man like Max would be like trying to fly. Flapping your arms madly and hoping that you wouldn't fall flat on the ground.

She stilled. Loving *Max*? Whyever would such a thought enter her mind?

Shaking herself free of the notion, she opened her fan as if to shoo it away. Unfortunately, she was so taken off guard by the thought that she didn't notice Lord Markham's sly approach until it was too late.

"Lady Granworth," he intoned, bowing low and letting his gaze take the journey over her form at the same time. His brown hair was neatly trimmed, the cut of his clothes immaculate, and most discerning feature was the ever-present smug expression he wore. "How pleasant it is to see you here and with such a lovely companion."

Juliet bristled. Other than giving him the cut direct, there was no way to avoid the association. She would have to warn Gemma of him once he left their presence. He was one of the many gentlemen who treated women with utter disregard unless they might look well upon his arm. Unable to prevent it, she made the proper introduction.

"I am thoroughly enchanted," he said without batting an eye at the mention of Gemma's surname, which was a reluctant point in his favor. "I took notice of you when you first stepped into the room. I hope you forgive my boldness, but I also noticed how your brooch resembles an Egyptian scarab."

"You are correct, my lord," Gemma said with obvious pleasure as she touched the rose-tinted bronze with her gloved fingertip. "It is meant to symbolize good luck."

"How fascinating." Markham flashed a dazzling smile that truly made him appear quite handsome, but it was the cunning gleam in his gaze that never sat well with Juliet. She had encountered men like him far too often in Bath, the kind who possessed the detestable trio of wealth, power, and ego that made them immune to consequence.

Gemma did not seem to notice. "Are you a traveler?"

"I am. Perhaps we could speak of it more during this next set?" Then he bowed to Juliet. "That is, if Lady Granworth will permit me to dance with her companion."

Juliet knew that if she refused Markham, then propriety demanded that Gemma not dance at all this evening. Of course, her own method for refusing politely was to have a dance card filled with illegible names—and thereby a ready excuse. However, Juliet had not thought such a device would be necessary for Gemma this evening. And now it was too late.

Even though it went against her own inner warnings to allow him to touch her charge in any way, she inclined her head. "If Miss Desmond approves."

"I do." Gemma dipped into a curtsy and slipped her fingers into Markham's hand.

For the next handful of minutes, Juliet could not shake her wariness, yet she had no reason to feel this way. After all, the pair of them were simply dancing a quadrille, Gemma's curls bobbing against her glowing cheeks. And for all of it, she appeared content, which was the most important thing, Juliet supposed.

Watching them, she felt like a veritable dragon, looking for any sign of impropriety, and taking her employment seriously, as the dowager duchess, Zinnia, and Marjorie looked down upon the dancers from the arched gallery up above. Juliet had seen Max there, frowning at them, a moment ago too.

When the dance ended, a troop of giggling girls and their partners crowded the area in front of her. Juliet stepped to the side, peering toward the floor, waiting to see Markham escort Gemma to her side. What she saw sent her into alarm. Neither Markham nor Gemma were within sight.

Not wanting to reveal her panic, she opened her fan and slyly peered around to each corner of the room, skimming every wall, finding every shadowed alcove. She thought she'd caught a glimpse of Gemma's raven hair heading toward the refreshment table, but the gown of that debutante was a pastel green.

After checking twice more, Juliet turned her gaze toward the terrace doors. If memory served, this particular house had a rather extensive stone terrace that wrapped around in an L-shape before leading off into the garden.

Juliet would not put it past a man like Markham to convince Gemma to be alone with him. Even though Juliet hadn't been considered approachable by most of the *ton*, neither in London nor in Bath, she'd had experience with unsavory flirtations. Not only that, but she'd witnessed enough to provide ample warning in this circumstance.

She found them on the terrace. A misting rain had begun, and no one else was about, and they were standing close beneath an overhang of wisteria. As Juliet neared, she noted that Gemma had removed her brooch and held it in the palm of her hand, speaking animatedly, and apparently oblivious to the indecent direction of Markham's gaze.

"And before I left the bazaar, I had bargained the merchant down to one *para*." When Gemma lifted her face, her smile vanished, and she took a step back, as if only now realizing how close Markham stood.

Juliet hurried, the stones becoming slippery beneath her soles. "Ah, there you are, Gemma. I imagine, after a rousing dance, that you were in need of fresh air. But we must not tarry too long out of doors."

Gemma looked to Juliet, her expression more relieved than contrite, revealing that she had not come here for the same purpose that Markham likely had. "I was overwarm. I hadn't danced in so long that I'd forgotten what sport it was."

"Then we should dance again," Markham said, all charm and friendliness as he acknowledged Juliet's approach with a nod. Clearly, he was not intimidated by the presence of a chaperone because then he angled his head toward Gemma's ear and kept his tone low as he spoke again. "The exertion is half the fun."

Did he think so little of Juliet and of Gemma that he wouldn't even offer an apology for being caught alone with an unmarried woman?

"Thank you, but I had better not," Gemma said and took a step from beneath the wisteria.

Markham, however, set his hand upon her wrist, that smile still on his lips. "I hope you do not imagine you'll have a better offer. After all, a pretty woman with a tainted reputation only serves one purpose for a man, and that is not by becoming his wife."

He chuckled at both Juliet's and Gemma's gasps. As for Juliet, she was speechless, taken off guard by his callous insinuation. It was all too clear that he was speaking of making Gemma his mistress. The reason he did not care if Gemma was discovered alone with him was because another black mark on her reputation would not harm him in the least. She was already one smudge away from ruination in the eyes of the *ton*, and no one would expect Markham to marry her out of a sense of chivalry.

Gemma retreated a step, pulling her arm from his grip. But when he held fast, she jerked harder. "Unhand me."

Outraged by what she'd heard and what she saw, Juliet gripped her fan and stepped near them. It wasn't until Juliet glanced over at Gemma that she saw how her charge's face had gone pale, her eyes wide and staring down at the hand that restrained her. "Lord Markham, remove your hand from Miss Desmond, or I shall remove it for you."

He laughed. "You rail against my honesty when my only aim is to spare Miss Desmond pain. She has no future in society, no fortune, and nothing to appeal to a man with serious pursuits. And most of all, she comes from bad blood. There is no man who would willingly choose her to become his wife. At least I am offering her a chance to become something other than a shriveled-up spinster."

To Juliet, every word he spoke only reminded her of Lord Granworth's many insults that had chipped away at any self-worth she might have possessed. "*Your parents are nothing more than leeches who willingly sold their only possession on a whim. You were nothing to them but a lovely trinket to use for trade. At least I understand your true value. After all, men have offered me thousands of pounds to spend one night with you. Don't you see, my pet? You are quite valuable just as you are— unspoiled and beautiful. Make no mistake, however. When those offers cease, and their envy wanes, I will have no use for you, much like your parents and all of my followers who are pretending to be your friends.*"

She didn't know if rage emboldened her or righteousness, but Juliet closed the distance between them in two steps and repeated her warning.

Markham flashed another grin. "Be warned, Lady Granworth, if you should swat me with your fan, I might enjoy it."

Only now did she realize she was holding it open at her side as if the fan were claws attached to her fingers. She was so used to carrying one that it had become something of an extension of herself. She closed it and then did indeed smack the hand that lay upon Gemma's arm.

What happened next was a blur.

Markham moved suddenly, snaking his hand out toward Juliet. In turn, she wielded her fan against him, opening and then closing it sharply, his finger within the sticks and the guard. And then, she twisted it.

A horrible snapping sound followed. A sickening shudder tore through her, and she knew, even before he howled, that she'd just broken Markham's finger.

Max rounded the corner of the terrace just in time to hear Markham curse and hold his hand protectively against his chest. "Why, you cunning little b—"

"Markham," Max called out, earning an alarmed glance from Markham. Juliet and Miss Desmond were pale and still—and likely in shock.

Markham collected himself quickly, straightening his shoulders, but still clutched his hand. "I'm glad you are here, Thayne. You can serve as my witness to the extortion Lady Granworth was attempting, threatening to pull me into some sort of scandal, unless I show favor to her charge. I had no idea they were scheming together—"

"If you expect me to believe that, then you know little of my own character, let alone Lady Granworth's. You see, if she were to tell me that the sky is now cloudless and bright and that the dampness falling down from the heavens was ocean mist, I would believe her over any claim you might make," Max said, stalking closer. "And if she were to tell me that a duel at dawn was the only way to settle this matter, then I would comply. Most heartily."

Now it was Markham's face that went stone white. "That won't be necessary. I was just leaving."

As Markham skulked toward him, Max blocked his path and looked to Juliet.

Holding his gaze, her face illuminated by the ambient light from a street lamp beyond the garden wall, she looked heartbreakingly fragile, and his anger toward Markham grew. But as the moment progressed, that mysterious inner strength she possessed showed itself. Some mistook this part of her demeanor as coldness, a flaw that made her unapproachable. Not Max. He'd always admired her strength.

She straightened her shoulders. "Markham isn't worth the cost of gunpowder, as long as he stays away from Miss Desmond."

"Oh, he will." Max would make sure of it. But he'd wait until later to make his point perfectly clear to the viscount.

Markham's mouth twisted into a sneer. "You've become a right solid prig since you inherited. I liked you much better when I didn't know who you were."

Max nodded and let him pass, knowing that—later this evening—Markham truly would wish they'd never met at all. For right now, however, all of Max's attention was on Juliet and Miss Desmond.

Juliet turned to lay a comforting hand on Miss Desmond's shoulder, who by the appearance of her disheveled coiffure and distraught expression was still clearly shaken.

"I was told that men behaved with decorum in society," Miss Desmond said, her expression haunted, as if from a recurring nightmare. Stripping off her glove, inside out, she let it fall onto the wet stones and looked down at a series of long red impressions on her arm. "I should have kicked him when I had the chance."

Max looked down at those marks and felt a rage so powerful that he could barely think of anything other than ripping Markham's arms from his body.

"I'm afraid that some men never learn, dearest." Then Juliet drew in a breath. "I apologize. I should have warned you about him."

Gemma shook her head in a way that offered absolution. "It wasn't your fault. It is my father's doing, and now I know I will never be able to escape what he has done." She swallowed, turning rather green. "I-I think I need a moment alone."

"Of course," Juliet said, laying a protective hand over Miss Desmond's arm. "We'll go to the retiring room."

"No, I'd better not wait—" Miss Desmond covered her mouth with her bare hand, dashed out into the garden, and summarily bent over the nearest shrub. The harsh sounds of her retching punctuated the air.

Juliet watched over Miss Desmond, withdrawing a handkerchief and walking toward the garden steps, Max beside her. "She deserved so much more than Markham's unseemly offer."

Max clenched his jaw as grim understanding flooded him. He knew Markham was a cad, but he never imagined that he would openly proposition an innocent. His actions were unconscionable.

"Why is it that so many men refuse to acknowledge that a woman has a beating heart beneath her breast and a brain in her head, just as they do?" Juliet growled with vehemence, her own fist pressing against the balustrade. "And what's worse is that I have this raging desire to change those skewed opinions, even after years and years have taught me that it is a battle of futility."

Her declaration seemed to stem from something deeper than her anger toward Markham. In the past, Max might have taken this opportunity to ask her, to console her. This time, however, he feared that doing so would only bring forth more of the tender, protective feelings making a resurgence within him. And denying them was proving to be a hard-fought battle.

He reminded himself that he was not the fool who had once fallen in love with Juliet. That door was closed. Now, he was older and made wiser by circumstance.

And yet, when she lifted her face to his, looking at him with unguarded eyes, seeking solace, Max's heart could not resist. "You said it best already—those men are not worth the cost of gunpowder. Your arguments are too valuable to be wasted on the deaf. Instead, offer your words to the members of your own sex, for they are far more deserving."

A faint smile graced her lips. "At last, I approve of your argument."

He bent to retrieve her fan from the stones, only to realize the painted silk leaves and the ribs were rent in two.

"I thoroughly detest the man. He made me break my fan," Juliet said, taking it from his grasp. Her tone was almost flippant, yet a visible shudder stole over her, making her chin tremble. She swallowed. "The sound of it was quite alarming, actually. I don't think I'll ever forget it."

More than anything, Max wanted to pull her into his arms. But he settled for brushing his fingers over the sheen of mist covering her cheek. "You've been in the rain too long. Your flesh is cold."

"I don't feel it at all," she said and briefly closed her eyes, her cheek lingering in the cup of his palm. Then she drew in a breath and stepped back. "I suppose that is proof positive that I will not disintegrate in the rain like a plaster mold."

He needed to get her out of here before he gave in to the urge to embrace her and shield her with his coat. "I'll escort you through the garden gate to your carriage and send word to your cousin and Lady Vale before I take you home."

"You should stay and find a dance partner."

"I'm not leaving you." An uncontrollable wash of tenderness rushed through him. It was so powerful that he took a step closer without thinking. Alarm bells clamored through, warning him that it was dangerous to feel this way, that he'd been here once before, and it would end badly.

Their friendly animosity was suddenly under siege—at least on his part—by something more powerful.

"Come now, Max," she said softly. "We cannot leave the ball together without causing another scandal. I'm certain Zinnia will be ready to depart at once, as will Edith."

In the end, he knew that Juliet and those alarms were right. "Very well."

After taking a step down the stairs, she paused with her hand on the rail and turned to him. "Oh, and Max?"

"Yes?"

"Thank you for the book." She flashed a knowing grin.

Before leaving to fetch her cousin, he smirked back at her. "I have no idea to what you are referring, Lady Granworth."

CHAPTER NINE

The following day, Max rode to his solicitor's office, hoping that business matters would keep his mind from wandering to Juliet. Yet he wasn't holding out too much hope. Thus far, no distraction seemed to work.

After his *visit* with Markham, Max had returned home only to lie awake for half the night. He couldn't stop thinking of her and recounting all the things he wished he could have done to clear away the anguish from her expression. Even reminding himself of the animosity between them had not aided him. And it was because she had revealed her feelings to him that made it impossible.

She'd been open to him, even welcoming his touch upon her cheek. She had not shied away or pretended indifference either but offered a rare glimpse into the heart that she usually concealed so well.

For years, he'd convinced himself that he'd conjured romantic notions that had no foundation, that he had made too much out of every look, laugh, and effortless conversation, believing that they had shared one mind. But after last night, he'd begun to believe once more.

And that was pure folly. Proof of that was the fact that he'd left Harwick House before dawn, walked to his townhouse, and then roamed those halls where memories—both painful and poignant—kept him company.

It wasn't until he'd taken a good look at the man in the shaving mirror an hour ago that he realized an idiot stared back at him, and a familiar one at that. After all, he'd been here before, and he knew the inevitable outcome.

Juliet would sooner run—would even marry an old man she barely knew—before she would ever give Max a chance.

Leaping down from his horse onto the pavement outside his solicitor's office, Max warned himself to put her firmly from his mind. His determination was even marked in the firm manner that he looped the reins to the post.

In the next instant, however, all his efforts fell asunder.

Lifting his head, he caught sight of Juliet exiting the bank a few doors down. Covered from neck to ankle, she wore a modest white pelisse, which was not the type of garment that evoked a man's fantasies. And yet he was stirred all the same.

Perhaps it was the flash of red sarcenet, lining the underside, that made his pulse leap.

Why was he always so drawn to the barest glimpse of what lay beneath the surface with her? Even her white hat was trimmed in red silk on the underside. And all he could think about was stripping every bit of it away to discover what else he might find.

Here on the pavement, where dozens of people would bear witness, was certainly not the time to indulge in a foolish dream. Nonetheless, he found himself listing forward, prepared to take a step in her direction.

Thankfully, her tiger rushed around from the back of her carriage to open the door and lower the step. That red lining flashed once more as she gathered her skirts in preparation. Then, just before she slipped away, her hat tilted, and her gaze swiveled in his direction.

A smile graced her lips and held for seven full beats of his heart. In that time, he imagined striding up to her, hauling her into his arms, and lowering his mouth to hers to see if she tasted exactly how he remembered.

But then she was gone, nested inside the carriage, with the door closed behind her.

On a slow exhale, he reminded himself of the many times he'd watched her retreat. More than likely, it would happen again and again. And what Max needed was someone who would stay. What he needed was a wife. Therefore, it was time to turn his thoughts permanently away from Juliet and onto suitable candidates.

With that thought in mind, he pivoted on his heel and instantly collided with a passerby. The gangly man had his head bent in apparent study of the papers in his grasp.

"See here! Watch where you're—" Lord Pembroke looked up at him with a glower, but then his eyes went round, the whites seeming to expand to three times their size as his irises shrank. Stumbling back, he lifted his free hand to his hat, clutching it with a bony hand. "Forgive me, Lord Thayne.

Clearly I wasn't paying attention to where I was going. I was just reading these documents about that"—he swallowed—"venture I mentioned to you…at Lord and Lady Simpkin's."

Max held up a hand, not wanting to listen to an entire recapitulation of prior events. "This is not a killing offense, Pembroke, so you may relax and simply be on your way."

Surprisingly, Lord Pembroke listened and scurried off without another word. Max would have found the sudden exit out of character, or even strange, if he was not so grateful for it.

The sound of a chuckle from the doorway of Barnaby and Pluck drew his attention to North Bromley, the Duke of Vale, who met him on the pavement outside the solicitor's office. "I see our *friend* attempted to sell you shares of a silver mine too, Thayne."

They shared a smirk of exasperation. "What are the odds that he's changed his conniving ways?"

When asked a mathematical question, Vale always took the matter seriously. Even now, his dark eyes sharpened, as if he could imagine a slate before him, a stick of chalk in his hand. "Factoring in the length of time he has been alive, and analyzing the portion of when we were all at school together, I'd say nine-tenths of one percent. However, if you were merely asking theoretically, then I would say none at all."

Max agreed with a grin, a ready quip on his tongue. But then, the mention of calculations distracted him, suddenly reminding him of Vale's *Marriage Formula*.

Last Christmas, Vale had developed an equation designed specifically to find an ideal match. He'd even tested it on himself and had married within days of meeting his bride for the first time. By all accounts, Vale and Ivy were truly perfect for each other, two halves of one whole.

And finding his own other half was exactly what Max needed in order to put Juliet far from his mind. "Since we are on the topic of mathematics, how fares your plans for opening a registry service for those wanting to use your *Marriage Formula?*"

Vale shook his head and tugged on the lapels of his coat. "Abandoned, I'm afraid. With my first child on the way and my fellowship with the Royal Society, establishing those registries no longer seems important."

The news was disappointing. Yet Max was never one to give up without putting forth some sort of argument. "I'm certain there are many people who would benefit from it."

Vale looked at him with interest, his dark eyes sharpening. "Are *you* one of the 'many people'?"

"I have given it thought, yes," Max admitted, always having believed in Vale's concept from inception. In fact, he wondered why he hadn't thought of asking Vale sooner. "As you know, I intend to leave for Lancashire at summer's end. I would like to have the matter of a wife settled before I go." And if there was anyone who would not balk at marrying in such a short amount of time, it was Vale, who'd married by special license.

"As I recall, you felt it was a matter of duty. Yet now, I sense urgency more than obligation."

"The Season is nearly over, and I am running out of time."

Vale nodded, his expression one of thoughtful scrutiny, as if he were gauging Max's reaction. "And would it offend you to learn that I have already calculated your formula?"

"No, indeed, for I am most eager to learn the results." Knowing Vale, this should not have surprised Max, but it did. He had to wonder why Vale wouldn't have told him immediately.

Vale's gaze veered to the pedestrians stepping past them, and he bowed his head absently in greeting as a low laugh escaped him. "I think not."

"Truly, I cannot imagine any reason why I would not wish to know," Max stated. "I have no qualms over marrying for lack of fortune, family connections, or even beauty. So there can be no name you could utter of which I would disapprove."

When Vale arched a brow without speaking a word, Max suddenly understood why his friend had not told him the name. There could only be one reason, after all.

Because the formula had paired him with the single person whom the *ton* knew to be his bitterest enemy—*Juliet.*

Max clenched his teeth. "If that is true, then your equation is flawed."

Vale merely shrugged, not taking offense. "Which is another reason why I have discontinued my endeavors regarding the marriage registry. It was Ivy who made me realize that I'd disregarded the most important of all factors—love. That deep, abiding emotion overshadows all the other criteria, rendering them meaningless."

And Max knew better than anyone that Juliet could not give him love. Once upon a time, he had imagined that he could win her over, but no longer. He wanted more than mere glimpses.

A painful sense of longing pierced his heart. "Then I will simply find a suitable match on my own. There is always another way."

Later that week, Juliet and Zinnia dined at Harwick House.

Juliet found that she was not only well enough to attend but eager. In the past few days, she'd had no more pink spells but had grown rather fond of her sworn enemy. And she even imagined that they were back to becoming the friends they once had been.

She sipped her wine contentedly. The dinner was pleasant and cozy, accompanied by the patter of rain over the copper awning outside the dining room window and the crackle of a low fire in the hearth. Max sat at the head of the table to her left, Marjorie to her right, and Zinnia across from her, providing a taste of the life she'd wanted upon her return to London.

"Maxwell has decided to become serious about finding a bride," Marjorie said as the footmen brought in trays laden with capons, roasted potatoes, candied carrots, and also a fine aspic of pork and eggs.

All eyes fell on Max, waiting for confirmation. Juliet felt a sudden anxious rise in her pulse, though without cause. She already knew Max wanted to marry soon and had taunted him on several occasions because of it. At the moment, however, she could think of no suitable jest to cause him embarrassment.

"I had a recent conversation with Lord Ellery, who explained to me the logic of how hosting a party often brings to mind the ones, in particular, you wish to invite." He looked pointedly at Juliet, making her wonder if he knew this had been her advice to Ellery. "Of course, it is a rather rudimentary notion…" He let his words trail off as a smirk gave her the answer.

"And yet you still managed to understand the concept? Bravo, Max." She saluted him with her glass. "*Have* you made the list for your party?"

"He wishes to have a ball instead," Marjorie added, her tone shocked as she exchanged a glance with Zinnia. "As I said, he's quite serious."

The cozy, warm feeling Juliet had experienced only moments ago transformed into an unpleasant churning that made her wine taste bitter. She set her glass down, even while knowing that this sensation had nothing to do with her wine and everything to do with Max's decision. When he married, it would change everything about their dinners.

What if he chose to marry an idiot, or a shrew who had no sense of humor? Or some self-absorbed *cabbage* whose idea of intelligent conversation began and ended with her most recent purchase at the milliner's? If he made the wrong choice, these dinners would suddenly become a chore she would have to endure, rather than something she enjoyed.

"Actually, I have begun my list," Max said. "It is surprising how clear everything becomes, once you set ink to paper. Several young women have shown themselves to be quite intelligent, possessing varied interests and pleasing conversation."

Juliet clenched her fists in her lap but kept a congenial— if a bit strained—smile on her lips. "You failed to mention your requirement of one who relishes a good argument. Of all traits, surely that is on the top of *your* list."

"I will reserve all of my arguments for Parliament and offer my bride a perfectly agreeable home life."

And for some reason, hearing those words sparked Juliet's ire. Or perhaps it was the smugness in his countenance, as if he were issuing some sort of challenge, that he would make the best husband and his marriage would be the happiest in all of England. Essentially, he was promising this to a woman he hadn't even chosen, and—*drat it all*—Juliet might be the teensiest bit envious of her. Because if anyone was stubborn enough to make good on his promise and keep his wife happy all the days of her life, it was Max.

"Do you know I have never hosted a ball?" Marjorie asked, her question cutting through the sudden tension. "We've had parties and dinners aplenty, even with a bit of dancing in the parlor, but never a ball."

Zinnia lifted her serviette from her lap and delicately touched the corner of her mouth. "A ball is so much effort. And our houses are similar in the way that, to truly have enough room for dancing, we would need to use the first-floor portrait gallery."

"You are right, Zinnia. The gallery would be the only option, leaving room enough for a quintet in the adjoining hall." Marjorie relaxed, reclining back in her chair. "That is a relief, as I'd feared I would be forced to demolish a wall, as Maxwell has done at his townhouse."

Juliet's throat closed, and she was thankful that she hadn't taken another sip of wine or else she would have choked. "Demolished a wall?"

"Yes." Max cut into his capon as if the matter were nothing of consequence.

"A ghastly sight, to be sure," Marjorie said with a flip of her fingers in the air before she reached for her wine goblet. "I went to visit yesterday and saw the wreckage with my own eyes. Why, it is practically unlivable. I shudder to think how long it will take to finish."

"Mother, are you purposely trying to pique Lady Granworth's interest or unleash a tempest? As it is, dark clouds are forming above her head, and her stare is so cold that I am feeling chilled."

Only then did Juliet realize her smile had slipped. Not only that, but the flesh around her eyes felt tight and tense. She hadn't felt this exposed and under the glass since her marriage. Of course, during those years, she had never lost her composure. But leave it to Max to set her off kilter and then to be ungentlemanly enough to make note of it.

Drawing in a breath, she fixed an unruffled, pleasant expression in place once more.

"Of all people, she deserves to know what is happening with a property that could very well become hers in mere weeks," Marjorie reminded.

"That outcome simply isn't possible, as I am going to win the wager," Max said with such certainty in his steady gaze that Juliet doubted her own choice. "And regardless, the house is mine by right and by deed to do with as I choose."

"Not if you make it unlivable for me after I win. That isn't fair." A rise of anger—or perhaps panic—flooded her. Why was he doing this? After the other night at Lady Haguelin's ball, she thought there was a renewed connection between them. Yet this evening, it seemed that Max was doing everything in his power to sever that bond. It left her confused and hurt. And then—yes—decidedly angry.

"I am still complying with the rules of our wager." Again, he focused on his capon as if everything between them was only about the wager.

Was there not something more for him as well? But clearly, she had her answer in the gradual withdrawal of his usual challenging nature. It was replaced by a remoteness that not only made her worry about losing her home but losing her family, friends, and even her favorite enemy.

Until this moment, she hadn't thought his victory was even possible.

Max knew something had to change. He'd been falling back into the same behavior that had once left him standing in her foyer with a ring in his pocket and a crumpled missive in his hand.

These past months had been a trial for him, though perhaps also a way for him to finally put the past to rest. At every gathering, he had an uncanny awareness of her, his gaze knowing her exact location in a room. And even when he wasn't near her, his thoughts betrayed him by running in a constant loop of *Juliet*.

For his own sanity, it had to stop.

In fact, since the morning following the Haguelin ball, he'd nearly decided on a complete withdrawal from her company, but then Mother had surprised him with this dinner. And here Juliet was, filling his thoughts and his senses and making it impossible to forget her.

Hadn't she already claimed enough of his life?

"Maxwell, if you cut any harder into that poor fowl, I will begin to fear for my plate," Mother said with a laugh, edged with a modicum of tension.

Looking down at the shredded capon in his plate, he abruptly set down his knife and fork, then reached for his wine. "My apologies. My thoughts were distracted."

"I imagine so," Juliet chimed in, her smile brittle. "With a bride to procure, your own wedding to attend, and then your inevitable departure for Lancashire on the horizon, it is a wonder you'll even have time to arrange repairs to the townhouse."

She was goading him, he knew, but that did not stop the wayward thrill rushing through him. Damn but he loved to argue with her, loved to see that blue flame in her eyes. And even though he told himself that he would remain detached, he couldn't resist just one more row with her.

He took a sip of wine, savoring the heated discord between them. "The work is not so extensive that it will be neglected for any amount of time. If you like, I could arrange a tour for…say…the first of June." He paused for a moment, then feigned surprise. "Oh, but wait. You won't be in town by then. Pity."

With a cool gaze and steady hand, she lifted her glass to him. "We shall see."

CHAPTER TEN

After stewing all night, Juliet had come to a decision. She was going to ensure Ellery's victory by any means necessary.

In the beginning, her plan was simply to let Ellery's character speak for itself. After all, she'd done nothing to ensure his favor among the *ton* before the wager. And other than a lost fan in the shrubbery, she had done nothing since, yet she still expected to win.

Now, however, she would need to take more direct, even drastic, measures. While she didn't have a fully formed plan yet, she knew that it was her only option. She wasn't going to leave London. Her home was here, and she would fight for it.

But first, she was going to see what sort of disaster Max had made of *her* house.

Lifting the hood of her cloak to help shield her identity, she began an early morning stroll. It was not uncommon for Juliet, after all, though usually she did not leave at dawn. But since the reason for her trek was not entirely aboveboard, she required the certainty that most of the people in these houses were still fast asleep.

After all, the last thing she wanted was for her name to be in the *Standard* for sneaking into a townhouse that did not belong to her. Yet. And by all accounts, Max was still living at Harwick House, so she needn't worry about an encounter with him either.

By the time she finally arrived, her nerves were in a dither. She wanted to stand in front of the house and simply gaze upon it, cataloging how the years had pitted a few bricks and rounded the edges of the short set of stairs leading to the door. Amidst the glossy black paint was a familiar lion's head knocker. But as much as she wanted to linger, she was all too aware of the houses around her. Servants were typically the only ones awake at this time of day, but everyone knew that all it took was a whisper from a chambermaid, and the entire *ton* would learn of Juliet's criminal act by breakfast.

Therefore, Juliet kept walking until she rounded the corner. Then she slipped behind the house and through the garden gate.

The garden had overgrown. What was once pruned and manicured by their gardener—or even by Juliet's own hand—was now indistinguishable. It seemed as if the gentleman who'd purchased the house upon her parents' deaths hadn't tended the grounds at all.

She slipped in through the servants' door after discovering it was the only one unbolted. Inside the house, the clutter from laborers remained in the hall—various tools, pails, and brushes. The rooms were quiet, drowsing beneath dusty white sheets. Beneath the pungency of turpentine, the house still carried a familiar scent, as if she might see Father's pipe smoldering in a dish nearby or find Mother's lavender sachets within the drawers of the console table in the morning room.

As she traversed the ground floor, she felt fairly certain that the laborers would not arrive for hours to come. After all, the noise of the hammering, or whatever they did, would surely cause a fuss with the neighbors if it happened before eleven.

Of course, Max likely wouldn't care about bothering the neighbors. He did what he pleased, as the walls around proved. He hadn't cared about upsetting her when he bought the house out from under her nose. He'd done it to get under her skin, to make her angry enough that she would be willing to leave London. Yet with each step, she was pleased to find variegated wooden planks beneath her feet, telling her that he truly was making necessary repairs. There were also portions of the crown molding that had been replaced but not yet painted, along with fresh plaster to fill in the cracks on the walls.

Lowering the hood of her cloak, she lifted her gaze upstairs, hesitant about what she would find. Would it be the disaster that Marjorie claimed it was, or had that been an exaggeration?

Garnering her determination, she headed up the stairs to the first floor.

Her thoughts drifted to the dinner last night and how much it bothered her to think about him narrowing down his choices for a bride. What if he hadn't done any of this to get under her skin but had been sincere in the hope for a wife to live in this space with him?

That thought bothered her even more.

This was her house, and if anyone was going to live here, it would be her. *Not* Max and his new bride. Not Max and his family. She didn't want to think about him laughing here, loving here, or kissing someone else in the library. Her library—where everything in her life had gone completely, utterly topsy-turvy because of his kiss!

She couldn't stand the thought of him ruining someone else's life. She wanted to be the only one.

Her steps faltered on the top tread as she realized that—*drat it all*—she was jealous.

A frustrated growl left her throat. She stormed up another set of stairs to the second floor, angry with herself for feeling this way and even angrier with Max for causing it. How dare he constantly mention his need for a wife! Couldn't he be happy without one, at least until she got used to the idea?

Her irritation hadn't dissipated at all by the time she saw the gaping hole in the plaster at the end of the hall on the second floor. It was as big as a chair, revealing rows of grayish, broken lath behind it. With a glance around, she saw more of the same, along with some holes even larger and providing a clear view of the room beyond it.

She felt as if the blows he'd inflicted on the house were a personal attack. "What has that blasted man done to my house?"

"It is *my* house," Max said from behind her, startling her within an inch of her life.

"*Oh!*" She jumped, whirring around, her hand to her heart, pulse racing in her throat.

"And I can do whatever I like," he declared, casually leaning a shoulder against the doorway, arms and ankles crossed, as if he'd been watching her for some time.

He wore a pair of black trousers and was in his shirtsleeves, the neck gaping open as if he were in the middle of dressing. As if he'd *slept* here last night.

And seeing that he was standing in the bedchamber doorway that had once been her own, she was incensed. Her outrage came back full force.

"That has always been your problem, Max," she hissed, rounding the banister and storming toward him, armed with a pointed finger. "You've always believed you could do whatever you wanted and damn the consequences. Well, I'm not allowing it this time." She stopped within poking distance and did just that, her fingertip meeting the taut muscle beneath the fine lawn. "I expect you to have this completely repaired, or you can forget the fair price I was willing to pay."

He straightened. Uncrossing his arms, he leaned toward her as if he didn't even feel her assault. "Perhaps you don't recall, but I have *always* been fully prepared to face the consequences of my actions. You were the one who ran."

She scoffed and jabbed him again. "I was right! All along, this has been about what happened between us five years ago. Oh, I *apologize* for wounding your poor ego when I left, though it seems you've managed to recover, as you are busy *narrowing down* your list of bridal candidates."

"Ego?" He took her by the shoulders, his grip firm but not cruel, as contempt burned in his dark gaze. "I wanted to marry you. There was more than ego involved."

"That kiss happened because you were consoling me, and we both know it."

"Do we, Lady Granworth? Or is that something you told yourself to validate running away to marry a rich old man?" Gritting his teeth, seething as much as she was, he spun her around and pressed her back against the wall just inside the bedchamber. "And if you think for one instant that I'm going to sit back and watch you bring your next husband here to live, not four doors down from my mother's house, then you are sorely mistaken."

Then, without warning, he crushed his mouth to hers.

The shock of it made her grow still, her eyes still open, even as his closed and a groan tore from his throat. The sound of it woke her, startling her into a new awareness. Max was kissing her, his lips firm and familiar, his tongue bold and commanding, daring her to retaliate.

And she did, slanting her mouth beneath his, parrying with his tongue while clutching handfuls of his shirt in her fists. He groaned again, and the vibration of it had the strangest effect on her eyelids, for they drifted closed. Her head tilted, lips parting, allowing him deeper. She wasn't sure if this was part of a battle or a strange sort of truce.

Then again, weren't truces civilized affairs between warring factions with cooler heads? That was certainly nothing like her and Max and this heated skirmish of mouths and hands.

She didn't know what possessed her, but she pulled the hem of his shirt free of his trousers, and now her palms were pressed against the hard plane of his abdomen, her fingertips grazing a soft dusting of hair. It seemed the sensible thing to do—explore the terrain of her opponent's territory—and she refused to overthink her actions.

The clasp of her cloak slipped free from her neck, the garment falling away as Max's hands skimmed over her back, down the row of buttons descending to her derriere, then swept upward past the scalloped lace and to the bare flesh between her shoulder blades. His touch sent a shiver down her body, making her arch like a bow against him, poised to strike. Every inch of her skin suddenly felt taut, her breasts heavy, tingling. Her stomach dropped lower, weighted, emitting a sweet clenching sensation that seemed to deplete the air in her lungs.

She broke away from the kiss, turning her head, breathing hard now. Max did not cease his onslaught. He was battle ready, always, and far more skilled in this manner of warfare.

Even so, Juliet had no intention of surrendering. "You destroyed the walls because you're afraid that I will win our wager and bring another man here? My, my, Max, that sounds rather like a jealous man."

His attention shifted to the column of her throat, where his wet, open-mouthed kisses called attention to the steady throb at the apex of her thighs. She wanted to close her legs against it and squeeze tightly, but Max was there, the hard length of him pushing against her, driving her back against the wall. Her hips rocked against his in retaliation—or perhaps because she wanted to feel him once more. Suddenly, she wasn't sure that a battle was supposed to feel this good. But with Max, it was difficult to tell the difference. Part of her loved fighting with him. Every argument felt like a prelude to something more, something so near and yet still out of reach.

Her frustration mounted when he did not answer her taunt, and so she slipped her hands free of his shirt, took his face in her hands, and kissed him again. *Yes*, that would show him that she was in control. This time, her tongue swept into his mouth, and her hips rolled slowly against his. And because she wasn't finished proving it, she continued, even as he lifted her off the ground, his hands clasped over her hips and lower still, until he was cupping her bottom.

She found purchase on a demilune console, Max between her thighs, his position edging her skirts upward. But now the muslin was bunched between them. Parting her knees did nothing to bring him back to where he was a moment ago, to ease that insistent pulse. It was just like Max to give her a taste of something, only to leave her without. But she wasn't going to let him do that to her again. So just like in many battles, she took him prisoner, locking her legs around him.

Max set his hands over her wrists and slowly drew them down from his face, his gaze fierce. "I am not going to be the one to stop this, Juliet. Do you understand? It will be you, like always." He shook his head, pressing his forehead to hers. "I have reached my limit, and this game of ours must conclude, one way or the other."

Her first impulse was to challenge him in return, but when she read his expression, she couldn't. The edgy mockery she typically saw was no longer there. He searched her gaze, his dark eyes seeming vulnerable, and the furrows between his brows no longer angry but pained. He was open and exposed, revealing a raw desire so potent that it almost frightened her. Mostly because she felt it too.

She realized this was no longer about the house or any of their arguments. In fact, she wasn't sure if it ever was. No, this was about something more, that tangible thing between them that she couldn't shake loose.

If she chose to leave, she sensed that things would never be the same between them again. And if she stayed…things would never be the same between them again.

But she'd come this far, and running away was not an option. She'd had five years to think about Max's kiss. Five years of wondering what it might have been like if she'd made a different choice.

"I haven't once looked at the door, Max." And then she tipped her chin and pressed her mouth to his.

The battle lines disintegrated in that next kiss. He released her wrists, his arms engulfing her, his hands pulling her flush against him. The strength and sureness of his embrace made her breathless and hot.

In tune with her, as Max had always been, he worked the buttons free at the back of her gown, bringing the cool morning air through her chemise. Then, with one swift tug, he pulled down her sleeves and tapes, baring her breasts. He broke from the kiss, breathing hard, his mouth open, his gaze on the round swells of flesh bathed partly in the shadow of his body and partly in the golden light that filled the room. And with one single sweep of his thumbs over the dusky tips, they budded for him, sending a cascade of tingles through her.

She held her breath as his head dipped to claim her. The wet heat of his mouth covered her, his tongue a swirling sweep over the tip, right before she felt that first decadent tug.

His name left her throat in a rasp as her hands dove through his hair, drawing him closer. She hadn't even known how much she'd craved this, needed this. And when his hand slipped beneath her skirts and unerringly found the heart of her, she knew that Max had known all along. He proved it in the way that he touched her, stroking down the seam of her, drawing out the slickness that—up until this moment—she had been the only one to find.

But his ministrations weren't the hurried, frustrated fumblings of her own fingers. He knew exactly where and how to touch her, intermixing small decadent circles with sinuous caresses, and—*oh*—the sinfully slow slide into the undiscovered swollen tissue.

He lifted his head, seeking her mouth with urgent, demanding kisses. His hand was still between them, where the fall of his trousers touched her inner thighs, his knuckles brushing against her most sensitive flesh.

Seeking more, she spread her legs wider, tilting her hips toward him, a mewl of unabashed desire rising in her throat. What she wouldn't give just to tell him "Yes…*there*…" with confidence born of experience, and knowing the answer. But this was all new to her.

Even so, he answered her plea immediately, coming closer, stroking her slippery folds again, nudging that intimate opening. Instantly, she knew this was not his finger. This flesh was hotter, larger…*much larger*, already stretching her. A fleeting moment of panic struck her, making her wonder if she should say something about—

Max drove into her, impaling her, his hardness unforgiving.

A soundless gasp stalled in her throat. Clutching his shoulders, Juliet instinctively tried to lift away from the shocking invasion. Away from the stinging burn. How was she to know that it would feel like this? That he would fill her completely, forcing her to stretch around him? None of Marguerite's stories had prepared her.

Max released a low, gravelly curse, his face buried in her neck, his arms cinched around her, his body stiff and wedged deeply. Other than his heavy breathing, he went still but remained fully seated inside her.

She panicked, not knowing what to do next. Thus far, everything had been rather instinctual, with Max touching her in ways that made her respond. But now, he wasn't doing anything. Surely this was not the desired end result. There had to be more.

"Is this terrible for you?" she asked, feeling tears prick her eyes. How could she face him after such a failure? Perhaps she never should have crossed that battle line after all.

"You are perfect," he rasped. "Even more than I imagined."

Perfect? She'd heard the word before, countless times, referring to her outward appearance. But never for this. And *this* was quite something else entirely. With a small smile tugging at her lips, she pressed them to his shoulder, where the open neck of his shirtsleeves had shifted to one side, baring the tight cording of his muscles. Relaxing ever so slightly, her body gripped his as it pulsed, cinching around him.

Beneath her hands, she felt him tremble, revealing his restraint. He began to move in slow upward thrusts. He murmured against her neck, her ear, her temple—indistinct words that formed an intimately erotic lexicon.

She'd read about the particulars of the act, had seen lurid etchings and romantic paintings, but nothing had prepared her for the overwhelming intimacy. How there was a difference in his eyes now—a tender but untamed intensity that darkened his pupils. The way his arms held her with utter possession, made her want to offer more of herself. His scent filled her lungs, every breath hot and tantalizingly musky in the combined essence of their joined bodies. Those intimate whispers of how it felt to be inside her were like another caress, stroking her mind, permeating every thought.

This was far more than mere sexual congress. It was a life-altering, wholly necessary, completion of her being. In this moment, she felt as if she was born solely for him. This was the reason she had lips—so that Max could kiss them. She had breasts for him to taste, to tease, and to suck. And Max had arms so that he could hold her. Firm buttocks so that he could thrust, again and again. And her flesh was soft and yielding, solely for Max's hardness to plunge inside, filling her.

"Let go, Juliet," Max growled, a hoarse plea more than a command, the friction faster with each upward thrust.

"I am," she said, holding on tighter. Didn't he know that she'd let go of everything the instant he kissed her? She'd abandoned every part of her being, every minute of her past, as well as her future, solely for this present moment.

But the more she clung to him, and the more he thrust into her, the more she felt as if she were losing control. Something inside of her was building, coiling, tensing. That scream of frustration she always sensed inside her threatened to escape.

Unable to release it, she held fast to him, sinking her teeth into the crest of his shoulder.

He cursed again, a loud echo reverberating as he wrenched free of her body, and a torrent of hot fluid sluiced against her thigh. His breathing was hard, like a bellows, rasping out of his lungs.

And she couldn't help but smile. She loved the sound of Max coming undone.

"I did try, you know," Juliet said after a moment and with a kiss against his shoulder where her teeth had left an impression. An eager, buoyant thrill still throbbed where they had just been joined, and she closed her eyes to savor it.

Max brushed the hair from her face as he kissed the corner of her mouth. "No. You fought it the whole way. I could feel how close you were, and it drove me mad."

Only now did she realize that he was referring to *le petit mort*, what the French referred to as *the small death*, pleasure beyond one's control. Marguerite had explained that men who considered themselves good lovers paid careful attention to a woman's pleasure.

"Oh." She looked away, suddenly feeling shy. If she would have known how to *let go*, she would have. For him. Yet she wondered if she was so used to keeping herself in control that she would never be able to experience more.

He turned her face back to his and pressed his lips to hers in something far too tender to be called a kiss. "I was a brute with you. Can you forgive me?"

"Do not apologize for treating me like a woman made of flesh and blood." She swallowed down the sudden swell of emotion, her voice growing quiet. "You are the only one who has ever done so…as you likely know very well by now."

Chapter Eleven

The only one? Surely not, but yet…that would explain so much.

A pleased puff of air left Max's lips as he shook his head. He was doing his best not to grin from ear to ear, but it was difficult to hide the bewildered elation zipping through him. Therefore, to conceal it, he simply gathered her in his arms and carried her to the washbasin in the corner of the room. And what he enjoyed most of all was the way her head naturally fell into the nook of his shoulder.

Setting her on her feet, he let her dress fall to the floor. He took special care to cleanse her, not only her thigh and her sex but her breasts as well. He noted that with each brush of the cloth, her flesh responded, the dusky rose of her nipples drawing taut, each of her breaths becoming shallow, her flesh turning pink.

"Were you married to Lord Granworth in name only?" He had to ask.

"In the end, I suppose that is correct," Juliet answered, watching his ministrations with obvious fascination. "I was more of an *objet d'art* than a wife—his *Flawless Representation of Woman*. And there were times when I'd wished he'd found a flaw."

"He never touched you, desired you?" Max could not imagine that. Even now, he was making quick work of her stays and chemise, planning to make amends immediately for not having seen to her pleasure first.

"As you know, some men are driven by power, some by greed, jealousy, passion, or..." She lifted her shoulders in a delicate shrug, seemingly unaffected by her enthralling nudity. "Lord Granworth was obsessed with inciting envy in other men. He'd made it clear, nearly every day, that when I failed to do that, he would abandon me."

Max had spent years hating Granworth but apparently not enough. He almost wished the old blackguard were alive, simply so that he could throttle him within an inch of his life. "And none of those other men ever attempted to claim you?"

As he asked the question, he pulled her back into his arms, nibbling the silken flesh of her neck as he removed the pins from her hair and left them to fall heedlessly to the floor.

Her hands skimmed over his back, her body pressed intimately against him where his flesh was already thick and eager. "I wanted to take a lover, just to spite him. But there was always something missing, a void that I couldn't force myself to fill."

"I find that hard to believe. That night in the library you were so full of passion." Even now she touched and caressed constantly, brushing her fingers over his skin, gripping the muscles of his arms and chest. In turn, she seemed to thoroughly enjoy being petted, kissed, and fondled. And if he didn't get her to bed soon, he would take her standing up again.

So he took her hands, and even in this ordinary act of intimacy, he relished the sensation of her fingers twining with his. He always knew it would be like this with her. Only she shared this connection—this level of unspoken communication—with him. No other woman had ever affected him like this.

"I locked it away, I suppose, though not intentionally. I was the *hollow goddess*. I'd come to accept it," she said, returning to his embrace and slipping her slender arms around his neck. As she continued, she pressed her lips to his jaw in slow, tantalizing kisses until she reached his earlobe and tugged on it with her teeth. "Honestly, I don't know what came over me that night. I've blamed you for years, comparing your kiss to others, only to be left without having been stirred in the slightest. That night was the first time I'd ever felt anything that powerful, so potent that I was only aware of us and that kiss. It frightened me to know that there was a stranger living beneath my skin."

"You ran because I saw more in you? That I wanted you?" Max felt irritated, angered, and yet also elated. It was a puzzling mixture of emotions. "And then you tried to take a lover, but I ruined that for you as well."

He drew in a satisfied breath, feeling his chest expand as he lowered her to the bed and moved over her. He loved seeing her like this, so open and free with him, her golden hair fanned out on the pillow, her eyes heavy-lidded and drowsy from passion, and her lips swollen from his kisses. Not to mention the one he was going to give her right this instant.

She licked her lips when he finished and then grinned. "I wouldn't smile too smugly. I despised you for that, you know. That kiss of yours was a cataclysmic event in my life."

He'd felt that way too. In fact, he still did. Suddenly, it became all too clear that those years apart had only delayed the inevitable. When she returned to London, Max had sworn to himself that he would never fall in love with Juliet again. Never be vulnerable.

But damn, it looked as if the bells were tolling *never* right now.

Even though his scarred heart warned him to hold back, to proceed with caution, it was too late. He never stood a chance.

"And I'm certain part of me felt the daggers you were throwing all the way from Somerset. In fact, the cloud of hatred you hurled at me might have been the reason I never married. Perhaps *I* should start despising you."

She laughed, brushing a lock of hair from his forehead. "Oh yes, as soon as you've finished despising me for one thing, you must hoist the banner of a new cause."

He kissed his way down her body, caressing her, stroking her, paying close attention to those moments when she would hold her breath and her hands would still. Then he would linger, edging out her response, waiting for the shuddered exhale that told him all he needed to know. "Your skin is incredibly hot and turning a becoming shade of pink."

"This flush is also your fault—a recent affliction that I first thought was the result of too much sun at the Minchons' garden party. Then I thought it was because you incited my temper."

"And then?" He nipped at the velvet underside of her breast, where her flesh was even hotter.

"Let's just say that I can never look at cake without feeling a little flushed. Alas, there seems to be no cure, other than sinking into an ice-water bath."

"Is that right?" He grinned, taking pride in causing such a reaction in her, but suddenly wondering if there was another cure she had not considered. He moved lower, intent on discovering the answer. "And in all these years, you've never felt carnal desire, not even with yourself?"

When the last word left his lips, he skimmed his fingertips between her thighs, her downy curls as soft as kitten fur.

A shuddered breath escaped her. "I am a woman of seven and twenty. Of course I have explored my more intimate places."

He groaned, his mouth pressed to her hip. Fully, achingly aroused once more, he was eager to take her. It didn't escape his notice that she hadn't once stopped him from touching her or shied away. In fact, she was practically purring. "I don't believe you. I think a demonstration is in order."

"Absolutely not," she said with a scandalized laugh. "And I don't want you to imagine it either. So remove that look from your face."

"It's too late. I have already imagined it several times—you in the bath, you in the morning with the bedclothes rumpled, you in the carriage…"

She gasped. "*The carriage?* I would never."

"You could take a relaxing tour through the park, shades up, enjoying the scenery, and all the while your busy little fingers take a tour of their own. No one would ever know." And as he spoke, he began a tour of *his* own, nibbling his way down the curve of her hip.

"Max!" While her intention may have been to sound outraged, the bright excitement in her eyes and her throaty laugh banished it. "And what do you think you're doing?"

He continued on his course, sampling and examining every inch of her. "Your declaration of being an *objet d'art* has sent me on the task of unearthing a secret flaw to disprove you."

"I hope you are successful," she said, her head tilting, her fingers twirling locks of his hair.

"I think I shall be, for here is a very suspicious mark." He nudged her thighs wider and rubbed the tip of his finger over a spot. "It appears to be a freckle."

He did not mention, however, that it was the most flawless freckle in existence, perfectly round, and the dark, lustrous brown of a coffee ground.

She lifted up on her elbows, a beatific smile on her lips. "Truly?"

"Let me press my lips against it to be sure it is not a mark that will rub off." And as he did that, nestled near her sex, her lids lowered drowsily, and she let out a breath. He inspected the mark once more, quite intently, breathing in her sweet musk. "It is still there, proving you are a woman of flesh and blood."

"And not a flawless, *hollow goddess.*"

"No. Instead you are *my* goddess," he said in earnest, brushing his lips against the curls that guarded her sex. "And now you must allow me to pay homage."

Juliet's gasp filled the room as he closed his mouth over her. Boldly, she kept her gaze on him, watching him with an avid carnal interest, her skin glowing pink now. Sliding his tongue over the swollen folds, he laved her tenderly, telling her in low murmurs how decadent she tasted and how much he wanted to stay right here, worshiping her for hours.

She whispered her agreement on several shuddered breaths. Yet when he delved deeper into the slick, molten center of her, it did not take long. He tried to draw out her pleasure, take her to the precipice and back with slow, purposeful strokes against and around the tight bud of hidden flesh. But as the first tremors began, there was no turning back. He drew her into his mouth, flicking his tongue until he felt her convulse. Feeling her body quake, he held her hips steady and continued until, at last, her scream pierced the air.

It was the most cathartic orgasm of his life, and it wasn't even his own.

When he settled over her and moved inside her, he witnessed the pure wonder on her face. And he knew she was his now. In fact, from what she'd confessed, she always had been.

But he knew her well. When it came to romantic overtures, she became skittish and uncertain. He feared that her marriage had only intensified this inclination. Therefore, in that moment, he decided to take things slow.

No sudden movements. He just needed to bide his time.

At last, Juliet knew how to release that scream that had been trapped inside her. Though it was less scream and more keening moan. And Max had made certain that she never stopped.

He kept her in that bed all morning, tangled in each other, until they were both too weak to do anything other than doze off for a few minutes.

When she awoke, she went about making her wrinkled clothes as presentable as possible and dressed in quick order. With Max there to fasten her buttons, it took far longer than it should have because he kept trying to remove her dress all over again.

She was thankful that he never once mentioned marriage. That would have put an awkward end to their lovemaking. But then it occurred to her that he might have thought there was another reason for her to have been so accepting—nay, *willing*—to share his bed.

As he set her cloak around her shoulders, she turned, concerned. "I want you to know that this did not happen because I expect you to give me the house or that I planned to use sexual congress as a means of bartering."

He gave her a crooked smile that began as something adoring but then turned into something altogether naughty. "It never occurred to me, but now that you give me the idea…"

She laughed when he reached for her, no doubt ready to pull her back to bed. And she was tempted but also quite sore. "It's important—now more than ever—that we continue our wager. I do not want you to have any doubt."

That new smile returned, and he inclined his head in agreement. Taking a step toward her, he kissed the corner of her mouth. "I will summon a carriage and drive you home."

"No, you will not. Can you imagine the scandal? I will walk as if I have just returned from the park."

"You will not walk." Those three vertical lines between his brows returned but were accompanied by a rather arrogant smirk. "I am pleased to say that you are far too exhausted."

Exasperated but somehow still grinning, she laid her hand over his heart. "Are you going to argue with me, even now?"

This time, he pressed a kiss to the center of her mouth and lingered. "With you, always."

CHAPTER TWELVE

The Season Standard—the Daily Chronicle of Consequence

Lady F—th's concerto this evening is sure to impress. Rumor has it that our resident goddess ordered a length of crimson silk from the drapers. One must wonder what stunning creation Lady G— will display this evening.

In other news, our favorite Viscount E— was spotted in the park this morning...

Each time Juliet read the current issue of the *Standard*, she breathed a sigh of relief. There was only that brief remark but nothing more. Not even the barest whisper about her scandalous visit to Max's townhouse yesterday morning.

Of course, Max had been quite clever in his plan to make certain no one saw her. So clever, in fact, that Juliet had wondered aloud how often he hailed hacks and then asked them to drive around to the garden gate.

Finding her question amusing, Max had grinned, spouting some nonsense about believing her to be jealous, just before he'd kissed her. Soundly.

Even a full day and a half later, Juliet could still feel the warm, tingly aftershocks of it.

"Do you think Lord Thayne will attend Lady Falksworth's concert this evening, madame?" Marguerite asked with a saucy waggle of her brows as she put the finishing touches on Juliet's coiffure.

Even though Juliet had confessed nothing about the events of yesterday morning, her maid had known instantly. Of course, it was impossible to hide the remnants he'd left on Juliet's flesh, tender and pink from his ardent attentions. Even the way she'd walked had been slightly altered, hinting at a new awareness of muscles she never knew she had. Most of all, Marguerite had claimed that Juliet was glowing, her skin and her eyes emitting an ethereal shimmer.

Glancing in the vanity mirror, she wondered if it was still showing. Then again, perhaps her current iridescent state was the gleam of candlelight glancing off the deep blue silk. "As I told you before, I do not know Max's plans from one day to the next."

However, that did not stop her from hoping she would see him tonight.

"But you are his lover now, no?"

Juliet didn't know that either. The way things had been left between them, she was unsure of where they stood. She'd half expected him to propose to her. When he hadn't, she told herself to be grateful. Gone was the impulsive man from five years ago who'd turned her world upside down. Since she was just settling into her life, she didn't need any sudden alterations, which included changing the peculiarly tense sort of friendship that she shared with Max.

When he did not call upon her at all today, however, she began to worry that he regretted what happened. No matter what their history was, she counted on his being in her life. And she prayed that her act of impulsiveness had not ruined everything she cared about the most.

Rivalry or not, she didn't want to lose him.

"What I know is that I shall be late to the concert if I do not make haste," Juliet said, choosing an ivory comb from the collection on a tray. Although, given her destination this evening, she would almost rather miss the concert entirely. She truly loathed Lady Falksworth.

Marguerite made a sound of disgust. "That woman does not deserve your attendance with the way she spoke incessantly about your scandal when you returned, not letting anyone forget the reason you married Lord Granworth."

"Ah, but in doing so, she made me quite the celebrity, didn't she? I daresay, my name has not been absent from the *Standard* for a single day since," Juliet said in jest, pretending to enjoy being beneath the *ton*'s quizzing glass. Yet not even this was the true reason Juliet despised Lady Falksworth. The hatred Juliet felt had begun years ago, when Lady Falksworth was a guest of Lord Granworth's in Bath.

They were distant cousins but very much alike in nature. Even down to their exacting tastes in—what they considered—beauty. In the beginning, Lady Falksworth had suggested that Juliet not be allowed to drink more than one cup of tea each day in order to prevent her teeth from staining. Dark berries had been added to that list as well, and in a matter of days, Lord Granworth and his cousin had decided upon Juliet's entire daily rations.

From there, Juliet's life had been managed into quarter-hour increments, subject to change only on Lord Granworth's whim and Lady Falksworth's suggestions.

During all of it, Lord Granworth made sure to remind Juliet that she was nothing without her beauty, nothing without his money or his connections, and that without all of it, not even her parents would love her. And Juliet hated that she'd believed him for so long.

It wasn't until Zinnia and Lilah had written to her over a year ago, expressing condolences and asking after her well-being, that Juliet began to find her strength again. Out of all the people who had fervently followed Lord Granworth and professed to being her dearest friends, none had ever proven it. Only Zinnia and Lilah had inquired after her.

She still remembered the utter shock she felt. That initial gesture of kindness had filled her with such joy that it had snapped her out of her doldrums. She had spent far too many years living as an empty shell. But that was over and done.

The woman that Max had seen inside her, the same one he'd kissed in the library all those years ago, deserved better.

Since her return, and even in the months before, she had found her inner strength and also a sense of self-empowerment that had helped her learn all she could about art trading. By doing so, she had amassed a small fortune, far more wealth than Lord Granworth likely ever expected her to possess from his life's collection of beautiful objects. But above all, Juliet loved being a strong, independent woman.

Wasn't that the reason she'd entered into her wager with Max in the first place? Yet things had just become more complicated. She wasn't certain how to proceed with Max but knew that she needed to keep her plan firmly in motion.

Marguerite scoffed as she anchored the comb in place. "I still do not believe Lady Falksworth deserves your attendance."

"That may be true," Juliet agreed, pulling on a pair of long white kid gloves adorned with pearl buttons at the cuff. "However, I have a wager to win, and now is not the time to rest on my laurels."

"Lord Thayne would surely give you the house if you asked for it."

Undoubtedly. Juliet knew enough of Max's nature to believe him capable of sudden tender gestures. "Which is precisely the reason I must win on my own. I cannot have him thinking that I was intimate with him in order to win the house."

"And you told him that, *non?*"

"Of course."

Marguerite dusted her hands together. "Then the matter is settled."

Juliet shook her head, adamant. "A person proves her or his character through action and deed. If our situations were reversed, I would be offended if Max stopped trying to win, and a measure of regret or doubt might creep in as well. He has every right to be assured that what happened between us had nothing to do with the wager."

"Only passion," Marguerite said with another eyebrow waggle before reaching into the narrow, velvet-lined armoire for Juliet's sapphire necklace.

Juliet chose to ignore her maid. "With any luck, I'll encounter Ellery this evening and continue with my plan to showcase him in the best possible light." Since the rescue of her fan had been such a triumph, she concluded that the rescue of her person would be even more so. Therefore, she intended to feign a turned ankle, which would serve two purposes—the first being the obvious favor he would gain, and the second being an early departure for both of them from tonight's concert.

Marguerite clucked her tongue as she fastened the clasp, the blue stone winking in the silver taper light. "I do not like this plan of yours any longer."

"Whyever not?" Not that it would stop Juliet, but she was curious.

"What would Lord Thayne think to see you leave the concert on the arm of another man? Surely he would be jealous."

After yesterday morning, Juliet believed that Max knew better than that. Clearly, she was not one to take a lover on a mere whim. And at the reminder of what it was like to be in Max's embrace, her reflection smiled back at her. "I thought you once said that a jealous man made a wonderful lover."

"*C'est vrai.*" Marguerite offered a thoughtful nod, pursing her lips. "But passion born from jealousy is a poison, madame. A little can cause hot tingles all over the skin, but too much will murder your love affair."

The warning sent an ominous shiver through Juliet, and her smile faded, her expression uncertain. Turning away from the mirror, she stood. "You are assuming far too much. I do not even know if I am having a love affair."

Marguerite smiled and kissed Juliet on both cheeks. "Then for your sake, I hope Lord Thayne will make it perfectly clear tonight. *Vive la romance!*"

The receiving line at Lady Falksworth's concert followed the curved wall around the overly gilded, art-choked first floor hall and continued down the carpeted stairs. Like the surroundings, most of the guests fairly dripped with adornments—a profusion of jewels, tiaras, and turbans meant to impress their hostess.

Unlike the prediction in the *Standard*, Juliet had not gone to any particular effort. She dressed with the simplicity that she always preferred. A single jewel and a well-designed gown was all she required. When it was her turn to greet Lady Falksworth, however, Juliet felt a modicum of pleasure at receiving squinty-eyed disapproval.

"Lady Granworth, how good of you to attend," she said with a pinched smile. "I seem to recall admiring the cut of that gown Wednesday last."

It was no accident that Juliet was wearing the same gown she had worn on a prior occasion, which they'd both attended.

"Oh dear," Juliet said without an ounce of chagrin. "How very frugal of me."

Lady Falksworth's cold blue eyes turned icy, clearly perturbed by the slight. "Hmm…quite. One would have thought, however, that my cousin's fortune might have afforded you a new gown for such an event. Unless, of course, your father's affliction has turned into your own." She tsked, not bothering to lower her voice but adding a dusty chortle to remove the weight from the slanderous comment. The small titters from those nearest proved she'd effectively made it seem as if they were close acquaintances.

Juliet had expected such a retaliation and did not bat an eye. Saying nothing only made her hostess appear peevish.

Lady Falksworth continued. "Oh, but aren't we all gamblers from time to time? I myself enjoy a rousing game of whist. Though I must offer a word of caution because, as it is, I have no more cousins to spare you from ruin."

This time there were a series of sharp inhales of shock.

Not wanting to give Lady Falksworth the satisfaction of thinking that she'd struck a nerve, Juliet gripped her composure as if her life depended upon it. "It is fortunate that I have no need of assistance."

"Ah, then we must play sometime."

Juliet inclined her head and withheld further comment. It was far better to retain the high road than to lower oneself into the muck. For those who dwell within it are far too pleased when company joins them. And yet, Juliet wished she would have said or done something. Years of injustice were still raging inside her.

She knew very well that nearly all the guests in attendance had fallen victim to their hostess's waspish tongue at one time or another. Society, however, was a fickle beast that cared more for pleasing itself whenever possible than for slaying old dragons. Proof of that was in the crush gathered inside the ballroom.

The moment Juliet entered the room, she searched for Ellery, still hoping that she might accomplish the goal for which she'd come, sooner rather than later. If she could feign an injury before the performance even began, then all the better for her.

Unfortunately, he was nowhere to be seen. Worse yet were the whispers gathering like a gale wind through a rocky cove. Apparently, Lady Falksworth's invitation to the Duke of Vale, Ivy, and the dowager duchess purposely excluded Gemma Desmond.

Juliet was incensed. *That condescending shrew!*

If Juliet would have known about this, she would have declined to attend out of solidarity. Regret and disappointment filled her.

She looked to the exit, prepared to show her support, even if after the fact. Yet as the troupe of Italian opera singers began their performance, the French doors leading to the ballroom closed. A footman in scarlet and gold livery stood sentinel in front of them.

It was common knowledge that Lady Falksworth despised tardiness and disruptions of any sort. Priding herself on following the rules of society to the letter, she also demanded clockwork precision of her servants, as well as punctuality and perfection in her companions. She had been known to say, "A life is not worthwhile without order."

But now, Juliet was set on disturbing Lady Falksworth's order.

When the moment was right, Juliet stood. Pressing a hand to her temple, she knew that any onlookers would assume she merely had a headache. It worked for the footman, after all. He was even kind enough to show her to the retiring room, where she could wait until the end of the performance.

"Thank you, but I would prefer to leave," she said, with a smile to him once they were alone in the hallway.

The young footman blushed all the way to the tips of his ears and began to stammer. "Her ladyship wouldn't...that is to say...Lady Falksworth prefers for her guests to stay until the evening's...festivities have ended."

Feeling penned in, Juliet glanced to the stairs. "And if a guest desires to leave, regardless?"

"I'm afraid, my lady, that Mr. Bowson, at the main door, would only show you to the parlor."

The gall of that woman! Juliet was even more determined to create a little chaos. And she knew exactly how to do it.

Not revealing the animosity that rushed through her, she inclined her head, dismissing the footman as she stepped into the retiring room. The moment he was gone, however, she set a course for rebellion.

Traversing a corridor and a set of stairs, Juliet crept into the aviary and closed the door behind her. It took a moment for her eyes to adjust to the dimly lit interior. Only the soft, fuzzy gleam from a half moon filtered through the clear glass-dome ceiling. Potted trees, perfectly pruned into spheres, surrounded the exterior walls. In the center, five Moorish white-capped cages hung from chains, and within them, her quarry.

Another well-known fact about Lady Falksworth was that—much like Lord Granworth—she was a collector. Most of all, she adored her collection of over a hundred green and gold finches.

Rows upon rows of golden birds with pinkish beaks were sitting on perches, chattering and chirruping noisily. A few of them flitted restlessly about, their tiny talons strumming against the thin bars, dipping with a twist of the neck to sip a bit of water, or winnowing a seed, gnashing endlessly to find the meat within. But for the most part, they stayed on their perches.

Juliet looked over her shoulder at the door, to make sure she was alone, before preparing to lift the latch of the first cage. Already, she could imagine the birds flying about and leaving their droppings all over the floor and benches. Then, when Lady Falksworth next showed off her collection, she would be humiliated. It was the least she deserved.

Besides, the birds should not be caged at all. Lady Falksworth had no right to keep these beautiful creatures imprisoned for her own amusement.

Juliet knew too well what that felt like.

Night after night, she'd disrobed for Lord Granworth's inspection and admiration. As per the marriage contract, she had no right to refuse him. Payment of her father's debts and even her own settlement was contingent on her pleasing him. Her only reprieve from being a spectacle had been during her womanly courses. Lord Granworth had found that *unfortunate* and *unappealing* but often said that it was *"an ordeal one must endure when having living art within one's house."*

Of course, after her parents' deaths, Lord Granworth no longer had any hold over her. She'd thought about leaving hundreds of times in that last year before his death. At the time, however, she'd had nowhere to go, no family, no home, no money, and nothing to call her own. She was a prisoner in a gilded cage, wanting for nothing except for her freedom.

Standing in Lady Falksworth's aviary, Juliet smiled with delight as she stepped back, waiting for the birds to rush out and take flight, finding purchase on a branch instead.

Yet after Juliet opened the first cage, she noticed that something strange was happening—or rather *not* happening. The birds had gone quiet, all huddled together on the perches. There was no more chatter, no more flitting about.

"Come on," Juliet encouraged them, clucking her tongue in a staccato rhythm. "You're free now. Look." She slipped her hand through the opening and wiggled her fingers before withdrawing.

Then, guessing that these birds were not the brightest, she went to a different cage and did the same thing. But those birds went quiet too. In fact, all of the birds remained silent, watching her carefully, as if she were some sort of predator instead of their savior.

Frustrated, she unlatched all the cages, leaving the doors gaping like mouths open in a silent scream. She felt tears sting her eyes. "Damn it all, why won't you fly?"

Max arrived late to Lady Falksworth's soiree. He had a devil of a time trying to get in, since the man at the door refused him. The butler had made it clear that tardiness was not permitted beneath her ladyship's roof, and the concert had already begun.

Of course, he hadn't intended to come at all. He didn't care for Lady Falksworth, as she had been the main instigator that renewed the *ton's* interest in the *kissing scandal* upon Juliet's return.

Then, after learning from Mother that Juliet planned to attend, Max was astonished. Juliet had made her dislike of Lady Falksworth apparent to him on several occasions, so he could not help but wonder why she would make this choice.

Having the butler close the door in his face did not deter Max in the least. He would simply find another way inside.

Standing on the pavement, he took in the golden shimmer of candlelight warming the panes of white-trimmed box windows set in rows along the pale gray stone facade. Erected on a corner, the property hosted a garden wall that lined the pavement, the towering structure more like that of a rampart barring intruders.

With a quick pace, he followed the wall as it wrapped around the back, and there he found an ivy-shrouded gate. In no time, he swept into the garden and, after a few steps, met with the domed glass structure of Lady Falksworth's famed aviary.

As luck would have it, the narrow whitewashed door leading to the garden was unlatched.

"Damn it all, why won't you fly?"

Once Max stepped inside, he stopped short. "Juliet?"

There she stood, bathed in moonlight and tears glistening in her eyes.

She looked at him, blinking slowly several times, and then said on a sigh, "You came."

He didn't know what had happened, but he would find the culprit and murder him later. In the meantime, he simply strode to her, gathered her close, and tucked her head beneath his chin. "What is wrong, my goddess?"

"I wanted to cause a scandal, but it isn't working."

"Ah," he said, as if he completely understood and knew exactly why she was standing in the aviary. "But we are much better at causing scandals together. So tell me what I can do."

"Stay just as you are," she said softly, resting her cheek upon his lapel. "I don't even know why I came. I should have given Lady Falksworth the cut direct when she brought up my father's gambling debts. Not many knew about it or that it was part of the contract he'd signed with Lord Granworth."

"Your father's..." Max stilled, a memory assailing him. "So the rumors were true."

She nodded, expelling a slow exhale. "He'd been only days away from debtors' prison. That night, Lord Granworth offered him a life of luxury, travel, parties...and all for the price of one worthless daughter. All that man wanted was my soul."

Max tightened his arms around her and pressed his lips to her rose-scented hair. "But you fooled them all, didn't you?"

"What do you mean?"

"You never gave them your soul. You kept it locked away for safekeeping."

She scoffed and gestured toward the cages. "I think I was more like these birds—too foolish to fly."

When he glanced at the cages and saw all the doors hanging wide, he began to put the pieces together. Only now did he fully realize what it must have been like for her, all those years trapped in a life that was not of her making. She was born beautiful and to parents who did not cherish her as they ought to have done but instead sold her into a loveless marriage.

He couldn't help but think how different it might have been. How fiercely he would have loved her, leaving her without any doubts.

"They won't fly. They're just sitting there." She sniffed, continuing. "And they deserve more than this life in a cage."

He pressed a kiss to her temple and drew in the faint rose scent from her hair. "Perhaps they are afraid. They know what their life entails inside their cage—plenty of food, a dish of water, a community where they feel like they belong. It would take an act of bravery to leave and venture into the unknown."

She was quiet for a moment. When she spoke, her voice was as frail and stained as lace trim caught underfoot. "I'd always had the freedom to leave Lord Granworth. I thought about it every moment of every day. I could have found employment as a companion or even a governess. Instead, I stayed and blamed my fate on my father's debts. When the truth was, I was afraid of what was waiting beyond my own cage. Most of all, I feared learning that everyone was right about me—that I possessed no true value."

"How could you have ever believed that?"

Again, her head rested against his shoulder. "Far too easily."

More than anything, he wanted to press his suit, to tell her that he thought she was brave for returning to London and especially for facing her opposition—*him*—head on. He hadn't made it easy on her. Yet through all their squabbles, she never once conceded to him, and that—he realized now—had made him love her all the more. The feelings that he'd always had for her were still with him. But as much as he wanted to tell her, he also didn't want to frighten her.

"When you're ready," he said, "I'll escort you back inside."

She lifted her face, her spine abruptly rigid. "You know very well that we cannot be seen together."

"Whyever not?"

"Someone will surely notice how well we"—she broke off, her gaze flitting to his and then away—"walk together."

He nodded sagely, trying not to laugh. "It is true. You and I have been walking for many years now, and I do believe we are experts."

"Be sure you do not say that with Zinnia nearby. She would be crushed to learn that she is not the leading example," she teased in return, relaxing into his embrace once more. "But all jesting aside, I think you understand my meaning."

"Yes, we do *walk* quite well together." He studied her carefully and risked stealing a kiss. "It is a pity that you would give us away, unable to keep from caressing me with your gaze. You ought to learn to control that, you know."

She grinned, and the moonlight reflected in her eyes was soft and tender. "I shall put forth an effort, but I cannot make any promises."

And with so little, she filled him with the hope that, perhaps, she might not be as skittish as he feared.

Chapter Thirteen

The following morning, Juliet met with her solicitor and went over her accounts.

Young Mr. Sternham stood on the opposite side of her desk, his gloved hands clasped in front of the brown suit hanging on his boney frame. Like his father, the elder party of Sternham & Son, he wore a monocle, pinched beneath a lowered wiry gray brow and a lifted cheek that caused an arc of wrinkles from one side of his nose to his jaw. The fact that she'd never seen either gentleman without his eyepiece made her wonder if it was fastened upon birth. Though, regardless of the origin, that large monocled eye was now staring at her with undisguised impatience.

"I am nearly finished, Mr. Sternham," she said with an apologetic smile. She preferred to check the books herself and keep a close watch over her spending. Even though she had an immense fortune, she could never forget her father's inadvertent lesson to her—that poor decisions are often the result of desperation.

Unfortunately, she was not wholly able to concentrate on numbers. Not since last night. Neither she nor Max had returned to the concert. Instead, Max had driven her home, holding her close in the dark interior of the carriage. There was something simple and intimate about leaning against him, her head resting upon his shoulder.

The wonder she felt in that moment still lingered with her today. Likely that was the reason her gaze kept veering to every *M* on the page, her eyes seeing *Max* everywhere.

Max's Millinery Shop—straw hat, ribbon, gloves

Smythe's Florists—Max, Fern, and Gypsophila

Draber's Confectionary—Max

In fact, she had to blink several times to see what was actually there.

Merlin's Millinery Shop—straw hat, ribbon, gloves

Smythe's Florists—Myrtle, Fern, and Gypsophila

Draber's Confectionary—Macaroons

Perhaps she required a monocle too.

After another minute or so, she reluctantly gave up the effort and closed the ledger. Instead of adding up the column with her solicitor waiting, she simply handed it over to him, thanked him for his patience, and stated that she would come to his office on the morrow. She hoped her thoughts would be in the right place by then, yet she had her doubts.

She couldn't stop thinking about Max, wondering what he was doing and if he was thinking of her. Pathetic, really.

Her stomach fluttered continuously, as if she'd swallowed a hummingbird that was trying to escape. Her heart vacillated from a quick, light cadence to an irregular, anxious, and wary rhythm. And worst of all, she caught herself sighing— *sighing, for heaven's sake*—at regular intervals, as if she were on a schedule.

This morning, Zinnia had asked if she was coming down with a fever.

Readily denying it, Juliet had assured her that all was well, even though it embarrassed her to no end. Her only consolation was that she could blame Max for this too.

Nonetheless, as Zinnia left to pay a call on Marjorie, she had decided to stop by the apothecary to see if he had a powder to aid Juliet's breathing.

Now that Zinnia was gone *and* the solicitor was gone, Juliet had far too much time on her hands.

"Have any missives or packages arrived, Mr. Wick?" she asked as she stepped into the foyer.

"No more since a quarter hour ago, my lady." The butler's stately expression remained unchanged, aside from the slight lift of his brows as he glanced down to the empty salver on the rosewood table. "If there is an order you are expecting, I could send for a messenger."

"Thank you, no. That is not necessary, just a mere curiosity." Juliet fought a cringe, feeling as if she'd gone to Bedlam. "However, if anyone calls, I shall be in the parlor."

Mr. Wick cleared his throat. "Forgive me, my lady, but I was under the impression that you were not at home for callers on Thursdays."

"Oh, is today Thursday? Well, then, that explains it. I'm never quite myself on Thursdays," she said with a short laugh and wondered if she should feign a dizzy spell for better effect.

Thankfully, she was saved that decision when three sharp knocks rapped on the door. Mr. Wick turned to answer it.

"Delivery, sir," a boy wearing a carmine felt cap said, lifting a rectangular package wrapped in brown paper with both hands.

Juliet felt a smile tug at her lips as hopeful expectation soared through her. She wasn't expecting any deliveries, and from what she knew, Zinnia wasn't either. But since a similar instance had happened twice before, she could not help but wonder if this might be for her.

It seemed to take forever for Mr. Wick to check the card attached and turn around. All the while, Juliet held her breath.

Then, at last, Mr. Wick inclined his head and stepped toward her. "For you, my lady."

The plain white card with the familiar scrawl greeted her as she grasped the edges of what felt like a shallow box. It was quite light, as if it contained no more than air, and she would be just as content as if that were all that lay inside.

"Thank you, Mr. Wick," she said, breathless, ready to rush into the parlor to open it.

That goal altered suddenly when Mr. Wick turned back around to pay the lad. That was when she discovered that the boy was no longer the only one standing on the other side of the threshold.

Max lifted a gray John Bull from his head, his unerring gaze pinning her in place before he looked to Mr. Wick. "Is Mrs. Harwick here by any chance? I was informed that my mother was paying a call on Lady Cosgrove this morning."

"My apologies, Lord Thayne. I'm afraid that Lady Cosgrove left a short time ago in order to—I believe—pay a call on Mrs. Harwick," Mr. Wick said, a puzzled inflection to his tone. Poor Mr. Wick. He was likely to believe that everyone became out of sorts on Thursdays.

Max clucked his tongue in regret. "I must have misunderstood. My thoughts have been somewhat distracted of late.

The only thing I seem to recall is that Lady Granworth is not at home on Thursdays, so I suppose I shall have to return from whence I came. Good day, Mr. Wick."

Astounded, Juliet watched Max turn without even sparing her another glance. She was torn between outrage and laughter. How dare he come all this way, see her standing not four steps from him, and not even ask to see her! And yet, she had the distinct impression that he had not come here for his mother, especially when he had never done so before.

"Mr. Wick, you may inform Lord Thayne that I am, presently, at home," Juliet said, speaking loudly enough to call attention to Max, who then glanced over his shoulder with a smirk on his lips. "Unless, of course, he has a more pressing engagement."

She turned away, not waiting for his response.

Inside the parlor, Juliet closed her eyes and did her best to quiet the thrumming of her pulse. She clutched the package to her breast and told herself that it was foolish to react this way simply because Max was here. He'd escorted his mother here on several occasions this Season.

Then it occurred to her that this was the first time he had come *alone* and, presumably, to see her.

Happy—simply for the sake of being happy, she supposed— she crossed the room, sat on the settee, and placed the unopened package on the table, the card beaming up at her.

Mr. Wick appeared at the door, somewhat befuddled. "Lord Thayne to see you, my lady."

Then Max emerged, his hat and gloves absent, his dark hair slightly mussed and curling at the peak of his forehead in the shape of an apostrophe. He bowed, his gaze never leaving her, not even to shield the blatant passion burning in his eyes.

"Thank you, Mr. Wick. That will be all," she said, hoping the tremble in her voice was not detected.

The butler left without a care, while Max, on the other hand, seemed to study her even more closely.

"How good of you to see me," he said, taking the chair opposite her. "You are looking quite well. Far better than the impression Lady Cosgrove gave."

Ah, so he had known she was here alone. "And what did she say, mere moments ago when she came to call on your mother?"

He grinned unabashedly. "That you were near death's door, likely stricken with a fever, a breathing ailment, thoughts adrift, unable to focus on a single task…"

"She did not." At least, Juliet didn't think it sounded like Zinnia to reveal so much.

"Then perhaps those are my ailments alone," he said with an absent shrug, as if he hadn't revealed something so monumental that it stole her breath.

"I am in perfect health at the moment," she proclaimed, simply because it pleased her to contradict him.

He sat forward, elbows on his knees, fingertips pressed together. "Are you certain? Because I do see a package on the table, and you seem to have forgotten all about it."

She suppressed a smile. "It would be rude of me to open it with you present."

"Why? Afraid it is from an admirer and that the contents might be of an intimate nature?"

Her own curiosity spiked, her flesh tingling and drawing taut. Could that be the reason Max had come this way, precisely when the package was delivered? Did he want to witness her discovering the contents?

Unable to resist the challenge of drawing out the suspense, she reached out and brushed her fingertips over the string. "There is no way of knowing. This very thing has happened twice before, and the card was not signed."

"Hmm…So there is no telling who the sender is or what could be inside."

"None at all." She withdrew her hand and clasped it in her lap.

Max narrowed his eyes. "And you aren't the least bit curious?"

"Me? You know that I would never reveal such a shortcoming in my character. Since it is you, however," she whispered, "I will tell you a secret. If curiosity were a rash, I would be covered in spots from head to toe."

He gritted his teeth but smiled at the same time. "Then open the blasted package."

"You would not mind?"

"I insist."

Lifting the package to her lap, she tugged on the string, her heart beating madly beneath her breast. As always, she took her time in parting the paper, savoring the moment, and…just perhaps prolonging the torment of her audience on purpose.

At last, she reached the box. Then, lifting the lid, she discovered what lay within the blue felt lining.

Her breath stalled in her throat.

"The door of a birdcage." In fact, she would guess that it was one of the doors from Lady Falksworth's aviary, as it looked the same, with slim metal bars painted white and curled at the corners for decoration.

"And now it is always open," Max said, his hushed tone proclaiming his sincerity and something more.

She laid her hand over it, tenderly, as one would touch a priceless treasure. Unlike the two gifts that had come before it, this was not meant to incite either her ire or her amusement. It was far more tender in sentiment and something only Max could have given her. Because only Max knew her intimately. He had been her friend, her enemy, and then her lover. And now, even though she wasn't sure what they were any longer, she was certain of one thing. She was falling in love with him.

The sudden realization terrified her.

Looking to Max and seeing the tenderness in his gaze only made matters worse. Before now, the only man she'd ever thought she loved had been his brother, Bram. The result of that experience had left her defenseless.

With Max, she shared a history, a deeper connection that was more than smiles and flirtations. Somehow, she knew that loving him would be worse when it ended. Catastrophic, in fact. After all, he needed a wife before he left for Lancashire, while she…did not need or want a husband. She enjoyed her new life of independence. Loving Max put that in jeopardy. He was the type of man who would want everything she could give.

Slipping the box to the cushion beside her, she stood, her gaze darting to the window and then to the door.

Max stood too, his brow furrowed in concern. "Are you unwell?"

She shook her head, trying to hold on to her composure, even as she began searching for her fan, crossing the room to the milieu table and opening the drawer. "Just a trifle warm. There doesn't seem to be enough air in the room."

Of course, she could be worried for no reason at all. It was entirely possible that nothing would change between them. But even as the thought formed in her mind, she knew it wasn't possible. Max was looking for a wife and maybe even thinking that she would be willing. Oh, she hoped not. She hoped he knew her better than that.

Max came up behind her, a comforting presence at her back, his hands tenderly skimming down the length of her arms. "But your skin feels cool."

"Does it?" She closed her eyes, relishing the feel of his hands on her and wanting to lean back against him so badly that it nearly caused her pain not to do so.

"I do not think you are overly warm. In fact, I think the gift upset you. If that is true, then I will remove it at once."

"The gift was perfect." As of yet, he had not admitted to sending it, but she no longer wanted to keep up this pretense between them. "You understand me better than anyone."

And because it seemed like a need she could not control, she turned in his arms and kissed him.

The touch of her lips released a whirlwind of hope and desire inside Max. Everything between them was finally coming together. Not pressing his suit seemed to be working. If this was his reward, he would give her all the time she needed, even if waiting went against every instinct to claim her as his own. He wanted the entire world to know that she was his at last.

He wasn't going to risk losing her a second time.

Breathless, she pulled back from the kiss, her hands poised against his chest. "What do you want of me, Max?"

He could see the panic in her expression. And while he liked that they were always straightforward with each other, he knew it was still too soon to tell her the truth—that he wanted all of her and for each and every moment, for the rest of his life. "Only what you are willing to give."

His answer seemed to soothe her fears, because she twined her arms around his neck and pressed her lips to his again. This time, her kiss was eager, searching, and fervent, almost desperate, as if she needed something more from him. Assurance? Clarity? He wasn't sure. So he gave her everything he could in that moment.

Knowing exactly how she liked to be kissed, he grazed her mouth with his and ever so slightly nipped her with his teeth in the way that always made her tremble. She clung harder to him, parting her lips on a soft moan. And he lost himself in that sound, that admission of intimacy not even she could conceal. He walked her backward so they were shielded behind the open door.

Like days before, they wound up against the wall, ardently kissing and groping. Her hands slipped beneath his coat and down his back. She surprised him by gripping his arse and pulling him closer, her body welcoming the thrust of his hard flesh against her. Through the yellow muslin, he palmed her breast, worrying his thumb in circles over the pert tip. She gasped into his mouth and reached between them to the fall of his trousers.

But just then, he heard the sounds of a door opening, followed by Mr. Wick's voice as he greeted Lady Cosgrove in the foyer.

Max stayed her hands. "Your cousin has returned."

Juliet blinked, her eyes going wide, her gaze darting around as if only now coming to the realization that they were standing in her cousin's parlor. "Quick. You must pretend you were just leaving."

He laughed, looking down at the blatant evidence of his arousal. "I will need a moment or two."

"Oh dear." Her wispy golden brows lifted, and a small puff of air left her swollen lips. "You will need to carry something in front of you. Something quite large."

He grinned. "I could carry you out of here and solve two problems at once."

Her gaze lifted to his, lingered, and for an instant she appeared to give the thought consideration. But then, alas, she shook her head. "It would create more problems than it would solve. Here." She reached for her fan and opened it with a snap. "No. That won't do. We need something larger. Perhaps you could pick up a chair and pretend you are moving it about the room."

Knowing they were running out of time, Max took her hand and led her back to the settee before sitting in the chair across from her. He dared to press one kiss upon her cheek. "You may want to open your fan, for you are displaying a lovely shade of pink above your breasts and along your throat."

No sooner had Juliet opened her fan than her cousin walked into the room.

"Good morning, Lord Thayne, Juliet."

They returned the greeting as if it were typical to encounter them alone in the parlor. Max supposed they were fortunate that Lady Cosgrove appeared distracted, her hands worrying the knot of her reticule.

"I am glad you are both here for I have some news. Your brother," she said to Max, "the Marquess of Engle, has just returned to London."

Instantly, Max looked to Juliet to read her expression. Her gaze darted to his and then quickly away, as if to conceal her reaction. He did not want to think about why the mention of his brother's name would make her do so.

He swallowed. "That is excellent news."

"Not entirely," Lady Cosgrove added with downcast eyes and a sorrowful shake of her head. "It is with my deepest regrets to also inform you that your sister-in-law, the Marchioness of Engle, has died."

Juliet covered her gasp with her fingertips. "That is dreadful news. Oh, Max, I am so sorry. Please extend my deepest regrets to your mother and to Bram."

Bram. She still referred to him by his given name, as if there were still a familiar sentiment between them. Now, his brother was a widower. And Max was suddenly wishing he'd carried Juliet out of here when he had the chance.

CHAPTER FOURTEEN

By the time Max crossed the threshold, Harwick House was in utter chaos. Servants, both familiar and foreign, were scurrying about the hall, carrying in trunks, and forming ascending and descending lines on the stairs. Saunders's face and pate had gone red, his mouth a tight grimace. It was clear that the family were not the only ones taken off guard and besieged by this unexpected visit.

At least, Max hoped it was a mere visit. After all, Bram had been abroad so long that surely he would want to retire to his own estate in Devon, and London was a mere stopping point. Yet even while the logical conclusion formed in his mind, a cold shiver of foreboding snaked down his spine and settled into the pit of his stomach.

"By the looks of things, it appears as if my brother has every intention of staying," Max said under his breath.

"Indeed, my lord," Saunders answered and then cleared his throat. "You'll find Lord Engle and Mrs. Harwick in the study."

When there was a break in the line at the stairs, Max headed up to the first floor, his legs filled with lead. He had to remind himself several times that he was no longer the discounted little brother but a marquess in his own right. Not that Bram had sent word of acknowledgment to that fact.

Regardless, it was time to put the past to rest and extend the hand of compassion to his brother. This was surely a most difficult time for him.

Max opened the door to the study and spotted Bram facing the sideboard, his blond head bent. Across the room, Mother frowned, her arms crossed and toes tapping on the hardwood floor.

When her gaze alighted on him, she expelled a breath. "Max, help me force your brother to see reason. We are in a state of mourning. I cannot possibly host a party announcing his return." And then her expression softened to one of pity. "Of course, you realize that we can no longer host your ball either."

Max nodded in understanding. Besides, the ball was the last thing on his mind. "Of course not. We are all in mourning now." He crossed the room and stood next to Bram. "Allow me to extend my sincerest regrets, brother."

"Regrets? Whyever would you have any of those? You weren't married to her. I'm the only one allowed to have regrets." Bram slurred his words, his breath pungent as vinegar and fire. He pivoted toward Max, pointing at him with a brim-filled glass, scotch sloshing over the side and onto the toe of Max's boot.

Since the decanter on the tray was still moderately full, Max could guess that Bram had already been foxed by the time he arrived. The red-glazed eyes and ruddy cheeks were also an indication. "She was your wife. It's only natural to mourn her loss; however, now is the time to make arrangements for her burial."

Bram scoffed wetly, teetering where he stood. "Her lover took care of that. Already buried her in his family plot, the blighter."

Mother gasped. "Oh, Bram. I'm so sorry. You never said anything in your letters."

"Yes, well, it wasn't worth the mention, was it?"

Max didn't approve of the disrespectful nature of Bram's response and was about to say something when Mother shook her head and held out her hand in a gesture that suggested a need for patience. Even though Max felt he'd been patient enough for five lifetimes, he conceded to her wishes with a nod.

"If you can bear to tell us," Mother said, "what exactly happened to her?"

"Died in childbirth, so I'm told."

Both Max and Mother went still, the air stolen from the room. He knew better than anyone how much Mother had wanted a grandchild.

"And the baby…" she asked, clearly holding her breath.

"Mine, though one can never be too certain. My *wife* was increasing—five months—when she left, so the odds are in my favor."

Mother's eyes began to well with tears. Seeing her distress at the news of losing not only a daughter-in-law but also a grandchild, Max went to her side. He wanted to rail at Bram for his callousness, but such would be unseemly at this time.

Whatever ill will might still be between them, Max would never wish such a loss on anyone. "Then I am ever sorrier for both your losses."

"Both?"

"Your wife and child."

Bram drank a hearty swallow and flipped his fingers inconsequentially in the air. "The child survived."

Mother's handkerchief paused. "Pardon me?"

"The child is a girl," Bram said with a shrug. "Came in another carriage. Cries a great deal and never goes hoarse, if you can imagine it."

And just as he was complaining, Saunders appeared in the doorway, his eyes strained with jagged red lines, revealing that he might have reached his limit. "A *Miss Slade* is here with a child in tow, my lord. She claims to be the nurse of Lord Engle's child."

"Just so." Bram lifted his glass in a salute and then slumped down into the leather winged chair by the hearth.

And then, before their eyes, a shy young woman with a ruffled cap over her pretty blonde head stepped out from behind Saunders. The woman—who couldn't have been more than eighteen years of age—possessed an uncanny resemblance to the former Miss Leonard, the late Marchioness of Engle. And sleeping against the crook of her shoulder was not an infant but a downy-headed child with limbs long enough to dangle beside Miss Slade's hip and wrap around her neck.

Miss Slade curtsied and bowed her head but did not speak.

Mother stepped forward as well, inspecting the child and looking first to Max, with her brow wrinkled in confusion, and then to Bram. "Surely this child, which is hardly a new-born, could not be yours," she whispered.

"She was born a year ago, Tuesday last," Bram announced, rising from the chair. But at the sound of his voice, the child stirred. Lifting her head, her mouth puckered into a frown that dimpled her chin. In response, Bram scoffed in disgust and returned to the sideboard.

"Do you mean to tell me that your wife has been dead a year, and I have had a granddaughter for all that time, and you never bothered to mention it?" Mother's rightful outrage was palpable, though not at all like her. The woman, who was all ease and nurture, seemed to age in that moment. A spindly spray of lines creased the corners of her eyes, which dimmed and turned darker as she glared at Bram's back. "Does she have a name?"

"Patrice," Bram spat, as if the name tasted of venom on his tongue.

"Named after her mother," Max said absently, reeling somewhat from the news he'd learned in the past quarter hour.

"My late wife's lover named her. He thought to raise the child as his own, but after a time, the fond memories of his affair seemed to fade, and he was no longer so keen to raise another man's spawn. So he shipped her off to me"—he spread his arms wide, glass in one hand, decanter in the other—"and now here we are."

The child's chin trembled, her face reddening. Miss Slade instantly began to pat her back, making shushing sounds before the inevitable wail.

And what a bellow! Max stared, dumfounded by the volume such a small creature could emit. He was torn between wanting to cover his ears and wanting to add his own hand to the patting process in the hopes that it would soothe his niece.

His niece.

The words that carried a familial bond stalled his thoughts. The brother, of whom he'd never been particularly fond, now had a child. And by all accounts, an unwanted child. Max felt his heart squeeze in sympathy for little Patrice. Fate had already cast a black mark against the child for having been born to two exceedingly selfish people. There was no need to add to her life's burdens. Therefore, Max stepped forward, his hands outstretched.

After a clumsy exchange, he took the child in his arms, resting her tiny bottom on his forearm as he walked into the hall, Miss Slade's footfalls close behind.

"Perhaps it is time that we took a stroll to the nursery," Max said to his niece, keeping his voice low. Whether it was the movement or the alteration in the environment, he didn't know, but little Patrice's cries quieted to air-sucking sniffles through her tiny, upturned nose.

At the end of the hall, Saunders appeared again. "I'm having the nursery prepared, Lord Thayne."

"Thank you, Saunders. Would you be so kind as to do me one more favor?"

The butler didn't hesitate. "Certainly, my lord."

Since Max could see that the strain of the day was practically cracking the man in two, he decided to send him on an errand of peace and quiet. "I'm unsure of how many bottles of port we have, and I find myself rather curious at the moment. I would appreciate it if you would disappear into your pantry for an hour or so to sort that out."

The tight flesh around Saunders's eyes seemed to soften as he bowed. "Very good, my lord."

As Max made the climb to the nursery, he continued to speak to his niece, whose hands had now found his face and who kept a close, wide-eyed study of his features.

"You are quite fortunate to be blessed with the finest grandmother for whom one could ever hope," he said to her. "Barring recent events, she is rarely cross and has a warm, affectionate nature. I'm sure that once she overcomes her shock, she will be more herself."

When he reached the nursery, he'd concluded his speech with the certainty that she understood everything he said the moment her head bobbled in a nod. "There's a good little sprite. Now, stay with Miss Slade, and I will visit later."

Leaving her with the nurse, Max went back to the study, no longer feeling so compassionate toward his brother. By the time he heard their voices in the hall, he was prepared for battle.

"I thought I made it clear that we are past any period of mourning. Therefore we can have a party, and the sooner the better," Bram said, continuing the same argument as before.

"That may be true in fact; however, *we* are only now learning of her death. Surely there is a precedent to follow under such circumstances."

"Why do you think I stayed away so long? Hell, why do you think I never wrote to you about her death?" Bram shouted. "That whore didn't deserve any outward display of respect after what she had done."

Max stormed in, appalled and outraged, then closed the door behind him. "But our mother deserves respect, so mind your language in her presence. And for that matter, cease this despicable drunken display. You've made it clear that this vice is not due to grief."

Bram trained his squinted eyes on Max and tossed back the last of his drink. "Traveling here, I'd imagined this sort of unwelcome reception when I brought the sordid news. Likely that is why my nerves are in a lather, and I required a medicinal tonic to soothe them. Nevertheless, little brother is right. My apologies, Mother."

Mother walked over to the chair and laid a hand on Bram's shoulder. "The news must have been difficult for you to bear alone. It is good that you are here at last."

Max fought the urge to roll his eyes as Bram lifted his gaze and smiled sweetly to her. When she patted his cheek, apparently all was forgiven.

"Why is the party so important to you?" she asked.

"As I said, the child wails incessantly. Miss Slade knows not what to do and seeks my counsel."

"Perhaps if you'd hired a nurse who was a little older and with experience…" Max murmured before both Mother and Bram interrupted him with a warning glare. Suddenly, it felt as if the past were being played out before him with few alterations.

"What I need," Bram continued, "is a wife to see to these trivial matters. I have an estate to run. Surely even Max can understand the importance of that."

Mother offered a resolute shake of her head. "Unfortunately, with this recent news, even your brother's plans to find a bride must be delayed, perhaps until next Season."

"*Next Season?*" the brothers parroted in simultaneous incredulity.

"The custom is for a mother-in-law to be in mourning for six months and for a brother-in-law, six weeks." Mother dusted her hands together. "I'm afraid this Season would be over by then. Most of the families will be away from town by the middle of June."

Bram sat up straighter and cast a smirk to Max. "As I have already observed my period of mourning, and I have a child in need of a mother, I see no reason why I cannot begin the hunt immediately."

Mother pursed her lips in consideration and then nodded. "It is true. A widower with a small child would be expected to remarry, posthaste. However, *none* of us shall venture into the social sphere until a suitable time has passed. There will be no balls, parties, dinners, picnics, teas, or"—her gaze veered to Max—"paying calls."

In other words, no Juliet for the time being. Not seeing her for a full week? Impossible. How would he survive it?

"For many gentlemen, those customs are pushed aside, as they have responsibilities and business to attend." Max felt that old sting of unfairness well up inside of him, even as guilt assailed him. Battling with these inner demons, he promised to grieve for his sister-in-law but not when he was so close to getting what he wanted most.

"Of course you can attend to business, and you should keep Bram with you. It would do you both good."

"You seem awfully eager," Bram said, eyeing him. "I suspect that you have settled on a bride, and now I am curious to learn her name."

Max wasn't about to make any bold declaration at this time. Nor was he going to hint at her name, especially not when he wasn't even certain he could convince her. "It is no one you know and therefore none of your concern."

CHAPTER FIFTEEN

The Season Standard—the Daily Chronicle of Consequence

The prodigal Marquess of E—e has returned! Once a great favorite of this page, Lord E—e arrived yesterday but with the dreadful news of his late wife. Whispers abound of the scandal that kept Lord E—e in mourning for a year without even speaking of it. Shocking, indeed! The hushed nature has set many tongues wagging. What's more was the sighting of a child entering H— House. We are all eager for our next glimpse of Lord E—e and are left to wonder if he will don the black cravat of mourning or the snow white one of courting.

In other news, Lady F—th has recently reported a theft at her residence. Apparently, her famed aviary was breached by an intruder...

"Lady Granworth, perhaps this concept is beyond your understanding and best left to your man of accounts," the banker, Mr. Woldsley, said with a condescending sniff through his bulbous nose.

Juliet had encountered many men who detested doing business with a woman. And certainly there were bankers and tellers enough for her to find one more amenable to working with her. However, it was *because* of Mr. Woldsley's supreme distaste for women in his establishment that Juliet found it rather necessary to work with him.

On previous occasions, she had even heard him make derogatory comments about Lady Jersey's operation of the Child & Co. bank, declaring that she was "quite good at being led by the men in her employ."

And while Juliet did not think that she could alter his opinion, she would do her utmost to irritate him.

Smiling, she spoke calmly. "I believe it is more a matter of recollection—yours, in particular—Mr. Woldsley. I have told you many times that I prefer not to deal in banknotes but gold and silver instead. It really is that simple. And *if* you would do as requested, just imagine how much sooner you could be rid of me."

He snickered at her. "Oh, Mrs. Granworth—"

"*Lady* Granworth, if you please."

"Yes, of course," he drawled. "What you are failing to grasp is that the banknotes are equivalent to the gold and silver you deposited."

She held accounts in a handful of banks, but her fortune was not singularly invested. Juliet took pride in her own autonomy, knowing that her success had come from seizing control of her own destiny.

She folded her hands in her lap. "Do you believe that men are perfect?"

A confused sort of frown removed his smirk. "No man of any sense would make such a categorical proclamation."

For the first time since she stepped foot inside this institution, Juliet's smile was genuine. "If men are fallible, Mr. Woldsley, then certainly that which they have created may fall under scrutiny. Therefore, I retain my preference for gold and silver over your institution's notes." She slid her written request across his desk. "If you please."

At her irrefutable logic, he no longer argued. Either that, or she had given him a megrim.

Nevertheless, moments later, she left the bank with her coin purse full but, most of all, with a priceless sense of satisfaction.

"Lady Granworth, as I live and breathe." The familiar smooth cadence stopped her instantly on the pavement.

Slowly, she turned around. *Bram.* There he stood, handsome and fit as ever, his pale features angular, his frame lean. The only sign of wear the passing years had given him was in the first strands of gray threaded with the blond at his temples and loss of luster in his irises. He looked dashing in a way that had always made her heart beat faster. She waited to see if it would happen again...

"You are even lovelier than my fondest memory," he said, removing his hat and placing it over his heart. His broad grin revealed a set of dimples that had once fueled her dreams.

She smiled, pleased by the compliment that implied she had entered his thoughts a time or two over the years, as he had hers. "And you are still as charming, I see, Lord Engle." Then, suddenly, she remembered the reason for his return to London, and her smile fell. "I was terribly sorry to learn of your wife's passing. I hope you received the letter that Zinnia and I sent."

"I did, thank you." He nodded somberly, curling his hands over the brim of his hat. "Though it is somewhat odd, albeit warming, to receive condolences under such circumstances."

Juliet nodded, finding it more prudent to say as little as possible. Marjorie had already sent a missive to Zinnia, listing the worst of the news regarding his late wife's indiscretions. "I have also heard that you have a daughter. Congratulations."

Bram chuckled. "A prayer for my sanity would be more apt, but thank you nonetheless."

She wasn't certain what he meant but supposed it was a jest of his own. At one time, she might have understood those small asides, after having spent so much time in his company. But that wasn't the case any longer. In fact, she didn't even know how to reply.

It felt strange to stand there with Bram and not have Max nearby. Thinking back, Max had always been there, through every party, every dinner, every moment…And without him, there was a void that she never fully realized before. Now it seemed so clear.

"I am surprised not to see Max with you this morning, as his solicitor's office is only a few doors down." Though just when she finished her sentence, she caught a glimpse of him beyond Bram's shoulder, emerging from that very doorway.

Now her heart did indeed race. The urgency of every beat drowned out whatever response Bram had made, forcing her to nod absently in response. And then Max saw her. The tight expression he wore instantly fell away, replaced with something more intimate. That was, until he noted to whom she was speaking. Then his eyes hardened, and his mouth set in a grim line.

At last, when Max stood beside his brother, he removed his hat and placed it over his heart. "My lady."

Not *Lady Granworth*, Juliet noted, pleased not to have the reminder of the mistake she'd made five years ago. "My lord."

The tension in Max's jaw eased noticeably, and the smile he gave her was so enthralling that she was tempted to repeat herself.

"As I was saying," Bram continued, "Mother is still sorting out matters of decorum after learning of…the news. For the time being, however, she has declared that we shall observe mourning for a week and then half mourning."

"And for the next seven days, she has requested that Bram and I only leave the house for business matters," Max said, a wealth of hidden meaning in his gaze. In other words, there would be no social calls, no hurried parlor moments, and likely no visits to the house they were fighting over either.

She felt the loss keenly. "Your mother is all warmth and compassion. Her example makes us all the better for it."

"Hmm…yes," Bram agreed. "Though I must say, my little brother is positively stewing over the imprisonment. Just last night, he complained that his courtship of a certain young debutante would be stalled."

Max cleared his throat and shot Bram an obvious look of warning.

"Just last night, you say?" Inwardly, Juliet started. Though why this news surprised her, she didn't know.

After all, Max had made no secret about wanting to find a wife before settling into his home in Lancashire. Yet up until now, she was under the impression that Max was still in the process of making a list for a ball, hoping to narrow down his choice.

And suddenly, she wondered if the intimate collision between them had been a mistake. It had happened rather unexpectedly, after all. In fact, Max might have already had a bride in mind.

Juliet glanced away toward her waiting carriage and down to the folding step that her tiger had just lowered. She wished to flee as soon as possible. With effort, when she turned back, she had a smile in place. "Congratulations, Max. Is your bride-to-be someone I know?"

Max gritted his teeth and kept his response brief. "Likely."

And there was her answer.

A swift, keen pain filled the spaces between every beat of her heart.

Since she planned to win the wager, however, she knew they would see each other in town, even at his mother's for dinner. She didn't want any strangeness between them. After all, he was an important part of her life, and she was determined to keep their friendship. *And—oh drat—was that the sting of tears behind her eyes?*

"And what about you?" Bram asked. "Surely you have returned to London to cast a wide net on the most eligible."

On a steady inhale, she tucked the ache away and focused her attention on Bram. She shook her head. "I have no plans to marry."

"You must come to my house and meet my daughter," Bram said, flashing those dimples once more, "for I am eager for your opinion." And he said it with such ease that she wondered if he'd heard her response at all.

This was never something she'd noticed about Bram before. In the past, he'd always seemed attentive. But perhaps his thoughts were just as distracted as hers. One thing was for certain, however; she needed an end to this encounter before her spirits plummeted any further.

She'd been right all along. Being in love with Max felt exactly like flailing uncertainly with no end in sight.

"I will respect your mother's wishes and wait this week before I pay a call." She did not linger but curtsied to them. "Good day, gentlemen."

"My, my, my," Bram said, staring after Juliet's carriage as it pulled away. "What a difference five years can make."

"She is the same as ever. I do not see why you are so flummoxed." Max gritted his teeth. It was obvious, in this first meeting between Bram and Juliet, that his brother was overcome by her beauty. Then again, who wouldn't be?

Even so, a surge of jealousy and bitterness flooded Max, putting him in an even fouler mood. Of course, he wouldn't have been in a temper at all if not for Bram's announcement that Max had found his bride.

Juliet's eyes had dimmed, and her entire demeanor turned cold in less than a single second. He could only imagine what she must have thought and how Bram's declaration cast a tawdry light on what had been the best moments of his life.

More than anything, Max wanted to tell her the truth, that he had every intention of marrying her if she would have him. But it was that "if" that kept him silent.

"Obviously you are not a man who notices the importance of a serendipitous meeting," Bram said, turning away from the street and studying the brick façade of the bank, his hands clasped behind his back.

A frisson of warning burned through Max.

"A woman who does her own banking tells me two things," Bram continued. "One, that she must have something of a fortune. And two, that she requires a man to look after it."

Max didn't like the palpable greed in his brother's countenance, the cunning glimmer in his eyes. Earlier today, the steward informed him that Bram had inquired after Mother's accounts, which only added to the mystery of why Bram had come home.

After all, if his wife's affair had humiliated him so greatly, then why risk such a public return now? He could have easily gone back to his country estate and sent for Mother to visit. Instead, he'd come, with his own servants and child, to Harwick House.

By right, the manor belonged to Max, as it was *his* father's house. But for Mother's sake and for little Patrice, he did not press the point. He would allow his brother to stay under his roof, even though Bram had never asked for permission.

However, with the news he'd received earlier from the steward, and now Bram's interest in Juliet's fortune, Max wondered at the true reason Bram had decided to come to town.

Instinctively, he knew he would not like the answer.

CHAPTER SIXTEEN

Juliet arrived at Zinnia's townhouse later that morning, still feeling distraught after her encounter with Max and Bram. Had Max truly found a bride? And had he known about his choice *before* their shared intimacies?

It was one thing to be Max's lover, but if he had already settled on a bride, then that made Juliet feel as if she were his mistress. Which was not something she could abide.

As for Bram, this first meeting after five years had been so overshadowed by his loss and Max's news that she'd hardly paid attention to him. Since she abhorred that trait in others, she would set her mind to being a more attentive conversation partner when next they met.

When she stepped into the foyer, Mr. Wick greeted her with a bow. "Lady Locke is in the parlor, my lady."

Lilah was here? The happy news could not have come at a better time. A sigh of relief left her at once, and she was half tempted to press a kiss to the butler's cheek but settled for squeezing his forearm before she hurried into the parlor. "Thank you, Mr. Wick."

The moment she stepped into the room, she saw her cousin's radiant face, her mahogany eyes gleaming, her brown hair framing her heart-shaped face in gentle curls. "Lilah, is this truly you, or am I merely dreaming?"

Lilah embraced her with affection. "Do I seem all that different?"

"I would not have known you, if not for Mr. Wick's introduction," Juliet teased.

"And I had been about to call the guard when this stranger appeared." Zinnia gestured with a wave of her hand, offering a highly uncharacteristic quip that only proved how pleased she was about Lilah's return as well.

"I hope that I am not terribly altered," Lilah said with a coy bat of her eyes.

Juliet slipped her arm through Lilah's and led her to the violet settee. "You are simply glowing. Wouldn't you agree, Zinnia?"

"Indeed." In ever regal fashion, Zinnia descended into her jonquil upholstered chair.

Lilah looked around the cozy violet room, eyes round with awe as if she'd been away from it for ages. "There are moments when I still cannot believe how much my life changed in such a short time. Of course, it did take over twenty-three years." She laughed, her warm gaze resting on Juliet and Zinnia. "I look in the mirror and see the same face and features that had gone unnoticed for most of my life, and yet now there is a subtle difference. How I see myself on the inside has changed. And I thank both of you for my first glimpse of that person."

"It was there all along, you know," Juliet said, understanding the difficulty in seeing beyond the self-deprecating ideas one tends to believe. "But you've not said a word about your husband. How is Jack?"

"Magnificent." Lilah blushed in the way that most new brides did. "These weeks have been quite the revelation, though I suppose that is the way it is with married people."

Not for Juliet, but no one other than Max knew her secret. However, this was the first time in her life that she could begin to imagine what caused that happy glow.

"Seeing your expression reminds me of the joyful years I spent with Lord Cosgrove," Zinnia said with a smile and then glanced to Juliet. "Every woman deserves a great love."

A terrible twinge of longing pierced her heart. It was so sharp, so painful, that it likely ripped a hole in that fragile organ. After Max's declaration, she was sure of it.

Dismayed once more, Juliet nearly sighed aloud but caught herself in time. Not wanting to talk about love—great or otherwise—she slyly changed the subject. "Since you have been away, there has been much news."

"I happened to glance at this morning's *Standard*," Lilah said with an eager nod as Mrs. Wick entered with the tea tray. "I read that the Marquess of Engle has returned."

So, for the next few minutes, they spoke in hushed whispers about the scandal. When Zinnia mentioned how the late marchioness had been the one to claim the *Original* title during Juliet's last Season, Lilah gasped. "I'd always wondered but never wanted to ask. Were you…friends with her?"

Juliet stared down into her teacup, forming a kind reply. "We had attended many of the same parties, and I was quite familiar with her."

"Strange," Lilah said. "That is the same way I speak of Miss Leeds and Miss Ashbury, and you know my feelings toward them."

"Quite." Juliet offered a nod of agreement, thinking of the pair of termagants. There were definite similarities between them and Miss Leonard. "She and I were rivals for Lord Engle's affections."

Lilah's cup stalled. "And he married her instead. How awful it must have been for you."

"At the time, but no longer," Juliet said with the ease of hindsight. So many years had passed, and worse disasters had come and gone since then. "I daresay, not many debutantes were unaffected by his charm. Though to his credit, he made no formal declarations to court either of us." Though, on her part, his attentions were somewhat misleading.

"But now he has returned, and so have you. It almost seems as if fate has put him in your path once again."

Juliet smiled reflexively but without giving an answer. Zinnia carefully sipped her tea, her gaze distant, as if she were distracted by the idea. Instantly, Juliet knew that it was time for another change of topic, and began regaling them with her encounter with Mr. Woldsley.

Then, all too soon, their visit came to a close.

"I wish I could stay longer, drink tea, chat, and even walk in the park," Lilah said, standing, "but I have ordered furnishings for Jack's townhouse, and they are scheduled to arrive at precisely twelve."

"And when do you suppose that you'll have your home ready for company?"

Lilah laughed. "Surely by day's end. Jack is rather impatient to have all the *frippery and nonsense*, as he calls it, settled. So he hired an entire army of men to see it happen."

Zinnia squeezed her hand and smiled. "Send us a card, Lady Locke, and we will pay you a call."

"But for now you must go," Juliet teased, walking her to the door. "Zinnia and I are eager to lay the calendar on the tea table and speculate on when we might expect a new addition to the family."

Lilah said nothing but—once again—blushed furiously as she left them in the foyer to speculate all they liked. And though Juliet didn't want to feel this way, a terrible envy rose within her.

Unfortunately, she was unable to abandon that feeling. In fact, by the afternoon, it only worsened when she received a somewhat urgent missive from the Duchess of Vale, requesting Juliet to help plan a nursery. She might have laughed at the note altogether if not for the final words: *"I would hate to inconvenience you on such short notice, but I must seek your counsel."*

Believing there was more to the missive than met the eye, Juliet departed posthaste and went directly to the townhouse in St. James.

"I am so glad you have come," Ivy said to Juliet as they walked together up the wide marble stairway, their slippered steps muffled on the aubergine and gold runner. "Though I must confess to a partial deception because your advice on nursery décor is not the only reason I wanted you here today."

"Since I am hardly an expert in such matters, I had assumed as much." Juliet squeezed Ivy's hand in reassurance. "Whatever it is, I will do my utmost to help."

"You see, it is regarding Gemma…" From there, Ivy went on to describe Gemma's despondency of late. Since being snubbed by Lady Falksworth, Gemma had received no invitations. Even paying or receiving morning calls to friends of the dowager duchess had diminished.

"She confessed to me that she feels like a burden to us," Ivy continued. "Not only that, but she is considering giving up the idea of marriage altogether and taking orders instead. And while I've only known her for a short time, I do believe she is stubborn enough to do it."

This news was heartbreaking indeed. "I quite like her obstinacy. In this circumstance, however, I fear it will not serve her best interests."

"I wholeheartedly agree. It drives me mad to think of how her determination not to be held back by her father's reputation is being thwarted again and again."

Juliet firmly believed that any amount of courage or determination should be nurtured. "Then I think distracting her thoughts with planning the nursery is a brilliant idea."

"She is in the attic now, scavenging for ideas." Ivy looked up toward the coffered ceiling once they reached the tapestry-lined hallway on the third floor. "She is not one to remain idle for any length of time, which must stem from a life of constant travel. Though I fear this trait may encourage her to set a course to a destination from which she cannot return. Her maid even informed me that Gemma keeps a packed satchel in her wardrobe."

"Oh, dear. Then we must come up with an idea quickly."
Juliet thought of mentioning her desire to introduce Gemma
to Viscount Ellery, but it seemed too self-serving now. She
would wait until her wager with Max had ended before intro-
ducing Gemma to the man who was sure to be named this
Season's *Original*.

And honestly, Juliet didn't even want to think about the
wager or about what she learned of Max this morning. So a
distraction was essential for her as well. "Did you happen to
see Lilah this morning?"

Ivy nodded, her white teeth flashing in a broad grin that
lifted her cheeks. "She stopped for a moment to tell me of
her return and then professed that she should be fully prepared for callers tomorrow. Though if anyone can conquer an
impossible task, it is Jack. He has already proven he would do
anything for Lilah."

"Very true." And in Juliet's opinion, her cousin deserved
every happiness. "Perhaps we can persuade her to host a small
gathering. It would give Lilah the opportunity to have her
first party as Lady Locke but also provide Gemma something
else to think upon."

"I think that is a splendid idea. Then again, who am I to
say, when it is not my home that will be invaded?" Ivy laughed,
opening the door at the end of the hall. "And here we are—
the realm of the heirs of Vale, as my husband proudly declared,
moments after the physician first confirmed the news our
happy arrival."

Juliet might have laughed as well, if not for her pleased
gasp upon seeing the room. At first glance, the large rectangular room wooed her with the warmth of hardwood floors

the color of dark honey, a cozy rocking chair beside a white brick fireplace, and two pairs of arched windows at either end, with wrought-iron hinges on the shutters.

"It's lovely," she whispered.

Ivy led her into the room, pleasure glowing in her cheeks and in her winter blue eyes. Absently, she laid a hand over the tiniest bump in her middle. "What do you think of something whimsical? Bright colors. I do not know if Gemma paints at all, but her sketches are quite good. Perhaps I can persuade her to draw a pastoral mural on this larger wall, giving little Northcliff the notion that he is ruler over a great enchanted land."

"Do you have a sense that the baby will be a boy?" Juliet asked, charmed by the idea.

Ivy grinned but shook her head. "Not yet. *Little Northcliff* is a moniker that North's cousin gave the child. Lord Wolford was merely jesting, of course, but we have grown fond of it."

Juliet was immeasurably happy for Ivy and the duke. She wanted all that was good and bright in the world for her friends. And yet, with a great jolt of surprise, she realized that she also wanted it for herself.

Then again, perhaps she'd always wanted it but had never felt worthy of it before.

Juliet wondered what it would be like to have life growing inside her and to feel the sense of awe that was evident on Ivy's face. All she'd ever hoped for, when she was married, was to have a life of independence. To do as she pleased. To answer to no man. And she finally had that. Yet now she wanted more. The question was, however, was she ready to pursue it?

Juliet tucked the thought away for later. "And if it is a girl?"

Ivy sighed, her shoulders rolling forward marginally. "Ugh. There are so many from which to choose—our mother's names, his aunt's, Lilah's, yours—the list is endless."

Emotion welled in Juliet's throat. "You have considered my name?"

"Well, yes. You are one of our closest friends, silly."

Ivy embraced her, and in that same instant, the oddest thing occurred—a tear slipped down Juliet's cheek. Usually, she kept herself more composed than this, but the drop slipped free before she was even aware of the need to cry. What was happening to her? Usually, it was only with Max that she'd let down her guard.

Wiping the dampness from her cheek, she returned the embrace. "And you are mine as well."

"I do hope it isn't true what Edith told me," Ivy said with a frown. "That you have wagered with Thayne again, and this time you signed a contract, stating that you will leave London if you do not win."

Juliet nodded solemnly, suddenly knowing how much more she stood to lose. "In my own defense, I never imagined that Max could win. I still don't. In fact, I'm certain that my candidate will become the *Original*."

"Indeed?" Ivy lifted her pale brows and, after Juliet's affirmative response, continued. "Then what will happen to Thayne? He will be homeless."

"Hardly." Juliet laughed. "He may purchase a house anywhere. I have no qualms over where he lives. Just as long as it is not *that* house in particular."

And yet, the idea of encountering him in the future with his wife and their children sat sourly in the pit of her stomach, and she doubted the existence of a remedy.

"Anywhere? You are quite generous to your enemy. What if he purchased the house next to yours? Would that spark your ire?"

Juliet swallowed, almost wishing things were as simple as being Max's enemy again. "No, for I would simply buy the most beautiful cannon for my garden."

Ivy grinned and then turned thoughtful. "And in less than a fortnight, it will all be settled."

"Yes." Though it was a frightening notion. How would it be to live in that house, where there was so much history between her and Max?

CHAPTER SEVENTEEN

$\mathbf{M}$AX stared down in utter astonishment at the documents his steward had spread before him. A fortune of thirty thousand pounds had been squandered in the course of five years—or rather, four. This past year in France, Bram had lived on credit and the monthly offerings of their mother. "How can this be?"

Obviously sharp enough to understand a rhetorical question, Mr. MacDonald remained silent but merely lifted his brows in a shrug. After all, the evidence spoke for itself.

The final page was even more damning. According to a letter from the caretaker, the tenants at Bram's estate in Devon were living in squalor and sickness. Bram had disregarded every appeal for assistance and had chosen instead to live lavishly in France. Until recently, he was even keeping a mistress in a fine house with a slew of servants. When the shop owners and jewelers had closed their doors on him, however, he immediately booked passage to England.

It was even worse than Max imagined. "Have you contacted all of Lord Engle's creditors?"

His steward nodded but with measurable hesitation that sent a bolt of wariness through Max. "I should have a total for you by Friday next, my lord."

"Very good, Mr. MacDonald," he said. "After your exhaustive efforts this week, I shall see that you receive suitable compensation."

"Thank you, my lord."

"I do have one additional request, however," Max said with a glance toward the rosewood clock on the mantel. It was still early. Yet ever since Mother had told him that Lady Cosgrove and Juliet would call around eleven, anticipation made each minute stretch into an hour. "Later this morning, I would like to schedule a meeting with both my brother and you to go over the entries within this ledger, which you and I have already discussed at length."

Mr. MacDonald's copper-penny eyes squinted in confusion. "I'm not certain I understand, my lord."

Max knew he sounded rather cryptic, but it was desperation driving him. "In a few hours, I would like you to keep Lord Engle busy, here in this study, while I am…attending an errand."

He cleared his throat, hoping he didn't have to be more specific. He needed to see Juliet for the sake of his own sanity. And *without* his brother there to spoil anything.

This past week, Max had been driven to the brink again and again with every moment spent in his brother's company.

Then, during the few moments they had been apart, astoundingly enough, Bram had managed to accrue more debts.

He'd sent his own servants on errands, having them gad about town and then sneak back here. Word from the servants loyal to Harwick House was that Bram's tailor was fashioning seven new suits. Not to mention the constant deliveries of top hats, boots, walking sticks, and other baubles for a gentleman's *every* occasion.

During that time, Max had drafted at least four dozen letters to Juliet, trying to explain that there was no debutante. But every letter he wrote ended up sounding like a proposal of marriage. In the end, he knew it would be better to speak with her face-to-face.

With any luck, he would have that chance soon.

Juliet had spent the rest of the week planning the nursery with Ivy, visiting Lilah in her new home, and keeping Gemma distracted with shopping excursions and morning calls. Peculiarly, even while in the company of her friends, these had been the longest seven days of Juliet's life.

The balls and parties she'd attended were completely dull affairs. The rain, having been steady all week, kept her from enjoying her walks in the park. And each time she was alone in her bedchamber, she would stare for moments on end at the birdcage door that she'd hung in front of her vanity mirror.

"And now the door is always open," Max had said.

At the time, Juliet had imagined a greater meaning to his words, believing that Max was saying that he wanted more between them. Yet apparently she'd been mistaken.

Still, she missed Max. Since her return to London, this had been the longest period of time she'd gone without seeing him.

"Madame," Marguerite said from over her shoulder as she fastened the buttons of Juliet's gown. "You are sighing again."

"I was?" Instantly, Juliet straightened her shoulders and drew in a deep, cleansing breath. Of late, she'd been revealing far too much of her thoughts. She'd always prided herself on her composure, but now she didn't know what had come over her. "Forgive me, Marguerite. I have turned into a stranger, both to you and to myself."

She tsked. "You are the same madame I have always known, but *he* does not deserve your sighs. A man who would take you to his bed when he is planning to marry another deserves your spite."

Juliet agreed. She only wished she could convince her heart to hate him again. "What happened between us wasn't planned. In fact, we were in the midst of an argument."

Marguerite harrumphed. "You needed to put the past to rest, and now that is done. But I still do not like him."

Put the past to rest. Hmm…Was that the true reason behind their intimate clash? Perhaps the pent-up emotions and animosity over the years had all come out in a rather unexpected way. Juliet was mature enough to understand how something like that *could* happen, she supposed. And yet, she had been certain there was more than that between them. At least for her.

Apparently, the same had not been true for Max.

Juliet drew in another fortifying breath instead of listlessly exhaling. This morning, both Zinnia and she intended to visit Marjorie at Harwick House. If Max should happen to be there, then Juliet would simply greet him as she had done prior to their…collision. As always, she would conceal the truth of her feelings and the raw wound he'd left upon her heart.

The only problem was that she wasn't at all certain she could control her emotions as she once had. For some reason, she felt as if Max had unlocked something within her and then had taken the key with him.

CHAPTER EIGHTEEN

Full mourning was at an end at Harwick House, and Marjorie, dressed in lavender, greeted Zinnia and Juliet in the foyer. Then, pulling them quickly into the blue parlor, she began to discuss recent events as if half starved for gossip.

Discussing the latest society rumors was merely an appetizer. By the time tea arrived, they had moved on to the main course, which included whispers of Lord Pembroke's silver mine venture and how scores of people had already bought into it. Juliet, while having opinions on the matter, made no comment because she wanted to move on to a more important topic. She only wanted to hear about Max.

"I imagine you are all eager to venture out of doors," Juliet said to Marjorie.

"Oh, heavens yes! Even though I love having my boys at home once again, they behave like caged animals most of the time, always grumbling and growling at each other." She laughed softly with a shake of her head that sent a pair of garnet earbobs swaying. "In fact, I was certain that today they both would have left the instant the sun rose. Instead, Saunders informed me that they are in the study."

Juliet tried not to be distracted by the knowledge that Max was here and *not* visiting his debutante. Her gaze, however, might have flitted to the door once or twice as their conversation continued.

A few minutes later, the nurse tapped on the door to inform Marjorie that her granddaughter had finished her meal and was dressed for company. Shortly thereafter, they ascended the stairs to the third-floor nursery.

Marjorie bounced Bram's daughter, extolling her many accomplishments, not the least of which was how she constantly babbled sounds while pointing to different objects, as if having a full conversation with them. "Mark my words; she will speak early, like her father, fully prepared to charm us all."

"And what of Max as a child? Did he speak early as well?" Juliet found herself asking before she thought better of it.

Neither Marjorie nor Zinnia seemed to think it was out of character for her to ask, and the former answered immediately. "No, indeed. He was quite late. I'd worried over it so much that I was about to call upon a physician. But then, just as I had him bundled in my lap as the carriage set off, he pointed out the window and said *bird*, clear as day. I'll never forget it. I even asked him what he said, and he pointed again and said *bird...fly.*" Marjorie shrugged. "I suppose he was simply waiting until he had something to say."

Juliet smiled, entranced by the story and wishing Marjorie would continue.

But in the next instant, the conversation took a turn when Marjorie asked her, "Have you ever given thought to having child?"

"I...well, that is to say...one is usually expected to be married to entertain such notions..." Juliet's throat closed around her response before she could add *and I have no intention of remarrying.* Which effectively left the most important part unsaid.

Her truncated answer seemed to please Zinnia, for she smiled and then cast her next remark to Marjorie. "Juliet has been assisting the Duchess of Vale with her nursery this week. Edith tells me that it is coming along rather splendidly."

"Is it?" Marjorie asked absently. A peculiarly blank expression crossed her countenance, as if her thoughts had drifted from the room. She blinked at Juliet and then looked pointedly at Zinnia. "Forgive me, but I just recalled that I forgot to speak to Mrs. Shelly regarding the linens I ordered for Patrice. One must stay on top of these things, after all. But I should like your opinion, Zinnia. Would you be so kind as to accompany me?"

"Of course."

Then Marjorie hesitated another moment, clucking her tongue with an impatient glance at the door. "I cannot imagine where Miss Slade has run off to. Juliet, you would not mind holding my granddaughter while Zinnia and I rush downstairs, would you?"

"I'd be delighted." And before Juliet knew it, she had her arms full of sweetly fragrant little girl. As they left, however, she found it rather suspicious that no one had bothered to use the bell pull to ring for Mrs. Shelly instead. In fact, Juliet found these last few minutes altogether odd. It was almost as if Marjorie hoped to spark a motherly interest on Juliet's part.

"*Ma...mon...ma...mon...ma...mon...*" Patrice babbled, patting her chubby little hands against Juliet's cheeks. The centers of the child's palms were warm and slightly damp, creating a suction. "*Maman.*"

Hearing the child's words with a French ear, Juliet heard, "*My mother,*" and her heart stuttered to a complete stop. She stared, transfixed by a pair of innocent blue eyes.

Oh dear...

It was possible that Patrice was speaking already but in her own dialect of French. Then again, it was equally doubtful. Considering where Juliet's thoughts had been all week, her mind was simply causing her to hear things. Though, suddenly, the words that Lilah had mentioned, about *fate* and *Bram* filtered into her thoughts. Pairing that with Marjorie's strange behavior, Juliet couldn't help but wonder if Marjorie desired a match between her and Bram.

Her thoughts aimless, she wandered around the room as the child bobbled her sleepy little head. Looking to the rocking chair, she decided to put it to good use for both of them.

It was after Patrice had fallen asleep that Juliet finally spotted Max. He had paused just inside the doorway, staring at her quietly. Since he was in shadow, she couldn't read his expression or determine whether he was pleased to find her here.

"Good day, Max," she whispered, not wanting to disturb the sleeping child. "How has your week fared?"

"The seven longest days of my life." Even when he spoke, he drew the words out on a lengthy exhale as he moved closer.

"If it had not been for Mother's demand that we only attend matters of business, I hope you know that I would have called upon you."

The news made her giddy. Until she remembered his debutante.

She affected nonchalance with a tilt of her head. "I have been away, regardless, spending much of my time with Lilah and also at Vale's townhouse with Ivy and Gemma. We have been choosing swatches for the nursery." Then she looked down to Bram's child and stroked the fine, wispy blonde strands on her little head. "It seems my entire week has been one long siege of infants."

"Have you ever given thought to having your own children?"

Juliet might have laughed at having the same question posed to her by two different members of his family but found herself distracted. Because in that moment, she imagined what it might be like to hold Max's child in her arms.

She did not look at him when she answered. "That would cause quite the scandal."

"Not if you were to marry."

If you were to marry…not *if we were to marry*, she noted with a twinge beneath her breast. Then again, she didn't expect him to propose. He knew her too well.

"If I were to remarry, how would the *Standard* stay in business?" She laughed softly and then, at last, met his gaze.

He stared at her for a moment. "There is no debutante, you know. I only mentioned that I was courting someone in the hopes of earning leniency from Mother's recent demands. Unfortunately, my efforts failed."

"*Oh.*" Her breath fell out of her body all at once, leaving her lightheaded and with the strangest desire to throw her head back and cheer to the heavens. The good news was that she hadn't gone completely mad and managed to suppress that impulse. "I never gave it a thought."

The corner of Max's mouth twitched. "Of course not. Otherwise, that might have meant you were jealous."

And if she admitted to being jealous, then she might as well just tell him that she loved him. But knowing how complicated that would make everything, she managed to suppress that as well. "And how is your candidate faring?"

Slowly, Max released another long exhale, shook his head, and crossed his arms, as if she'd issued another challenge. "Very well. Yours?"

"All I'll say is that you'd better hire more laborers to finish the repairs on my house by month's end."

"Is that so?" His gaze suddenly heated as it dipped to her grinning mouth. "Perhaps we can continue this discussion in a more private setting as soon as the nurse returns."

Her stomach flipped, her pulse beating madly in response and more than a week's worth of longing. A week's worth of doubting she'd ever be in his arms again. "Will this be a *lengthy* discussion?"

"Most assuredly," he promised, his voice turning husky as he took another step toward her. "In fact, you would have to stay for dinner and then allow me to drive you home."

She was about to remind him that Zinnia was here as well, but they were interrupted, making the point moot.

"Lady Granworth, you are looking quite at home with a babe on your lap," Bram said as he strode into the room. Not bothering to keep his voice low for the child, he said, "Max, why didn't you tell me we had guests? Your steward and I have been waiting a quarter hour for you to fetch the ledger you said you'd left in your chambers."

Max shrugged. "And when it wasn't there, I thought perhaps that I'd had it with me when I last visited my niece, but I do not see it in this room either."

Bram frowned, appearing skeptical, but then turned his attention back to Juliet. "Mother sent me to ask if you would return for dinner this evening. Apparently, Lady Cosgrove is amenable."

Juliet opened her mouth to speak, but Bram interrupted her.

"And since we have had no company all week, I hope you will consider it." Then, he took the liberty of bending down and scooping his daughter into his arms. He didn't even ask Juliet to relinquish her hold first. Bram's hands brushed the underside of her arm and the top of her thigh as if he had the right to be familiar with her.

The entire exchange made Juliet uncomfortable. And when she looked to Max, he was glowering, his jaw clenched.

Once free of the child, she slipped out of the chair and stood between the brothers. This scene, aside from the child in Bram's arms, seemed all too familiar. The only difference was that she'd never felt so much tension between all of them before.

But with Bram coming here at his mother's request, it felt far too much like Marjorie was trying to play matchmaker *and* with the wrong brother. Perhaps Max realized it too.

Rather than ponder the magnitude of this discovery, she inclined her head and moved toward the door, wishing that her discussion with Max had not been interrupted. "Thank you for the invitation. I will think on it and give Marjorie my answer."

Surprisingly, Max caught up with Juliet just after she rounded the first corner. It was almost as if she were walking slowly for the sole purpose of waiting for him.

Since that thought put him in a better mood than the one he had been in moments ago, he decided to keep it. He altered his footfalls to land in step beside hers. Then, clasping his hands behind his back, he offered a nod as one would to a fellow traveler. "Are we practicing pedestrianism?"

Her lips twitched, but she kept her gaze on the path ahead. "Zinnia often states that *'there is no purpose of walking unless one approaches the task with excellence.'*"

"And your unhurried pace must be why you have not ventured too great a distance from where we last saw each other," he mused. "The reason could not be because you were waiting for me to join you. Or even that you were hoping that I would secret you away into one of these rooms so that we could continue our…discussion."

A shocked laughed escaped her as her head whipped in his direction. "You know very well that we cannot."

He grinned, noting how her voice had turned breathy and slightly hoarse. The flesh on her throat and down to the lace edge of her lotus-embroidered dress began to glow carnation pink too. "*Cannot?* My, my, that does sound like a challenge. After all, we know that we *can*—and quite well too."

"*Max*," she warned but without any censure.

When she cast a glance over her shoulder, it reminded him that Bram could be upon them at any moment. When Max had left with a ready excuse of looking for the ledger, his brother had already rung for a servant to take Patrice. Looking around, he quickly spied the door to a room where they would be undisturbed for a time.

He held out his hand in offering. "Would you care to see where I hosted my first debates?"

She didn't hesitate to curl her fingers into his palm but asked, "Is that really where you're taking me?"

Without answering, he drew closer and brushed his lips over her knuckles. It meant a great deal that she would trust him this much. There was not even a hint of guardedness in her gaze but just a soft smile on her lips. If she knew how quickly he could imagine bolting the nearest door and keeping her sufficiently occupied for hours, she might be a little wary.

Since he valued her trust, he steered her down a short hall and into the room where he'd spent much of his youth. Closing the door behind them, he turned the lock, more so for the sake of her reputation than for purpose of seducing her. He knew they didn't have much time before someone would become suspicious of their absences.

"This is our room of *odds and ends*, where cracked urns, clocks that do not keep time, and chairs that require new upholstery come to await repair." He gestured to the various items cluttered about the outer edges of the room. And even though he had not used the large square desk that sat in the center of the room for some time, Saunders always made sure that it remained clear of debris.

Juliet's fingertips glided over the surface of the faded leather blotter. Then she moved to stand on the opposite side and, facing him, lifted the lid on the birchwood box with brass hinges.

"There is a Bible inside." With her discovery, her gaze met his, her expression both amused and curious. "Is this your despatch box, like the ones they have in Parliament?"

He shrugged. "Of course. This was *my* Parliament. Every minister and shadow minister were expected to uphold the honor of their appointments."

Silhouetted by the window behind her, a faint hazy glow settled around her, and a soft smile touched her lips. "You truly used this room to practice your debates, didn't you?"

"Do you doubt it?"

Slowly, perhaps even fondly, she shook her head. "Not at all. In fact, I can picture you standing here as a boy, with your hair falling over your brow as you rail at your imaginary opponent. I'd wager you were completely adorable."

He cleared his throat and straightened his shoulders. No man, no matter his age, wanted to be labeled *adorable*. Yet even though he put on a frown, his heart thrummed with pleasure. "I was fearsome, spending many an hour wearing down the opposition."

"But was it a fair fight?" she teased, pointing across the desk to the empty space before him. "After all, I see no despatch box for your opponent."

"There is a second box. Only now, the slips of paper holding the names of our candidates are tucked inside, and

Saunders has it locked away in his pantry, awaiting the end of our wager." A heavy silence fell between them, weighted with expectation. Their wager would soon be over, and the binding twine that had brought them together would be severed. Max hoped that all the other strands woven around them would hold fast. Though this lack of assurance frustrated him. "Nevertheless, I always argued both sides, out of fairness."

Her brow delicately furrowed. "Did you have no one to argue with you?"

While his heart warmed at the evidence of her concern for his younger self, he did not want her pity. "I preferred this space to myself. Besides, Father was usually on an outing with Bram, instructing him on how to be a marquess and uphold the Engle line."

"And what about teaching you how to uphold the Harwick line? You were his only son, after all."

"And Bram was the son of the man he'd admired most," Max said matter-of-factly. "Besides, it was long ago."

She lifted her chin, her mouth set in a firm line. "If it is so ancient, then why does it anger me to learn of it?"

Looking down at the way her delicate hand had curled into a fist, he realized she was not pitying him. She was defending him. His breath halted in his throat. Her vehemence on his behalf birthed a hope so fragile and sharp that it caused his chest to burn. He rubbed his hand against the buttons of his waistcoat just over his heart.

Years ago, he had shared his thoughts with her, his passions, and his pursuits, but he had kept this part to himself. Now, things were different. He wanted to tell her the things that he'd never told anyone else. But later.

"Likely for the same reason that I would rail at your parents for not having treated you as you deserved." Walking around to her side of the desk, he set his hands on her shoulders and turned her toward him.

A breath shuddered out of her at that first touch. He felt it too. Seven long days of needing to touch her...

His thumbs strayed to the bare flesh beyond the ribbon trim, stroking the smooth ridge of her collarbone. She closed the space between them, her arms wrapping around his waist as she rested her cheek against his chest. "Oh, Max, I missed you."

He held his breath as the quiet admission clamored through him in a noisy, rambunctious burst of joy. The Juliet of old would never have revealed so much and so openly. Even though it was not a declaration of love, those words were the nearest thing to it.

"I even missed arguing with you." She laughed softly and lifted her face.

He could hardly breathe. It felt as if his dreams were finally coming true. "I can think of no reason to argue at the moment."

"Well, I certainly can."

He felt the flesh of his brow pucker in confusion before she continued.

"You have yet to kiss me."

He grinned, his hands slipping down her back, following the enticing curve of her spine as he pulled her hips flush against his. "I could say the same of you."

Her gaze drifted to his mouth and held. He waited for her to take what she wanted. And smiling, she rose up and brushed a tender kiss across his lips.

Then, before she could get away, his mouth covered hers with more urgency. And that was all it took. The desire between them ignited like tinder, those fast flames feeding on their combined yearning. Her lips plumped beneath his, parting in sweet invitation. Welcoming his tongue with hers, they tangled together as if forging knots to keep them here, like this, for hours.

Their bodies moved as one like the steps of a dance—him forward, her back—until she met with the desk behind her. He lifted her, nudging the despatch box to the side as he stood between her thighs, the eager iron-hard length of him wedged against the heated nook of her body. Their hips rocked simultaneously, paying no attention to the few layers of clothes between them. They simply wanted the release denied to them from more than a week of longing.

But Max wanted more than a quick release. He wanted all of her. His deft fingers moved to the row of buttons at her back as he dragged his mouth down her throat to the spot that made her whimper.

"What are you doing?" she asked between shuddered breaths.

"Removing your dress."

"And what makes you think I need to be *un*dressed in your Parliament?"

That taunt set off a burst of fantasies that they would have to explore later. But for now…"Because when I'm inside of you, I don't want anything between us. And neither do you."

She moaned her agreement as she sealed her lips to his. Just as he reached the last button—*damn these tiny pearls*—a sudden wail pierced the air. The sound of it was so close that it was no surprise to hear Miss Slade's voice in the hallway, shushing Patrice and promising to find her father straightaway.

Even though the cries dissipated as they drifted by, most likely toward the stairs, Max and Juliet's happy reunion was interrupted.

Again, Juliet laughed softly and rested her forehead on his shoulder. "For a moment, I'd forgotten that people were waiting for us. I suppose we should be grateful for the reminder."

"No, we shouldn't," he grumbled, knowing that the opportunity was lost. While he would surely be able to coax her, the moment of unreserved and vulnerable passion was gone. Even more than he wanted her body, he wanted her heart completely open to him.

Framing her face, he kissed her brow, her nose, and both corners of her mouth. Then, holding her gaze, he took her hand and placed it over his heart.

"I missed you too, Juliet." Said with the same quiet promise that she had done, he let the words settle between them, wanting her to understand and testing the waters to see if she was ready to hear the actual words he wanted to say. *I love you, Juliet...*

She looked down to where her hand rested and back up at his face, her eyes widening ever so slightly. A pretty pink flush still clung to her skin, but her breasts were rising and falling in quick, panicked breaths.

"I really must go. Zinnia will worry, and as it is, I'll have to figure out an excuse." As she spoke, she nudged him back a step before she set her feet on the floor.

"Don't run"—he dared to keep her hand, gently restraining her—"not this time."

"I will return this evening." She offered him a nervous smile. Then she squeezed his fingers before slipping from his grasp, and turned so that he would button her dress.

Obviously, it was too much, too fast. But *bloody hell*, how long was he supposed to keep this locked up inside? Reminding himself to be patient was even more difficult now that he sensed she was closer than ever to accepting the truth—she was *his*.

The only problem was, he needed her to see it on her own.

When he finished, she turned. She must have read the doubt and restlessness in his expression because she placed her hand on the despatch box. "I promise."

It wasn't the answer he was hoping for, but it was what he had for now.

Later that evening, when Max strode into the parlor and saw Juliet, he felt like a man who had the whole world within his grasp. Everything seemed possible. She had not run after all.

Standing near Lady Cosgrove and Mother, Juliet wore a silver gown that cascaded sinuously over her form. The blue ribbon bordering her bodice was the exact shade of her eyes when they were dark with desire. And it had been far too many hours since he had seen that particular hue.

"And what has you so pleased, Max?" Juliet asked, taking a step toward him. Behind her, Mother continued to show off Patrice to her friend, while Miss Slade stood near the door, likely waiting for Bram to make an appearance. "Or is it surprise that I am seeing?"

He met her gaze, wishing he had the freedom to take her hand, to pull her closer. "Is a man not allowed to express pleasure without requiring a reason?"

Her lips twitched in a wry grin. "I pity your opponents in Parliament, for they will never receive a direct answer to a question."

Perhaps, he thought, admiring her clever wit. Yet any candid response he might give her would likely end up with him on bended knee. "Sometimes it is better to circumnavigate than to land directly on the argument."

"You prefer the endlessness of a circle, do you? Always finding yourself back at the beginning?"

He took a moment to consider. "Revisiting the start of something allows for better perspective."

"Hmm...I believe you have the right of it. After all, that is why I want to live in my townhouse. I should like to recapture a certain part of my life." Opening her fan, her gaze drifted to the door, coincidentally in the moment that Bram walked into the room. "However, it would not mean as much if I did not have my independence."

A low groan of frustration escaped Max, though no one could have heard it because Patrice's sudden wailing filled the room. Even so, all Max could think about was that somehow he'd wound up stuck at the beginning with Juliet, when that was the last thing he wanted.

Instead of taking charge of his daughter, Bram walked toward the sideboard, Miss Slade on his heels, asking what she should do. In response, the sound of Bram's oath carried overhead.

"The sound travels well in this room, does it not?" Juliet whispered from behind her fan and cast a sympathetic glance toward the child. "Excuse me, Max. I believe Miss Slade would benefit from some instruction."

On impulse, Max reached out to stay her, but she slipped past him before his hand connected with hers. Thankfully, it did not appear that anyone noticed.

Across the room, Juliet whispered something to Miss Slade, who curtsied and then took the steps to remove the child from the room. It was all done with grace and poise. Yet for some reason, it made Max cringe at how effortless it was for her to take charge on Bram's behalf.

After their brief conversation, a familiar sense of foreboding filled him, no matter how hard he tried to shrug it off. Most of all, Max hoped that his plan of waiting for her to be ready would work and that the lure of reliving the past would fade.

Since Bram's return, however, Max's instincts were telling him that it wasn't a good idea to leave matters unresolved between him and Juliet. He didn't trust his brother's agenda.

CHAPTER NINETEEN

The Season Standard—the Daily Chronicle of Consequence

The date we have all been waiting for is nearly here, dear readers! In one week, we shall know the name of our Original. And, of course, for those who have been invited to Lord and Lady B—cke's gala, they will have a final opportunity to speculate on who will be crowned. Thrilling, indeed!

For now, we are ever watchful over the Marquess of E—e who was spotted in the park looking dangerously handsome atop his new phaeton...

In the morning, Juliet took her daily walk near the fashionable hour so that she might encounter Ellery. Thus far, he'd been making a splendid showing, but she didn't want his favor to fall beneath the shadow of Bram's return. Therefore, she decided to make sure that he did something truly remarkable to keep him firmly in the hearts of the *ton* and, with any luck, the anonymous committee members as well.

Normally, she stayed away from the Serpentine and kept to the less-traveled paths. However, she knew that Ellery frequently took this winding road toward Rotten Row for his horse's exercise. And sure enough, not far in the distance, she saw him riding high in his glossy black phaeton, his silvery gray top hat and coat looking like shining armor in the sunlight.

When the moment was right, she would pretend to trip and twist her ankle, barely catching herself with her parasol. Looking down, she saw the perfect spot where she could avoid any shrubbery.

But just when she lifted her gaze, she saw the blur of another phaeton whipping around Ellery's. The driver's head was turned to look back over his shoulder, and Juliet knew in an instant she would be crushed beneath the immense wheels.

Fearing for her life, she dashed to the side of the road. Then, tripping over a branch, she landed on all fours in the dirt. *Drat it all!* But at least she was alive. Taking a quick accounting, she found that she was unharmed, for the most part.

Behind her, she heard several shouts and a scream. Suddenly, she knew that the graceful trip she'd planned had turned into a clumsy, public incident. Instead of merely losing her footing—and thereby procuring Ellery's gallant rescue—she'd been nearly bowled over by a madman.

By the time she righted herself and began brushing the dirt from her poor ruined skirts and gloves, she heard the voice of someone quite familiar, only it wasn't Ellery.

It was Bram. "Lady Granworth, you should take care. Why, the Serpentine is no place to walk."

Looking past him, she saw that the madman's phaeton was now empty, the horse's reins tied to a nearby branch just off to the side.

"Were you the one driving that menace?" she asked, sounding like a harridan and not caring a whit.

Bram had the nerve to laugh at her. In fact, he didn't bother with an apology. "Allow me to escort you to Hanover Street. I will have you home in no time at all."

Considering the way he drove, she did not doubt it.

Though, remembering her purpose, Juliet cast a somewhat panicked glance in Ellery's direction. He too had left his phaeton and was striding toward her.

"Lady Granworth, may I be of assistance?" Ellery said, coming upon them. His expression was concerned when he looked at her but turned hard when his gaze landed on Bram.

"And who might you be?" Bram asked rudely.

Juliet made the introduction, each man nodding curtly. She had no intention of ruining her plan and nodded to the viscount. "Thank you, Ellery, that is very kind—"

"However, she already has an escort," Bram interrupted, putting his hand on her elbow.

Ellery, standing a few steps away, waited for her response. And since there was a curious crowd gathering, and it would not suit either her cause or Ellery's character to allow a battle to ensue, she abandoned her venture. "Lord Engle will see me home. Thank you again, Ellery. You were kind to stop."

But if she thought her terror was at an end after nearly being trampled on the path, she was a fool.

She felt an even greater risk while Bram tore through the streets all the way to Hanover Square. He paid no attention to her requests for him to slow, and she feared that she would be sick.

Then, to further her humiliation and dismay, when they finally arrived, Max was just coming down the steps of Zinnia's townhouse. Messy, disheveled, and thoroughly embarrassed, Juliet wanted to hide.

He rushed to the pavement, tossing his walking stick to the ground. "What happened? Are you hurt?"

She stopped, clutching the side rail of the driver's perch, and sat up straighter so that he could see that she was well. "I am fine, Max. A little dirty, but alive." No thanks to Bram.

Before Bram could even set the brake, Max had climbed up to assist her, his hand seeking hers with care, as if she were suddenly an ornament of blown glass. If they were alone, she would have scolded him, even if she found it rather sweet.

Still feeling unsteady once he had her on the ground, she held onto his shoulders a little bit longer for support. "Thank you," she whispered and forced herself to release him and step back. She missed the feel of his hands on her waist instantly.

Bram hopped down and stood beside her. "And why are you here, little brother?"

Max's shoulders went back, and he clenched his jaw, causing a muscle to twitch. "I came to pay a call on—"

"On my cousin," Juliet finished for him in a rush, casting a look of reprimand. He looked positively territorial, and she ignored the responding pulse that quickened in her own body. She felt as if Max were engaged in some sort of medieval joust against his brother for the honor of wooing her. Ludicrous! Yet part of her was afraid of how much it pleased her and how much she wanted to be claimed by him. "I believe I heard Zinnia mention that your mother was sending something over."

Bram chuckled. "You are still Mother's errand boy, I see."

Max gave her a dark look but answered his brother. "Apparently so. There could have been no other reason I was here."

She swallowed, feeling guilty. But really, did he expect to announce to the entire *ton* that he was now paying calls on his sworn enemy? She wasn't even ready to tell him how she felt. The last thing she wanted was to have the gossips announce it before she did. Already, it seemed that a parade of carriages had converged on the square to watch the spectacle.

Thankfully, Mr. and Mrs. Wick appeared on the stairs, rushing down to the pavement. Zinnia was framed in the doorway.

"Good day, gentlemen," Juliet said, taking hold of Mr. Wick's arm, eager for this entire episode to end.

The following morning, Bram strode into the breakfast room, all smiles and brimming with pleasantries. "Good morning, Mother. And little brother, how fares your courtship of that debutante?"

Max was tempted to tell him to bugger off but thought better of it. "It is promising."

Or at least it was until Bram had returned. Now, Max felt as if he'd stepped in mud up to his knees, and every step forward was interminably delayed.

Bram continued on as if Max's response was of no importance. "I have an announcement that I'm certain you are both eager to hear. I have decided on a bride—or courtship, rather. But it is my guess that, soon enough, Max and I will have a new battle, and that will be to see who claims the first wedding day at St. George's."

Mother shook her head. "Bramson, we've been in mourning. Surely you could not have decided on a bride as of yet."

"It has become quite clear to me since yesterday. Can you not guess?" Bram puffed out his chest and gripped the edges of his lapels. "I mean to marry Juliet Granworth."

Max frowned. "Have you spoken to her about this?"

"I did not even need to because it was she who made the suggestion to me in the carriage."

"She said she wanted to marry you?" Max was stunned, but before he jumped to conclusions, he would find out from Juliet.

"Not in those exact words, but she did agree that I should take a wife soon for Patrice's sake. And I shall."

At Bram's ridiculous assumption, Max wanted to relax once more. With the history between them, however, he couldn't let go of the reminder that Bram had usually gotten everything he wanted.

The *ton* was enthralled by Bram, carefully watching his every move. And Max felt the stirrings of a peculiar sensation of déjà vu.

Too sore for walking, and frankly too embarrassed to return to the park yet, Juliet stayed in. Unfortunately, word had spread about her brush with death, and nearly every gentleman of her acquaintance came to call, in addition to a few ladies, including Lilah, Ivy, and Gemma.

But not Max.

Worse was the audacious bouquet that Bram presented to her. The flowers were so large and so many that she had to hold them with both hands when he thrust them at her. She tried to smile, but it froze when she spied several ants climbing out from the centers.

"Peonies. How lovely," she cried but tried to hide her alarm. "Myrtle, could you please take these to the upstairs sitting room." And she quickly handed them off to the maid.

Then the next day, he brandished another bouquet of peonies, of such magnitude and quantity that they ended up in this morning's *Standard*.

"*The Marquess of E—e hefted another armful of enormous peony blossoms up the stairs of a certain Hanover Street house,*" Juliet read aloud to Zinnia, who sat opposite her in the morning room.

"Mrs. Wick requested to keep the flowers out on the terrace, as the ants were spotted in the hall, in the parlor, and crawling out of the upstairs sitting room." Her cousin paused in the act of penning her letter and shook her head in disapproval.

They'd both thought that banishing them to the moldering sitting room, which they used primarily for the purpose of storing unwanted objects, had seemed the perfect solution. Juliet hadn't the heart to send those flowers to the sanatorium, as the patients had enough troubles without adding insects to injury.

"I'm not certain what I should do if this continues," Juliet confessed.

Zinnia gave a peculiar look, tilting her head to one side. "We can always throw them out."

Juliet laughed. "I'm not speaking of the flowers but of Bram."

"Do you not like Lord Engle's attentions?"

She hesitated before answering. "At first, I thought he was trying to make amends for having nearly killed me, but he never actually apologized. Then yesterday, it occurred to me that he might be courting me. Or at least *he* thinks he is. He never asked, and I would not have consented. What unsettles me most is that I fear Marjorie desires the match."

"With Lord Engle?" Zinnia blinked owlishly. "Not at all."

Before Juliet could ask Zinnia to elaborate, Mr. Wick cleared his throat from the doorway.

"You have a caller, my lady."

"I don't believe I'm at home today." Juliet checked the calendar to be sure she wasn't mistaken. Most people only had certain *at home* days when they were accepting calls. After all, no one was expected to be available on a whim.

"Yes, my lady. I said the same to your caller; however, he is rather insistent. His lordship states that you will make an exception for him."

Could it be Max? Her heart began to race. She hadn't seen him in days, other than the day she'd fallen in the park. He hadn't returned, even though she'd offered a perfect excuse to call. Running an errand for his mother was innocent enough, wasn't it? "Who is it?"

"Lord Engle, my lady."

That oh-so-brief elation abruptly vanished. "I am still not at home. No, wait. I will see him, but keep him in the foyer." Then to Zinnia, she added, "This will not take long."

It was time to be perfectly clear with Bram that she was not interested in courtship or marriage.

When she stepped into the foyer, she saw that he was holding not one but *two* bouquets of peonies. *Poor Mrs. Wick.*

"Considering how well received the other bouquets were, I knew you liked these the best," he said with a smug grin. "And did you see the paper this morning? The entire *ton* is quite envious."

Max would have known that her exclaiming *"peonies"* in such a shocked tone was not necessarily stating a preference. In fact, she had told Bram quite plainly that she preferred roses. But he had not listened.

He was entirely too much like Lord Granworth in that regard. In fact, he was too much like Lord Granworth in many regards. Complimenting her clothes and how well she looked, and then complimenting himself and how well they looked together.

At one time, it might have thrilled her to know that Bram was courting her, like having a second chance to relive the past. But if she could go back in time, she would not return to the days when she wrote his name in her diary.

No. There was only one day from her past that she would revisit, and someday she would tell Max about it.

Taking the flowers, she set them on the table. No doubt ants were now crawling out of the petals and onto the rosewood. Thankfully, Mr. Wick was ready and armed with a crumb broom and pan.

"Lord Engle," she began, "I have enjoyed your return to town. You are as charming and entertaining as ever. However, I want to make sure you know that I have no intention of marrying." And then to be perfectly clear. "I believe, and I'm fairly certain that the *ton* believes, you are courting me, but I cannot allow it to continue."

"This was all in good fun. Nothing more." Bram smiled and offered a nod of understanding, before he bowed and took his leave.

Well, that was a relief. In fact, it was so simple that Juliet wondered if she'd misread his intentions.

Somewhat uncertain, she made her way back to the parlor with the hope of returning to her previous conversation with Zinnia. With any luck, she would find out what Zinnia had been about to say—regarding the matches Marjorie wanted for her sons—before they were interrupted.

Chapter Twenty

The night of Lord and Lady Babcocke's ball had arrived. After escorting Mother to the gallery, Max stood near the doors to the card room, his gaze straying to Juliet too often.

This evening, she was a vision in dark red silk, with gussets sewn into the fabric beneath her breasts and molding to them like worshiping hands. The single ruby pendant that rested in the hollow of her throat winked in the light of the chandeliers whenever she turned his way. And he was happy to note that it winked quite often, because she watched him too, gracefully maneuvering her fan to disguise the direction of her gaze.

He hadn't seen her in days. Max ached for her and would have moved a mountain to see her, if she'd only given him one small reason to believe she wanted him to. But he respected her desire for independence and, perhaps, wanted her to *miss* him again. After all, the last time they were apart, she had expressed more about her feelings than she ever had before.

So instead, he read about her callers in the *Standard* and listened to Bram profess how eagerly she awaited his calls.

Max reassured himself that he was not being overshadowed by his elder brother, who now breezed into the room, grinning as if he owned the world. The truth was, Bram was in debt up to his eyes and didn't own much of anything, other than an estate he kept in near financial ruin.

"What, no peonies in hand?" Max asked when Bram stopped beside him.

Since there was no change in his expression, his brother likely didn't hear the sarcasm. "They did cause quite the stir. It is a shame they will not be in bloom much longer."

"A shame, indeed." But Max wondered if Bram had ever bothered to figure out that Juliet liked roses. Velvety pink roses that were the shade of her lips, to be exact.

"But it is all part of the game," Bram said. "She is almost mine. In fact, she made a point of telling me that she was not interested in marriage."

Max grinned, more certain than ever about his course. Yet out of curiosity, he asked, "But why should this please you?"

"Because when a woman mentions marriage, she is thinking about marriage. Of course."

"Or perhaps she was actually telling you that she had no intention of marrying."

Bram shook his head against such logic. "All she needs is someone to change her mind."

"And if she already knows her own mind?" Max knew this about Juliet as well. She knew exactly what she wanted. And Max believed—*hoped*—she wanted him.

"No wonder you are still unmarried." Bram laughed. "You have far too much to learn about the fairer sex. You must guide them."

Unlike his brother, Max had learned something from Juliet. She revealed herself in actions more than in words, and she responded to gestures, more than bold declarations. And tonight, he was going to give her every opportunity to show him what he meant to her.

Tonight, he was going to ask her to dance.

"What a complete crush, my dear," Lady Babcocke said to her husband as they lingered near the open doorway that led to the balcony.

Juliet did not mean to eavesdrop, but she was standing on the other side, applying her fan to cool her cheeks. She'd been staring at Max quite often this evening, and in his gaze she saw so many promises that it made her feel flush with eagerness. If only he would cross the room to her.

Then again, that was likely not a wise decision, for surely everyone would know what was between them the moment they breathed the same air. That was the only thing that kept her from crossing the room to him. Because of their wager, nearly *every* eye followed their *every* move.

Even if she could wend her way through the crowd, the gossips would label her as Max's lover by morning. And what frightened her most about that was that it didn't frighten her nearly as much as it should.

"It may be a crush," Lord Babcocke murmured to his wife, "but we are not likely to see Pembroke here, are we?"

"Is Pembroke unwell?" Lady Babcocke asked.

"He should be, after what I heard. He's been trying to get everyone to invest in his South American silver mine, but word has it that it never existed."

"*No.*"

"It's true, my dear. Though I pity anyone who fell for it because the lender closed his doors today, without a word. Just took the money and fled."

Juliet hid her astonishment with her fan, waving it swiftly and pretending to be distracted by the clasp of her dance card chain at her wrist. This time, instead of filling her card with illegible names for every dance, she took special care to write down one name in particular for the waltz. *Maxwell Harwick, the Marquess of Thayne.* If only he were to ask her.

"What will happen to all those who were swindled?"

Lord Babcocke shrugged. "Ruination. What else?"

The conversation earned the attention of others passing nearby. "What were you saying about ruination and Lord Pembroke?" With the question, more guests stopped and gathered. And soon enough, there was such a crowd around the balcony doors that Juliet could not escape.

"Surely, there will be banking institutions that will help those who were cheated," someone said after the news had been repeated several times over.

"Not likely," Lord Babcocke said, puffing out his chest and rocking back to the heels of his shoes. "But if there were, would *you* be eager to trust those bankers who may have had a hand in it? I'd have a mind to withdraw all my funds."

Juliet shook her head, no longer hiding the fact that she'd been listening. "No, I'm certain that is not the answer. After all, imagine if everyone went to the bank and demanded all their money at once." She shuddered, knowing the banks could not support it.

She never went into any of her lenders and demanded her entire fortune. No, she simply took out what was needed, a few pounds here and there. Because she knew that her gold, in part, helped fund those banknotes Mr. Woldsley was so fond of, and since many people carried those notes, there needed to be gold in the vault to support them.

Unfortunately, her words of caution fell on deaf ears. The crowd was far more eager to hear Lord Babcocke's dire warnings.

Juliet managed to extricate herself from the mob but wound up stopping short when Bram stepped into her path. He was the last person she wanted to see. She thought she'd made herself perfectly clear.

"Why, Lady Granworth, you are a sly one. Have you happened this way during the waltz to procure a dance partner?"

Her gaze searched for Max. "No, indeed."

"Ah, waiting for a formal offer, I see." He bowed, ignoring her headshake. "Would you do me the honor of this dance?"

Unbelievable! Had Bram always been this obtuse? If there weren't so many people watching with avid interest, she might simply have walked past him. But causing a scandal would only spoil her hopes for the remainder of the night.

"I'm sorry, but this dance has already been promised to another..." she said, searching for her dance card even now but finding it absent from her wrist. Drat! She must have dropped it over by the balcony doors.

"Surely the gentleman should have come to claim you by now."

She tried to be patient with Bram, but quite honestly, his manipulation was wearing on her nerves. "He is likely making his way to my side right this instant."

"Then allow me to escort you to him." But instead of proffering his arm, his slipped his hand around her waist and began the steps of the waltz. It was in those few seconds, before she turned away and left him alone on the ballroom floor, that she spotted Max across the room.

The hard look he gave her was something she would never forget. Only now did she realize how often she'd seen it in the past but dismissed it as a product of Max's argumentative nature. And she noticed how much pain was there too.

Because of it, she knew she would have to do something drastic to get Bram out of her way once and for all.

Max left the ballroom a much wiser man. At last, he realized that Juliet would never give him everything he needed. He'd been patient, with the great hope that she would soon be ready. But now he knew differently.

"Max," Juliet said, out of breath as she emerged from a narrow passageway beside the main hallway. Lifting her hand, she absently smoothed back a lock of hair that had slipped from her coiffure. "It was not what it looked like."

He gritted his teeth. He'd had experience enough with exactly what it looked like. She'd saved the waltz for Bram. "The past has taught me differently."

"Please," she beseeched him quietly, glancing down the hallway to the trio of guests who were walking toward the ballroom, their backs to them. "Come away from the main hall so that we can talk privately."

Of course, she would not want anyone to see them together. Not even now, with so much more between them. He'd had enough of being cast aside by her, and it was time she knew.

Stepping into the narrow corridor, he opened the door to the nearest room. Thankfully, it was not a library but a small sitting room, swathed in the flickering light of the garden torches beyond the window.

"About the dance," Juliet began.

Max shook his head and held up a hand immediately. "This is about more than a single waltz. This is about patience and things that we've concealed from each other. And perhaps I am as much to blame because I haven't been completely honest with you."

She went still. "You haven't?"

"No," he said, drawing in the breath he needed for strength. "Five years ago, the day after I proposed to you, I went to your house and found a letter waiting for me instead of my bride. That event is something you likely imagined would have happened.

"But what you don't know is that my proposal was not given on impulse," he continued, baring it all. "I had already planned a life with you hundreds of times in my mind. The morning after, while you were in a carriage preparing to wed Lord Granworth, I was standing in your foyer, arguing with your butler. I carried with me every farthing I possessed in the world, along with a ring in my pocket and the determination to make you happy for the rest of your life."

Silvery light glinted off the moisture gathering in Juliet's eyes, but she said nothing.

He handed her his handkerchief and closed his eyes briefly when their fingers brushed, leaving his skin aching for more. Instead, he took a step back. "Of course, I know your reasons now and understand that yours was not an easy decision. Perhaps I should have told you how much I loved you." He steeled himself to continue. "How much I still love you and want to marry you."

She gasped, putting his handkerchief to her mouth as tears began to slip down her cheeks. And for a moment, he hoped that those were tears of joy.

But her next words proved otherwise. "You know how I feel about marriage."

"All too well." He jerked a nod. "The idea frightens you. And it should because I would want everything you could give. Not only your love but children too, and decades of your life until we are both too old to remember those five years we spent apart."

He waited a beat for her response, until he remembered how long he'd been waiting already. Looking up to the shadowed ceiling, he let out a breath, feeling like a fool.

But before he set his hand on the door, prepared to leave, she spoke. "Max, I don't think I'm ready."

"And I don't think you ever will be."

CHAPTER TWENTY-ONE

News of the *South American Stock Swindle* spread like wild-fire through London late Friday. Fortunes were lost, without any hope of recovery.

Juliet knew precisely how it felt to have no hope. She'd felt this way since Max had walked away from her last night. Worse than that, he'd ignored every missive she'd sent today, returning them unopened. She didn't know what to do.

"A panic has ensued," Zinnia said, as if reading her mind rather than the newspaper. "Many have rushed to their banks to remove all their funds, only to find the institution locked and a notice of bankruptcy on the door. Rumors are even spreading that smaller banks have borrowed money from other banks."

"In such a crisis, those notes will be in excess of the amount that can be ensured," Juliet remarked absently, the business portion of her brain filling in while the rest of it was distracted on thoughts of Max.

This entire ordeal was all Bram's fault. He simply refused to take no for an answer and did not care one fig about listening to her either.

After Bram called the other day, Zinnia had told her of Marjorie's concerns about his estate falling into ruin. Ever since, Juliet suspected that his fascination with her was mainly financial. True to form, however, while appearing to court Juliet, he'd also been wooing a slew of debutantes, keeping the *ton* wondering whom he favored. Not surprisingly, he switched his attentions between several who were the prettiest but who also had large dowries.

Juliet wished he would abandon his pursuit of her and go after one of them.

"Lord Pembroke fled the country in the dead of night," Zinnia continued, having moved on from the *Post* to the *Standard*. "Rumor has it that he'd been part of the scheme all along."

"He used people for their money."

Zinnia issued a hum of disapproval. "He should have relied on the standard practice among our set—to marry well."

Juliet scoffed, despondency making her bitter. "For some men, one fortune is not enough. Take Bram, for example. Not only did he gain his wife's dowry but also the inheritance her aunt left her. Now he is looking for more. In my opinion, he is no better than Pembroke. And it pains me to think that I once cherished him above all others. I was such a fool back then. If I had only seen…"

"That Lord Thayne loved you?"

"Yes, I—" Juliet stopped. "How did you know?"

After all, her cousin had not been in the room last night to hear his confession. She hadn't even been in London five years ago but in mourning for Lord Cosgrove. In fact, she hadn't returned to town until Lilah's first Season.

"Marjorie told me." Zinnia lowered both papers, her expression soft. "When Lord Thayne inherited and was intent on finding a wife, I'd asked her why he hadn't married before."

Juliet swallowed down a lump of guilt. "Because of me?"

Zinnia didn't respond, her silence like a cog in the wheel of Juliet's thoughts.

"I feel so powerless," Juliet said after a moment, propping her elbows on the table and burying her face in her hands. "I cannot give him what he wants."

"Then perhaps you should offer something else until you don't feel so…" Zinnia paused and then cut directly to the heart of the issue with one word, "afraid."

Juliet growled to herself in frustration. A woman could be madly in love but still not ready to marry, couldn't she? The terrified strumming of her heart told her that it was possible. After all, hadn't Max warned her that he would want everything she could give?

And what she could give him now was reassurance that she cared nothing for Bram, but Max had refused to read the letters she'd sent. So what was she to do? Storm over to Harwick House and tell Bram once more that she did not intend to marry him? He likely wouldn't believe her and would only be encouraged by the gesture.

In fact, she imagined that the only way to be rid of him was if she suddenly lost her fortune.

Juliet lowered her hands, inspiration dawning through the gloom. "I think I have an idea that just might do the trick."

Leaving Hanover Street, Juliet's carriage lumbered toward one of her banking institutions. Standing on the pavement outside his bank, his head bowed and his cravat askew, was none other than Mr. Woldsley. He was staring at the notice of bankruptcy hanging on the door as he withdrew the key from the lock.

Juliet tapped on the hood and asked the driver to stop. "Mr. Woldsley," she said from the window. "Surely, you are not closing your institution."

He turned, his eyes bloodshot, his nose red. "Oh, it's you. If you've come for a withdrawal, then read the sign." He hitched his thumb over his shoulder to the notice fixed to the other side of the glass.

"I have not come for a withdrawal," she assured him, feeling more confident in her plan by the moment.

He sneered at her, but there was more exhaustion than vehemence behind it. "Then to gloat?"

"Not at all. In fact, I believe I can help."

"Help. Ha! The likes of you have caused this to happen—people demanding all their money at once, not understanding how lending institutions work."

"Mr. Woldsley," she said patiently. He, more than most anyone, knew that she had never once demanded all of her money but only the interest accrued. "How much does your bank need in order to remove the sign from that door and open on Monday?"

Knowing a bit about business and seeing the catastrophic nature of this occurrence, she felt certain that the Bank of England would step in by then to lend funds to many of the smaller banks to prevent a complete collapse.

He straightened his shoulders and pulled sharply on the lapels of his coat. "Amusement at another's misfortune is petty indeed. I don't think you understand the scope of this disaster—"

"I am prepared to lend your bank fifty thousand pounds."

Thankfully, her statement closed his mouth with a snap. Otherwise, she would have driven onward.

He went white, his bottom lip working against his teeth as he stuttered, "F-fifty th-thousand pounds? But how could you…manage to procure such an amount?"

"I manage my money quite well, Mr. Woldsley," she said. "Now, if you would care to remove that sign, I believe we may have a business arrangement to discuss."

"And what do you want in return?"

"My money returned to me eventually, of course. In addition, I would ask for two favors. The first being that no one knows of my involvement in saving your bank, to which I am certain you are already amenable. And the second, I would like a statement of my account, listing the amount of two pence and no more." *Yes. That should do the trick indeed.*

He stared dubiously at her, his eyes crossed as if a horn were protruding from the center of her forehead. "And whyever would you want such a document?"

"Those are my reasons alone," she said succinctly. "Oh, and I would add one more thing to the list. I never want to hear you say the words 'I don't think you understand' ever again."

Mr. Woldsley swallowed, looking sheepish—quite possibly for the first time in his life—and then he nodded.

Chapter Twenty-Two

The Season Standard—the Daily Chronicle of Consequence

At long last, we have our Original! I'm certain this name will come as no surprise to many of you, for haven't we all be watching her every step this Season? Surely our favorite goddess, Lady G—, is the most deserving of this coveted title...

Bram slapped the paper down on the breakfast room table. "What a triumph! Did you see the paper, Mother?"

"I am seeing it now on the table where it does not belong," she said sternly, eyeing Bram until he picked it up and placed it on the sideboard. "But yes, I am quite pleased for Juliet. I believe this honor has been long awaited. Would you agree, Maxwell?"

Max nodded absently, pretending that his focus was on the ham steak on his plate. In truth, he'd read the *Standard* first thing this morning. And since then, his stomach had churned with a sense of unease at the events that were about to unfold.

"It is fine for her indeed," Bram said. "But think of how it will be when I marry not one, but two *Originals*!"

Max knew Bram's announcement was forthcoming. His suit would be denied, of course. Yet even prescience in this circumstance did not take away the utter rage and despair he'd been feeling these past few days.

"That is in poor taste, Bramson, considering the fact that your first wife died giving birth to your child," Mother chided. "In fact, I find this whole rush to be married quite distasteful. And if weren't for little Patrice, I would forbid it."

"*Forbid*." Bram laughed and pressed a kiss to Mother's cheek, as if her words were a jest. Then again, Bram only listened to one opinion, and that was his own. "For now, I shall be off to pay a morning call. Are you not going to congratulate me, little brother?"

Max abruptly stood and then clasped his hands behind his back. Then, bowing to Mother, he said, "I will be in my study if you need me."

But before he could exit the room, Saunders appeared in the doorway, holding a missive in his gloved hand. "An urgent message from Lady Cosgrove, ma'am."

"Oh dear," Mother said as she took the note and then repeated herself several times as she read it, all the while shaking her head.

"What is it, Mother?" Max asked, fearing that something dire had happened.

"It is terrible news! Poor Juliet! She has lost everything, her entire fortune." Mother pressed the page to her breast, tears welling in her eyes. "The banks that closed, the ones that went under…Apparently, those were where she kept her money."

"No! That cannot be. She is rich as Midas!" Bram railed.

Mother drew in a breath, wiping her eyes with the crook of her finger as she settled her gaze on Bram. "You should rush over immediately, for your proposal will come at a most beneficial time. I will follow shortly, and we will begin to make arrangements."

Bram went white, his grin dissolving into a grimace, as if he were about to retch all over the table.

Max thought only of Juliet and what she must be suffering at this moment. More than anything, she'd wanted to be independent, to have control of her life. But with this news, she would soon be dependent upon her cousin.

Suddenly, Max knew what he had to do. He would give Juliet her house. He'd intended to sign it over all along, but after her stipulations following their intimacies, he hadn't wanted to leave her in doubt. At least with this, she still could have part of the life she wanted.

Then, by Monday next, he would leave for Lancashire, and finally be free of the hold Juliet had over him.

CHAPTER TWENTY-THREE

Juliet was surprised but elated when Mr. Wick announced that Max had come to call. Her first instinct was to rush to the parlor, but she was told that Max requested to wait in the study, with Mr. Saunders.

It was only the mention of Saunders that reminded Juliet of their wager. She hadn't even had time to read the *Standard* with all that had transpired, but Zinnia had given her the news.

The *Original*. What a shock, to say the least! It was strange how her return to London was like stepping back in time but making different choices.

"Good morning, Max," she said, trying not to smile too gaily in front of Saunders, and then she greeted the butler as well.

Bram had come and gone earlier. As expected, he'd explained that his affections had been caught off guard by someone else—Miss Leeds, apparently—and he was set to leave town for a few days to better acquaint himself with her family. Juliet had wished him well and, secretly, good riddance. Never in her life would she have thought how lucky she was to have lost him to Miss Leonard all those years ago. And this evening, she would say a prayer for the woman who had endured him for as long she could.

Max did not look directly at her when he offered his greeting but immediately gestured to Saunders to unlock the box. When Saunders did, he summarily left the room and closed the door behind him.

The box with their chosen candidates was before them now. Juliet stood beside Max as they both looked down at it sitting on the polished mahogany desk. "I can tell you right now that I did not win," she said with a small laugh, happy to be here with him.

"And I can tell you," Max began as he opened the box, "that I did."

He reached in and unfolded a slip of foolscap that carried a familiar slanted scrawl. *Lady Granworth.*

Instantly, tears gathered in her eyes, and she tried to blink them away. When she failed, Max withdrew his handkerchief and laid it on the desk before her. Still, he had not looked at her, but somehow he knew she was weeping.

"You chose my name, even when we were"—she sniffed—"enemies?"

Then, at last, he turned his gaze to her, and she almost wished he hadn't, because there was no hardness, no animosity, no heat, only emptiness, as if he felt nothing for her.

"You were never my enemy." He turned back to the desk and withdrew the other paper. One breath came out on something just short of a laugh. "Ellery. It makes so much sense, and yet I was blind to that. Blind to many things."

He closed the box and attached the lock once more. Then he withdrew a roll of parchment from within his coat and spread it out on the desk, angling it for her to see. "Here is the deed to the house. As you can see, I have transferred it into your name."

Confused, she shook her head. "No. The house is yours. You won our wager."

"I do not need the house as much as you do. Nor do I want it."

His coldness caused panic to rise within her. And when he took the box and turned to leave, she reached out and stayed him with a hand upon his arm. "Do you remember when I told you that kissing you five years ago had changed everything and also frightened me?"

The corner of his mouth twitched for an instant. "You said it was a *cataclysmic event.*"

"Yes, it was," she said on a breath, somewhat relieved that he remembered. "More than you know. That kiss was the reason the house was so important to me. You turned my world upside down in that library, and I have spent every day since wishing I could feel that way for the rest of my life. I thought that if I returned and started over in that house that I could capture the feeling of knowing that something else was inside of me."

He looked down at his arm as if waiting for her to remove her hand. "And now you have it. The deed to the house is yours so that you may start over or continue to relive your past. It does not matter to me anymore."

"No. I don't want the house. What I'm trying to tell you is that I found that feeling. And it had nothing to do with that house after all." She curled her fingers into the wool, holding tighter. "It was you, Max. It's always been you."

His head whipped up, leveling her with a glare. "That's rather convenient, isn't it?"

"What do you mean?"

"You are out of options. There is no Lord Granworth waiting in the wings or even—I expect—Lord Engle." He shrugged free of her. "I will not be held in your regard simply because you are without a fortune. I am no one's last resort, Juliet."

Why had she not seen it before? "Can't we go back to the way it was before your brother returned? If I would have known that you'd felt slighted in any way, I would have—"

"What would you have done? Made a public declaration of your affection? Come now, you forget how well I know you. And how much you prefer to stay inside that cage where your heart is safe."

"That is not true. Perhaps it was at one time but no longer."

"I am not going to argue the point." He blinked and suddenly that emptiness had returned to those beloved mud-puddle eyes.

"Max, you said the door was always open."

"I'm afraid that *always* has come and gone. Good day, Lady Granworth." And Max walked away.

"Don't go." Her voice came out raspy with unspent tears. But he closed the door just before she said, "I love you."

If he heard her, it was not enough to stop him.

Juliet remained in her chamber for the next two days. None of her dresses pleased her, so she didn't bother to change out of her night rail. No food tempted her, so she didn't bother to eat. And if it weren't for Marguerite, she likely wouldn't have even brushed her hair.

She did, however, find the shadows creeping along the ceiling in slow intervals somewhat fascinating. She spent the majority of her awake hours watching them and feeling as if that murky light now lived inside her. Despair moved in the same manner, slithering over one's soul to banish the light that once lived there.

"Enough, madame," Marguerite said, standing with her hands on her hips at Juliet's bedside. "You cannot let a broken heart linger, or it will become part of you."

Juliet thought of Zinnia and her midnight walks to her late husband's portrait. "My cousin fairs well enough with hers."

"And I have often thought the true reason she walks slowly is because she cannot find a reason to move forward with her life."

Marguerite was a little too wise for Juliet's tastes. "I'm sure she enjoys her independence."

"But she cannot rest her arm upon it when she walks or feel its warmth beneath her touch."

Juliet fought the urge to cover her ears but closed her eyes instead, blocking out the shadows and her maid's disapproving glower. Unfortunately, when she did, her memory forced her to see Max's cold expression as if the image were burned into her eyelids. She couldn't escape it.

"I made him wait too long," she said on a broken whisper. "I thought that by getting rid of Bram, I would have more time. But Max still believes that I chose Bram over him when it mattered—and for all the *ton* to see."

"Is it wrong for him to want everyone to know that you are his, even if he accepts that marriage frightens you?" Marguerite fussed with her pillows, piling one on top of the other until Juliet was forced into sitting upright.

Juliet's head spun, but she wasn't sure if the dizziness came from her new position or from what Marguerite said. "You don't understand. Max wanted me to make a grand gesture, declaring my feelings."

"And?"

There she went again, trying to make it sound so simple. "*And* what? I was afraid, and he knew it."

"Afraid that he does not love you in return? *Non*, for he has already told you that he does." Marguerite handed her a cup of tepid tea and then nudged her hand until she drank from it. "Then you must be afraid he is like your late husband and will treat you *abominablement*."

"Max is nothing like Lord Granworth," Juliet declared with utter certainty. "He is kind, patient, handsome, intelligent, tender..."

"*Quelle horreur*." Marguerite scoffed, took Juliet's teacup, and replaced it with a buttered scone. "I can see why you would not want to marry a man such as Lord Thayne."

Juliet took a bite without thinking, then another, and another until there was nothing left but a sprinkling of crumbs dusting the coverlet. She might have been hungry after all. "You don't understand," she said, reaching to the side table for her teacup. "Loving Max consumes me. He's all

I can think about. When I returned to London, I swore that I would never let another person rule my life."

"*Oui*, but those other people in Bath, and even your parents, they took from you, making you feel less and less. But with Lord Thayne..." Marguerite sank down onto the edge of the bed, her dark eyes warm and sincere. "Madame, I have never seen you so confident before."

Juliet nodded and felt the sting of tears again. "I know it. He has always brought out the best in me, even when I'm at my worst."

"There is a good chance he always will."

It was true. All of it. The reason she'd always had trouble concealing her emotions from Max was because they were connected. Not by mere attraction, or even friendship, but by a more intimate, ever-present bond. *Love*.

She needed to stop being so afraid of losing herself and instead realize what she could gain by sharing herself instead. But..."What if it's too late?"

"The more important question is—what if it is *not*?"

Suddenly feeling light and hopeful, Juliet embraced Marguerite and then shooed her off the bed so that she could get up and prepare herself for the day. Because today she was going to...

Her thoughts came up blank.

"I don't know what to do." Standing by the washbasin, she looked at her bedraggled reflection and cringed. "Of course, I'll need a bath first of all, but after that, I'm not certain. I suppose I could just march over to Harwick House and tell him."

"Ah, but he wants a bold declaration, *non*?"

Juliet rang the bell pull, considering her options. "There is another problem as well. He believes that I chose Bram over him."

Marguerite shook her head, murmuring in French about how she'd warned Juliet that jealousy was a poison. Once she'd finished her diatribe, she continued in English. "Then you will have to lure the brother back so that you can choose Lord Thayne over him."

"And how am I supposed to do that?"

"You will think of something, madame." Satisfied, she dusted her hands together. "Also, Lady Cosgrove wished to know if you will be joining her for tea with the Dowager Duchess of Vale."

Juliet's thoughts were headed in a dozen different directions, but at the reminder of how she'd agreed to help Gemma, they stopped. Thus far, Juliet had offered her new friend advice on how to approach the idea of marriage with an unfeeling, calculated heart. It was only in this moment that she realized what a disservice she was doing.

Instead of encouraging Gemma to find a man willing to marry her and to ensure that a marriage contract was firmly in place, Juliet should be instructing her to find value within herself. Only then would Gemma know what she truly wanted and deserved.

As soon as a woman understood her worth, she would be willing to risk anything in order to gain her heart's desire.

Anything, Juliet thought, even...cause a scandal.

Suddenly, she knew exactly how far she would go to prove her love to Max.

CHAPTER TWENTY-FOUR

Even after five days had passed, Max was hesitant to enter the study when he learned that Mother had invited Lady Cosgrove and Juliet to dinner. Saunders, however, informed him that Lady Cosgrove had come alone.

The tightness beneath Max's chest gradually faded. Or at least it lessened a degree. In time, it would fade completely.

When Max entered the parlor, he greeted Mother and Lady Cosgrove but did not ask after Juliet. No one seemed to notice. Therefore, he took the liberty of fetching their sherry from the sideboard.

"I have heard the good news," Mother said to her friend. "And I must say that I am heartily relieved to know that Juliet's tragedy was a mere accounting error. She must be glad to have her fortune once again."

Mother had told Max the news as well, and he was glad for Juliet. He would not have to worry about her in any way. She could do with her life as she wanted.

"I hesitate to tell you," Lady Cosgrove whispered, likely not knowing how well sound traveled in this room.

"It is fine," Mother whispered back. "Maxwell will not hear you from across the room."

A brief pause followed, during which Max opened the sherry and began to pour.

"This afternoon, Juliet informed me that it was all a ruse," Lady Cosgrove continued in hushed tones. "She never lost her fortune, not even for a single day."

"No!" Mother gasped quietly. "But what could have been her reason?"

Max went still, eager as well for the next words.

"And that is the reason for my hesitation. You see, it has to do with your eldest…"

"Say no more." Mother clucked her tongue. "I suspected that Bramson was only interested in her fortune, and that is why I pushed him to make a declaration that day."

Damn! Max looked down at the cabinet and saw that he'd spilled the sherry. Likely he'd drained half a bottle, and now it dripped on his shoes.

"But Maxwell saw to it that his debts were paid, and he was free to marry whomever he chose. And from what Bramson has told me, he has chosen Miss Leeds, whose dowry is five thousand pounds," Mother continued. "He is a few miles north of town at her family's country estate for a few days."

"Which is what I had heard; however, just before I left, Juliet received a missive from Bram. Apparently, he has had a change of heart and asked permission to renew his address to her."

"He has?" Mother's voice was slightly raised in surprise before she lowered it again. "And surely he could not have heard the news of her good fortune while he was away. So perhaps he does possess true affection for her."

"Perhaps. She sent a response to him immediately."

"Maxwell, what is taking so long?"

He nearly jumped at the louder sound, dropping the towel he was using to mop up. "A bit of a spill, but I have recovered now." He turned and crossed the room to hand them their sherry glasses. "Have I missed any important news?"

Mother blinked owlishly. "None whatsoever."

"And you, Lord Thayne—any news regarding your upcoming travels to Lancashire?"

He sat in the chair opposite and swirled his whiskey thoughtfully, wondering what could have been Juliet's reason for the pretense of losing her fortune. "My trunks are packed, and I am prepared to depart at first light on Monday."

"And what of your quest for a bride?" Mother asked.

"Halted for the time being. I think I would rather be settled into my estate. Then, in a year, perhaps…" He let his words trail off with a shrug. But he knew that it would be a long time before he would think about marriage again.

"You are not the only one planning a trip," Lady Cosgrove said after a sip. "Juliet has decided that she too will be traveling. Though not until the sale of the house is final."

"The house?" He frowned.

Lady Cosgrove looked to Mother and then back to him, her expression grave. "Forgive me. I thought you'd heard. She is selling the townhouse."

"Did she give a reason?"

"Her words were a mystery to me, but I believe she mentioned something about a painful lesson and a desire to let go of the past." Lady Cosgrove shook her head slowly. "Now that you have me thinking, I remember that I was to pass along a message to you, Lord Thayne, stating that she fully intends to have the bank draft made out to you, since the house was yours, after all."

Max gritted his teeth. He was not going to let her pay him for the house. If he allowed that, then it was like none of what had transpired since had even happened. And that Juliet was simply getting exactly what she'd wanted from him all along—to buy the house from him.

Now, the fact that she *wasn't* going to live in the house that was four doors down from his mother bothered him to no end.

"And you're sure he heard all of it? Every word?" Juliet asked when Zinnia returned later that evening, practically ambushing her in the foyer.

Zinnia nodded, removing her hat and gloves. "He spilled sherry everywhere."

Good. That was definitely a good sign. "What about the news that I'm selling the house?"

"Completely incensed."

Better and better.

"Was that muscle along his jaw ticking?"

"*Violently,*" Zinnia drawled.

Juliet smiled and embraced her cousin. "Now we simply have to wait for tomorrow."

Chapter Twenty-Five

Bram returned to Harwick House early Sunday morning as the family and servants were preparing to leave for church. Without any pomp or circumstance and still in his traveling clothes, he joined Max and Mother in the carriage.

While Mother was glad to receive him, Max would have preferred if he'd made an excuse to stay behind. After overhearing the conversation last night, Max guessed that Bram had learned the latest rumors from town and made certain to renew his addresses to Juliet.

And this time, Max was not going to be around to watch the spectacle.

"I did not expect your return for another two days," Mother said to Bram as he brushed the travel dust from his trousers and onto Max's shoes.

"I thought it unfair to accept Miss Leeds's and her family's hospitality when I am no longer certain she is the bride for me."

"This is news, indeed," Mother murmured with a trace of incredulity. "Have you decided to wait for a more appropriate time to marry?"

"Not at all." Bram offered a half a shrug. "The truth is, I find that my heart is engaged elsewhere."

This pretense of his brother's was testing Max's patience. "This does not happen to have any bearing on recent news regarding Lady Granworth, does it?"

"Recent news?" He lifted his brows in innocence and placed a hand over his heart. "I do not know what you mean. However, the name that you have spoken is the very same that plucks at the strings of this organ beneath my breast."

"Then you have no idea that her fortune has returned to her."

"No, indeed, little brother. I am merely here by her summons." He withdrew a letter from his inner coat pocket and unfolded it. "She writes: 'If you are able, then return to town at your earliest convenience, as I have an important announcement regarding my future marital arrangements.'"

Max reached across the carriage and snatched the letter out of Bram's hand, expecting it to be an invention of his brother's imagination. What he saw instead was confirmation of every word.

Juliet was planning to marry? No. This couldn't be true. Max knew her too well.

When they pulled up to the church, Bram removed the note from Max's numb grasp and slipped out of the carriage with a triumphant chuckle. "As I said before—when a woman mentions marriage, she is thinking about marriage."

All through the service, Max sat stunned, waiting for it to end. He didn't want to believe that Juliet had chosen to marry another, but her handwritten words proved otherwise. More disturbing was that she had sent the letter to Bram, as if she'd summoned him back to London with a single purpose in mind.

Then, at last, they were nearing the end of service. He could hear the restless shuffle of hymnals and reticules as the parishioners prepared to depart.

"This is the first reading of the banns," the reverend began, his voice booming from pulpit, "for a holy union between Lady Granworth of Somerset and..."

No! Max jumped to his feet in an instant. This couldn't be happening. Was she truly intending to marry Bram?

Max wouldn't allow it. Turning, he saw her sitting three rows behind in her usual place.

"The Marquess of..."

She smiled at him, her eyes beaming like gems in the sunlight. She looked so happy, so in love, the way he'd always wished she would have looked at him.

And suddenly he knew that he could not ruin this for her. If she loved...

"Thayne of Lancashire," the reverend concluded.

There was a collective gasp in the church that echoed up to the ceiling and down again, settling inside his chest. At first, Max didn't think he'd heard it correctly. His ears were suddenly ringing.

"Should you know of any impediment..."

Beside him, Bram stood too. "I believe you are mistaken, Reverend Thomas."

The reverend looked at the card again and adjusted his wire-rimmed glasses. "Lady Granworth of Somerset to wed the Marquess of Thayne of Lancashire. Lady Granworth, is this correct?"

Now, Juliet stood. The church had gone so quiet that he could hear the rustle of her pink skirts.

"It is," she said with a nod, still looking at him—*him!*— with that glowing gaze. "In three weeks, Wednesday next, I will marry the Marquess of Thayne. The man I love."

If his brain were functioning, he would have been stunned by her public declaration.

But his heart heard the most important part…she loved him.

"And Lord Thayne, is this correct?"

Max was already sidestepping his way out of the pew and striding down the aisle. He took her hand in his, feeling that this was exactly how it was always meant to be. "It is, but I might have to argue about the date."

Already he'd imagined a dozen ways to coax her to the altar sooner.

She laughed, squeezing his hand. "Would you care to wager on that, Max?"

EPILOGUE

The Season Standard—the Daily Chronicle of Consequence

Dear readers, the day we have been anticipating for three weeks is here at last! Doubtless, many imagined that news of an elopement between our Lady G— and the Marquess of Th— would certainly preempt this morning's planned ceremony. Reports abound of innumerable high-stakes wagers on the outcome. Scandalous!

This paper, however, suspected that our resident goddess and this Season's Original would have her grand day. For rumor has it that a length of the finest blue satin was delivered to a certain house on Hanover Street, which is guaranteed to draw many a passerby to catch a glimpse of the bride on the pavement in front of St. George's.

In other news, whispers regarding the sudden withdrawal of the Marquess of E—e…

"You cost me a hundred pounds, Thayne," Jack Marlowe, Viscount Locke, growled, gripping Max's shoulder with a broad fist. While his voice was gruff, the smirking eyes beneath his tawny brow were not. "Even Lilah thought you would elope with her cousin."

Standing beside him in the violet parlor at Lady Cosgrove's townhouse, Liam Cavanaugh, the Earl of Wolford, flashed a playfully threatening grin and clutched Max's other shoulder. "Aye. And I doubled the wager, as Adeline wanted a gambling adventure, so now I am out *two* hundred pounds."

Sensing a good deal of ribbing ahead of him, Max chuckled as he shrugged them both off and looked at the Duke of Vale standing across from him. "And I suppose, you're out *three?*"

Max glanced once more at the doorway, hoping to catch sight of Juliet coming down the stairs amidst the parade of trunk-toting servants. They had just finished their wedding breakfast, and she was now upstairs with the other wives, changing into her traveling clothes before their honeymoon.

His *wife* was upstairs... The thought sent warm currents of jubilation zipping through him.

"No, indeed," Vale responded with a smug arch of his dark brows. "I have *gained* three due to pure logic."

Turning his attention back to the room, Max eyed Vale skeptically. "Surely you could not have come up with an equation for the possibility of an elopement."

"Correct. I do, however, have a greater resource than mathematics, and that is Ivy." Vale offered a scholarly nod, as if this were a well-known fact. "She explained that a man who has patience enough to endure five years can certainly withstand three more weeks."

Max scoffed. "Then it was by pure chance that you won the wager, because patience abandoned me the moment the banns were read."

Locke and Wolford exchanged knowing looks and a grumble or two. Vale was seemingly pleased by the news. As for Max, even now his heart raced with anticipation as he looked at the clock on the mantel. While the long hand stated that Juliet had only been apart from him for ten minutes, to Max it felt as if ten days had passed. And if she didn't appear soon, he would climb the stairs, toss her over his shoulder, and carry her out the door.

In fact, the only reason he possessed enough sanity not to resort to a more primitive action was due to their frequent encounters. Calling hours, carriage rides, dinners, and parties had afforded them creative opportunities to indulge in intimacies. But those moments only whetted Max's appetite for more. He wanted her with him when he awoke, when he drifted to sleep, and for all the moments in between.

Yet there was also another reason he'd withstood these three interminably long weeks—his new wager with Juliet.

"You made another wager with Lord Thayne?" Lilah asked from the tufted bench at the foot of Juliet's bed. Adeline sat beside her, fixing the trim of Juliet's hat. Ivy and Gemma stood near the jewelry armoire in search of a sapphire hatpin to match the wedding ring on her finger, but at the question, they all stopped and waited for an answer.

Eager to leave the room so that she could be with Max, Juliet paused in the hurried buttoning of her pale blue pelisse to answer.

"A small one, yes." Yet the stakes were certainly nothing like their first wager or their second. "If he managed to wait out our betrothal without stealing me away to Gretna Green, then he would decide our honeymoon—the destination and duration. And if he'd failed, then I would."

Though the truth was, she never imagined he'd last a week, let alone three. And there were ample times when *she'd* been fully prepared to abscond with *him*. If not for their clever trysts, she never would have survived.

Tucking a butterscotch-colored lock behind her ear, Adeline came to her with the silk-lined hat. "Do you know where he's taking you?"

Juliet shook her head, even as eager anticipation caused her pulse to flit from one place to another. Already, she could feel her skin turning warm and pink. Thankfully, her pelisse was now buttoned up all the way to her throat and hid the evidence. "I was hoping one of you might know. Surely Max hasn't kept it a secret from everyone."

Her three married friends all shook their heads, each one in turn confessing that they had heard nothing from their husbands. In the next moment, however, Juliet learned about the wagers that had commenced between the gentlemen.

"I confess," Gemma said on a sigh, "that Ivy and I also…speculated on your actual wedding date."

"And I am pleased to say that Gemma has *agreed*"—Ivy flashed a triumphant smile—"to try one more Season before she gives up on the idea of marriage altogether."

"Though I don't believe it will do much good…" Gemma grumbled, lifting her myrtle green eyes to the ceiling.

Lilah laughed in clear understanding. "You may be surprised at the difference one Season can make."

"It's true. Sometimes love simply stumbles through your door," Adeline added with a shrug.

Juliet couldn't agree more. "One thing is for certain—love always happens when you least expect it."

She reached for the kid gloves waiting on her vanity. While putting them on, however, she found herself distracted by the lovely cabochon ring on her left hand. The same ring that Max had kept for her for five years.

"Madame," Marguerite said from the doorway. "The carriage is packed. You are ready for your honeymoon."

Her skin heated once more, her heart beating wildly. She was ready to spend the rest of her life with Max. She just wondered why it had taken her so long to figure it out.

"Marguerite," Lilah began, stepping toward her, "did Lord Thayne happen to mention where he was taking Juliet?"

With a sly grin, her maid nodded. "*Oui*, Lady Locke."

This gained Juliet's attention, as well as everyone else's. "Would you care to elaborate?"

"All I will say is that Lord Thayne's valet and I will not be following your carriage until tomorrow." Then that saucy minx simply curtsied and left them all to speculate.

"You won't be traveling far today," Ivy said as they all moved through the doorway, one by one.

Another palpitation fluttered beneath her breast as her hand curved over the banister. Hmm...just what had her new husband planned? She was only steps away from finding out...

"Oh, my dear, Juliet," Marjorie said, rushing out of Zinnia's chamber, her arms open. Her eyes shimmered with moisture, and her face glowed with her smile. "My daughter, at last."

Juliet returned her embrace, a wealth of tenderness overflowing inside of her. Not only for Marjorie but for everyone with her today. They were all precious to her—a true family. "It seemed to take me forever to find my way here."

Marjorie pressed a kiss to her cheek. "Never fear. The rest of your life can begin on any day."

Emerging from the doorway ahead of Zinnia, the Dowager Duchess of Vale cast a pointed look to her niece. "I completely agree, and one must always be prepared."

In response, Gemma crossed her arms. "As I have said before, Aunt Edith, I doubt there is a match for me."

Juliet, Ivy, Lilah, and Adeline all inhaled sharply, knowing better than to present a challenge to a trio of women who believed themselves to be matchmakers. At the breakfast this morning, Edith, Marjorie, and Zinnia had taken full credit for every happy union in the room. Juliet, however, hadn't felt guided into her match but more like she'd unwrapped it, bit by bit. Nevertheless, too content to argue, she had raised her own glass in the toast.

Now, however, the trio in question exchanged a look and then a nod. *Poor Gemma.* She would have not one but three women determined to find her a husband.

"And speaking of husbands," Juliet said with immeasurable pleasure, "mine is waiting below. So I will leave you to your discussion and bid you each a fond farewell."

Zinnia embraced her, tears welling in her eyes. "Promise you will write."

"Often," she promised. "And when we are settled in Lancashire, you must come and stay with us."

After Zinnia agreed, and Juliet pecked nearly every cheek in the hall, she finally swept down the stairs.

"Where are you taking me, Max?" Juliet asked from beneath the dark silk he'd tied around her eyes in the carriage.

It took every ounce of willpower to fight the temptation to kiss those pouting pink lips.

Soon…he promised himself and continued to guide her along the garden path to the doors of their townhouse. "You will see."

She huffed playfully. "Says the man who isn't currently blindfolded."

He stopped abruptly for effect. "Wait a moment. I thought *I* was the one wearing the blindfold, and you were leading me. I wonder where we could be."

"*Max*—"

Before she could scold him or swat at him, he bent down and swept her into his arms, laughing when she gasped and clung to him. He relished the feel of her in his embrace, the warmth of her body, the supple curves beneath his hands. Holding her close, he pressed his lips to her hair as he found the door latch and carried her over the threshold.

After he closed the door behind them, she lifted her head and breathed deeply. Then, with a smug grin, she said, "I know where we are. You have brought me to our townhouse."

Contrary to what Max had overheard between his mother and Lady Cosgrove over three weeks ago, Juliet never intended to sell the house. He knew this because when he'd threatened to purchase it from her and pay double the price, she'd laughed and confessed her entire scheme.

"Did you believe that I would want to spend my wedding day traveling in a carriage?" he asked, carrying her down the hall and then through another doorway before placing her on her feet.

"Hmm…" She laid her hands over his heart and lifted her pert chin. "I did not know what to think. After all, you have not seemed at all eager today."

"Not eager?" He scoffed tenderly, skimming his hands down her back and drawing her closer. "How could you doubt it? For someone who knows me better than all others, I am surprised by this claim."

"But you have not kissed me once since we have become married."

Slipping her blindfold over her head, he framed her face with his hands. "Because I wanted this first kiss to be right here."

Darting a glance around the room, she smiled, her eyes beaming with love when they met his. "The library."

Now, he too drew in a breath, finding the familiar scents of leather and citrus blended with rose water and sandalwood. This was the comforting fragrance of their home and reminiscent of many happy memories. Not to mention all the new ones to come.

He'd made certain that the laborers had restored this room to exactly the way it had been. Only now, a few more books were added, both his and hers, mingling together.

"This is the first stop on our honeymoon tour of exceptional libraries." Pausing between each word, he leaned in and brushed his lips across her brow, her petal-soft cheek, and both corners of her mouth before resting in the center.

For a moment, they both went perfectly still, eyes drifting closed. There was no rush. They had a lifetime to linger. And, at long last, she was his.

The End

AUTHOR'S NOTE

The Panic of 1825 was one of the first major stock market crashes. At the conclusion of the Napoleonic Wars, a period of rapid expansion followed. People were looking to the future, wanting a little nest egg, and ready to forge ahead with new ideas that would make their country stronger than ever. Investments boomed. From large cities to small hamlets, banks were writing checks (which they may or may not have been able to cash) to bring the railroad their way. It was surely an exciting time. In fact, the criminals thought so, too.

There were a number of swindlers who created "opportunities" for investment (such as the gold and silver mines of the fictitious Latin American territory of Poyais). This rush to riches and improvement created a bubble in the economy, filled with little more than false promises and hot air. Then one day, like one of Professor Faraday's balloons, it burst.

Once it was discovered that this territory never existed, let alone the abundant wealth investors would gain, panic ensued. People scrambled to the banks for their money all at once, the stock market crashed, and banks could no longer withstand the demands.

The Panic and subsequent recession lasted to the early part of the following year. Afterward, the economy started to grow again, but more cautiously this time.

Unfortunately, the fictional Juliet Granworth was not around to offer assistance. Otherwise, I'm certain she could have sorted out the whole mess much sooner.

ACKNOWLEDGMENTS

I've been incredibly blessed to write eleven titles for the Impulse imprint. The amazing people at Avon have only enhanced this dream come true.

I'm grateful to my editor, Nicole Fischer, for her easygoing nature and insightful notes in the margins. Many thanks to the entire art department for creating enticing covers and to the marketing and publicity teams for all their promotional endeavors.

Thanks as well to my agent, Stefanie Lieberman, for encouraging me to discover fresh ideas.

To the wonderful Lisa Filipe, your enthusiastic support has touched my heart.

And to my readers, it is because of your generosity that Max and Juliet's story became a reality. Thank you.

USA Today bestselling author **VIVIENNE LORRET** loves romance novels, her pink laptop, her husband, and her two sons (not necessarily in that order…but there are days). Transforming copious amounts of tea into words, she is an Avon Impulse author of works including *Tempting Mr. Weatherstone*, The Wallflower Wedding series, The Rakes of Fallow Hall series, "The Duke's Christmas Wish," and the Season's Original series.

Discover great authors, exclusive offers, and more at hc.com.

Give in to your Impulses . . .
Continue reading for excerpts from
our newest Avon Impulse books.
Available now wherever ebooks are sold.

INTERCEPTING DAISY
A LOVE AND FOOTBALL NOVEL
by Julie Brannagh

MIXING TEMPTATION
A SECOND SHOT NOVEL
by Sara Jane Stone

THE SOLDIER'S SCOUNDREL
by Cat Sebastian

MAKING THE PLAY
A HIDDEN FALLS NOVEL
by T. J. Kline

An Excerpt from

INTERCEPTING DAISY
A Love and Football Novel
By Julie Brannagh

When Daisy Spencer wrote an erotic novella about
the Seattle Sharks' backup quarterback and her
#1 crush, Grant Parker, she never expected it to
become a runaway bestseller. If anyone discovers
she wrote the sexy story, her days as a flight
attendant for the Sharks would be over. But once
she gets to know the real man behind the fantasy,
her heart may be in more danger than her job.

He could have hit the Stop button and kissed her in the elevator, but there was probably a security camera. He didn't really care, but she might not like being the center of attention when the snip of video got leaked to the local press or put up on YouTube. He wasn't letting her drive away without kissing her, though.

She paused in front of her car as she turned to face him.

"I had such a nice time. Thank you so much for dinner," she said. She shuffled her feet a little. He'd observed her so many times while she did her job. She always seemed at ease, even during the turbulence they'd experienced on the last Sharks flight. Maybe she had the same butterflies in her stomach that he had in his.

He moved a little closer to her and slid his arm around her waist. She tipped her head back to look into his eyes. He had to smile at the flush making its way over her cheeks as she licked her lips. Yes, Daisy wanted to kiss him too.

He touched his forehead to hers for a few seconds. Her skin was so soft. He could smell her perfume. He couldn't identify the flowers in it if someone offered him a million dollars, but it was nice. The parking garage was not exactly the backdrop for romance. Next time, he'd say good-bye to her at her front door instead.

"I had a great time too. I'm already looking forward to next Thursday," he said.

"Maybe we could go bungee jumping."

"Sounds perfect," he said. He heard her laugh again. "Right after that, we'll go zip-lining at Sharks Stadium."

He felt her shiver. He wasn't sure if it was the fact she was wearing an almost sleeveless dress, the idea she'd be that far off of the ground and speeding along a relatively slender cable, or that she was as attracted to him as he was to her. He needed to make his move, and he'd better do it before someone came screeching around the corner in search of a parking spot. He reached up to take her face in his hands.

"Maybe we should have a glass of wine in front of a roaring fire instead," he whispered, and he watched her eyelids flutter as they closed. He touched his mouth to hers, adjusted a bit, and kissed her.

She tasted like the wine they'd been drinking with a fresh, honeyed overlay that must have been all her. Her lips were soft and cool beneath his. He felt her arms slide around his waist as he deepened the kiss. He slid his tongue into her mouth, tasting her again. As he felt her tremble, he knew it had nothing to do with the cold. He pulled back a little and laid his cheek against her smoother one.

He wanted to kiss her until they both were breathless. He wanted to spend the rest of the evening with her, and maybe tomorrow too. Mostly, he wanted to figure out how to entice a woman into falling in love with him, and he wondered if he'd been going about it all wrong. The woman who currently regarded him with a soft expression as she reached up to stroke his face deserved more than he'd offered to women before.

"Thursday," he said. "I'll text you."

"Should I get more life insurance?"

"No. We'll have a great time." He pulled back a little and looked into her eyes. "I promise I'll figure something out that doesn't land us both in a body cast."

She dug through her purse, extracted her car keys, and hit the button to unlock her car. He made sure she was safely inside. She started her car, opened the driver's side window, and looked up at him again.

"Thursday," she said.

He watched the taillights of her car vanish around the corner seconds later.

An Excerpt from

MIXING TEMPTATION
A Second Shot Novel

By Sara Jane Stone

After a year spent living in hiding—with no
end in sight—Caroline Andrews wants to
reclaim her life. But the lingering trauma from
her days serving with the marines leaves her
afraid to trust the tempting logger who delivers
friendship and the promise of something more.

Oh hell, she should push him away. A better friend would demand that Josh Summers share his pies with a woman willing to daydream about a place in his picture-perfect future. She shouldn't let him waste his life waiting for her to make up her mind about a first date.

"You should do it," she said firmly. "You should buy the land. What are you waiting for?"

He cocked his head. One red curl fell across his forehead. His hair looked as if he'd rolled out of bed, run his fingers through the loose, wavy locks and prepared to face another day looking like an Irish god who'd somehow landed in rural Oregon. Though that might have something to do with the muscles he'd fine-tuned over the years of felling trees.

But right now she kept her gaze focused on his face, waiting for his answer.

"What if I decide on five bedrooms and the woman I want to share my dream home with thinks it's too much. I might have to settle for three in order to talk her into an outdoor kitchen that I'm thinking about building in addition to the monstrous one in the house."

"As long as you're not planning to turn half the house into some sort of man cave with beer pong tables lining the hallways, I think you'll find someone who will love your dream house," she said. "Of course to meet that special someone you will have to start dating."

And that was as close as she was going to get to kicking him in the butt and demanding that he turn his focus away from her. They could remain friends. But another kiss would just lead to a dead end.

His smile faded. "You think I should ask someone else to be my date to the wedding?"

She forced a brief nod and let her gaze settle on the half-eaten pie.

"No," he said slowly, lingering over the simple word. "I don't think so. But I might put in an offer on that land."

"You should do both," she pointed out despite the relief that threatened to turn to joy. "I can't move into your four- to five-bedroom dream home. Not when I'm still so . . ."

Scared.

Nearly fifteen months had slipped by since she'd run away from the military. She'd pressed pause on her life that day. There had been moments here and there were she'd felt ready to hit play again and move on. Each one revolved around the man standing across the stainless steel counter looking down at his pie.

"A couple of weeks ago you stopped wearing those baggy cargo pants." Josh dug his fork into the dish and glanced up at her. "I like the skinny jeans better."

Me too. And I like the way you look at my legs when you think I'm distracted . . .

"I stood out in the cargo pants and boots," she said with a shrug. "Lily said I'd blend in more if I dressed like the university students. And Josie had some clothes she didn't think would ever fit again even if she lost all the baby weight. She gave these to me."

"You stand out in those jeans too. I'm glad I only have to share the view with the dishwasher." He nodded to the machine. "And not all those young kids from the college."

"You're twenty-eight, Josh. Not that much older than those 'young kids.' Many of them are graduate students."

"More than half would love to have you serve their drinks," he said.

"I like it back here where no one will—"

"Notice you. Yeah, I get that. But my point is, you've changed since you first showed up here looking for Noah." He set down his fork and took a step back. "Who knows what will happen next?"

"Nothing."

I hope. I pray.

Because the only life-changing events she could imagine would land her in trouble. She'd carved out a safe place to hide. She had a cash job and a place to live thanks to her boss. If she lost this—

"Something always happens next." He turned and headed for the door.

She'd touched the hard planes of his chest when she'd kissed him, but the view of his backside left her wanting more. More pies. More conversation. More Josh.

One . . . Two . . . Three . . .

He turned and glanced over his shoulder. And then he

flashed a knowing smile. Oh, she'd seen plenty of hard-bodied men. She'd served alongside soldiers with drool-worthy muscles. There was nothing special about Josh Summers.

Except for his smile.

She was falling for that grin and the man who wielded it like an enticing treat. Tempted to trust in him. Believe in him.

"I'll see you at the wedding," he called and then he walked his delicious smile out the door of the bar's back room.

She abandoned her fork and dipped her fingers in the pie dish. Sugar. She needed a burst of sweetness to take her mind off Josh Summers.

Next time he asks you to lick the whipped cream from your lips, say yes!

Because Josh Summers was right. Something always happened next. And if she wanted to reclaim her life—or at least a small piece of it—if she wished for another chance to land in Josh's arms with his lips pressed to hers, then she needed to find out what happened when she said yes.

An Excerpt from

THE SOLDIER'S SCOUNDREL

By Cat Sebastian

From debut author Cat Sebastian, an
enthralling regency male/male romance about
a former criminal who has never followed
the straight and narrow and a soldier whose
experiences of war have left him determined
to find order in a chaotic world.

Jack could almost feel the heat coming off Rivington's body, almost pick up the scent of whatever eau de cologne the man undoubtedly wore. If he moved half a step closer he'd be standing between Rivington's legs. He knew that would be a bad idea, but at the moment could not seem to recall why.

"What I don't understand"—Rivington tipped his head against the back of Jack's worst chair as if he hadn't just been told to leave—"is why she didn't destroy the letters. If she knew the contents would harm her, why not throw them on the fire?"

Ah, but the ladies never did. Not in Jack's experience, at least. Mothers and governesses ought to spend more time instructing young ladies in the importance of destroying incriminating evidence and less time bothering with good posture and harp lessons and so forth.

Besides, that wasn't the right question to ask. The real wonder was that Mrs. Wraxhall hadn't kept the blackmail letter, the one clue that might lead them to her stolen letters.

Of course, people did all manner of foolish things when they were distressed, but Jack would have thought a woman who had the presence of mind to stay so tidy on such a muddy day wouldn't do something as muddle-headed as flinging a blackmail letter onto the fire.

Jack looked down at Rivington, who still hadn't moved. The man was apparently under the impression that they were going to sit here and discuss the Wraxhall matter, and really Jack ought to waste no time in disabusing him of that notion.

But instead Jack kept looking. A man this handsome was a rare pleasure to admire up close. He was younger than Jack had first thought—somewhere between five-and-twenty and thirty. Perhaps five years younger than Jack himself.

Yet he looked tired. Worn out. For God's sake, his coat was all but falling off him, despite obviously having been well-tailored at one point. "Shouldn't you be home, resting your leg?" Such a question might just be rude enough to send Rivington packing, and besides, Jack couldn't remember the last time he had seen a gentleman in such clear need of sleep and a decent meal.

Rivington opened his mouth as if to say something cutting but then gave a short, unamused huff of laughter. "If only rest worked." He didn't seem offended by Jack's rudeness. He was, Jack realized, likely a good-natured fellow. He had arrived here in a pique of anger—and likely pain—that had since worn off. Now he had the wrung-out look of someone exhausted by an unaccustomed emotion. Jack would guess that Rivington was not a hot-tempered man. And now he was contemplating his walking stick with something that looked like resignation bordering on dread.

"They always keep the letters," Jack said quickly, before he could remind himself that he ought to be ordering this man to go home, not engaging him in conversation.

When Rivington looked up, something flashed across his face that could have passed for relief. "Sentiment, I suppose."

Jack stepped backwards and sat on the edge of his desk to preserve the advantage of height. "I tend to think people hang on to love letters in the event they might choose to blackmail the sender." But then again, he never did quite expect the best from people. Maybe the lady was simply being sentimental, but in Jack's experience of human nature, people were more likely to plot and connive than they were to indulge in sentiment. Jack's experience with humanity was admittedly a trifle skewed, however.

Rivington's eyes opened wide with disbelief. "I knew a man who couldn't bring himself to sell his father's watch, even though he had creditors banging on his door at all hours. But he kept the watch because he couldn't bear to part with it. It may be the same with your Mrs. Wraxhall."

Jack shrugged. "Could be." Never having had a parent who inspired any feelings of tenderness or loyalty, or indeed any sentiment at all beyond a resentment that lingered years after their deaths, Jack mentally substituted his sister for Rivington's example. What if Sarah had a brooch or some other trinket—would Jack hesitate to sell it in the event of a financial emergency? He doubted it. Sarah would be the first person to tell him to sell all her brooches if need be. If she had any, which she did not.

"What will you do to recover the letters?" Rivington stretched one leg before him and started rubbing the outside of his knee.

Jack knew he ought to send the man on his way, but found that he didn't want to. Not quite yet. Maybe it was the dreariness of the day. Maybe it was the fact that this man clearly needed to rest his injured leg. Maybe it was simply that it had been a long time since Jack had been able to discuss his work with anyone. Sarah thought—correctly—that Jack's work was too sordid to be discussed. Georgie never sat still long enough to have an entire conversation. And nobody else in all of London was to be trusted.

Or, hell, maybe he just wanted to spend fifteen bloody minutes enjoying the sight of this man, appreciating the way the slope of his nose achieved the perfect angle, the way his eyes shone a blue so bright they likely made the sky itself look cheap by comparison. How often did Jack get an opportunity to admire anyone half so fine?

He pulled open the top drawer of his desk. "Care for a drink, Captain Rivington?"

An Excerpt from

MAKING THE PLAY
A Hidden Falls Novel
By T. J. Kline

T. J. Kline launches a brand new series with
the charming story of a NFL player who
finds love when he least expects it . . .

to say the least. A few of the other spectators agreed and began to applaud as the man caught the ball and jogged back toward James, tossing it to him gently as he came close. She watched him go to one knee in front of James and place a massive hand on his shoulder. She tried to fight down the overprotective instinct rising up in her. He obviously wasn't going to hurt James after he'd just, miraculously, avoided crashing into him. She caught up to where the pair were chatting like old friends.

"I'm so sorry." She gasped for breath, cursing the sandals she'd worn and her lack of aerobic exercise since moving to town. "I looked away and he'd taken off." She squatted down to James and grasped his shoulders. "What in the world were you thinking? You could have been hurt, badly. If this man hadn't seen you—"

"It's no problem, ma'am. He's just keeping me on my toes and prepared for anything." He smiled at James and gave him a wink before turning his deep chocolate brown gaze on her.

He rose slowly, unfolding his tall frame, to tower above her, leaving her eye level with his bared, sweaty chest. Bethany felt her mouth go dry, unable to speak even if she was able to get her brain functioning again, which it didn't seem inclined to do.

"**A**ny day, bro."

Grant McQuaid did a few ballistic stretches and picked up the football he'd brought along with him, tossing it toward Jackson, knowing his brother wouldn't turn down a quick game.

"How's that arm of yours?"

Jackson shrugged. "I guess that depends on your point of reference. I'm no Miles."

He meant Aaron Miles, the starting quarterback for the Mustangs, and the guy who'd rallied the team, taking them to the playoffs last year. The same game where Grant had sustained his last concussion, the one that might have ended his career. He crushed the thought before it sank in. He was *going* to play this season, there was no room for doubt.

"Let's see what you've got." He jogged down field from Jackson, effortlessly catching the ball. Grant had been a decent receiver in high school but his size had made the transition to running back a no-brainer in college.

The two of them played catch for the better part of an hour while Grant tried to ignore the people beginning to crowd under several of the shady trees nearby, watching. It wasn't unusual to see at training camp but here, in his hometown, he hated being a spectacle. He couldn't walk down the street without someone pointing, staring or asking for an autograph. Here he just wanted to be Grant, not Grant McQuaid, starting running back for the Memphis Mustangs.

"Last one," Jackson called, lobbing the ball down the field for a Hail Mary pass.

Grant went long, sprinting to make the catch. He was damned if he was going to look like a fool with this many people watching. It wasn't until the last second he heard the child's yell and the woman's voice calling for him to "Look out!"

"I've got it!" the boy yelled as he reached into the sky, a broad grin plastered across his face.

Grant glanced away from the ball in time to see the little boy run directly into his path.

Bethany couldn't watch. She'd looked away from James for two seconds to find a napkin in her purse to wipe away the ice cream dripping over his hands and the next thing she knew, she was chasing after him as he ran directly into the path of the two men playing catch. She should have known better than to believe James would sit still when someone was playing football.

The man who'd gone out for the pass barely flinched before he leapt over her son's head as if he was no more than a small hurdle, clearing James' outstretched hands by at least six inches.

Holy crap!

James might be small for his age but that was incredible,